Beast in the Bluegrass

Virginia Slachman

Copyright ©2023 Virginia Slachman
ISBN: 979-8-9877850-2-7
Cover design: Christine Holmes
Publisher: Cooper Dorian, LLC

Acknowledgements

As always, many folks helped bring this book to fruition. Per usual, my thanks go to Barry Irwin, for his many years of service to the Thoroughbred industry and the welfare of its horses, and for his continuing and long-standing support of my work. Then, without question, my thanks extend to Patricia "PJ" Cooksey, pioneering female Thoroughbred jockey, without whose generous time with me this book would not exist. To Hall of Fame turf writer Steve Haskin go my thanks for his lovely endorsement and interest in the book. In terms of specific research, I'd be remiss if I didn't mention Sandy Hatfield, Stallion Manager, Emeritus, Three Chimneys; and Richard Nolen, Broodmare Division Manager, Three Chimneys, both of whom opened their sides of the farm to me without reservation, and from whom I learned much about the challenges and care that go into breeding and raising happy, healthy Thoroughbred racehorses. In addition, Dr. Brad Tanner, DVM, DAVDC-EQ, Rood & Riddle Equine Hospital, was of great help as was Dr. Tom Riddle, co-founder of Rood & Riddle, for making his staff available to me. My thanks also extend to Ann Nicholas, proofreader. And to Shannon Huber go my thanks for her expertise in equine anatomy, equine injuries, Kajukenbo martial arts, as well as her sharp editing eye.

In terms of additional research on the veterinary side of the text, others who contributed to its accuracy include Dr Natasha Hamilton, Equine Genetics Research Centre Director; Bruce Howard, Equine Medical Director, Kentucky Racing Commission); Dr. Lawrence Bramlage, DVM, MS, DACVS, Rood & Riddle Equine Hospital; William Jones (Ireland), author of *The Black Horse Inside Coolmore;* and Adrian Beaumont, Director of Racecourse Services, for International Racing Bureau.

And of course, my thanks always extend to Becky Ryder, Director, Keeneland Library, and to Kelly Coffman, Research Service Librarian, Keeneland Library, both of whom are always of inestimable help, delivering just what's needed in a timely way and with great cordiality.

As for the policing side of the book, I learned much from Jay Beetz (Former Detective, Lexington, KY) and Garth Rogers (Former Detective, Mineral Area, MO). Drew Smith, Master Sargent, USAF, retired, was instrumental in helping me get the character of Wes right. And my brother, heart surgeon Dr. Frank Slachman, being an elk hunter of many years, advised on the hunt appearing in the prologue as well as on Cass' injuries.

Virginia Slachman, St. Louis, MO

Prologue

He took the mule because she was sure-footed and carried a heavy load. He took the big quarter horse because the gelding had suffered the worst of man and nature and did not complain.

He'd watched the elk herd for two weeks and knew their habits. He knew they'd be out at first light, so he left at 4 a.m., figuring to get to them by dawn. He saddled his red roan gelding in the dead of night, loading him last.

He ponied his pack mule, Dora, and took his time moving out, heading eventually to the ridge, moving silently and slowly through the scattered tall pines and aspens. The day, as it came on, was cold, just as he liked it. He'd been post-holing for most of the first few weeks in March, building strength in his leg muscles after the injury.

As the sun came up, he watched the light at first dawn, settling in as the wind died down and the forest came to life. Birds woke in the trees, the squirrels and chipmunks scattered beside their path as the trio moved forward silently.

The man squinted up through the deep green pines, their graceful, arced boughs gently shifting up and down as the wind softly picked up, ruffling through them. He'd scouted the possible approaches, taking the one downwind that also afforded deep enough soft snow to muffle their approach.

He should have taken the bull in the fall, but the injury prevented that. He'd subsisted fall through winter on the odd grouse shot on brief outings with his rimfire Ruger, or a hare caught in wire traps. The outings, keeping warm, and caring for the animals had exhausted him and prolonged his recovery. Now able to mount his big gelding, it was time for real meat.

Above the ridge, next to the forest's safety on the far side of the field, the herd shifted as one under a cold sun, munching the low, new shoots that held high appeal after the bleak winter. The largest bull moved with sinewy grace, slowly, gaining sustenance after the long, frigid months. There were a few other bulls, smaller, meandering among the heavily pregnant females.

Deep in the forest, as he and his pack mule made slow progress, he noticed the aspens were just budding out. This was good, promising an early spring. But the injury meant he'd missed the fall sunlight burnishing the tree leaves dappling the forest floor when the leaves turned on their stems in the wind, sending diffusing gold coins of light. Not like the harsh glare of Afghanistan killing fields.

He moved comfortably on his gelding, not rushing the horse's progress, glancing every now and then behind him to the ponied mule who plodded on, head low, silent, as was her job.

Once they left the forest he ground-staked the gelding and the mule, going silently on foot, slinging his field dress backpack and Weatherby behind his shoulder and slowly making his way up the rise. No need to hurry. He knew they'd be there.

Before his whole body became visible, he removed the backpack and rifle, then dropped to his belly in the scant snow, slowly scanning the herd. The Weatherby was heavier than his old 300 Win Mag, but this one was designed for accuracy up to 1,000 yards. The hunter ballparked the distance; five hundred yards would be no struggle for the big gun.

He'd already decided not to take the largest bull. It hadn't been a harsh winter, by most standards, but the herd wasn't at their full fall weight by any stretch. Even so, he couldn't pack all that meat out in one trip. Still recovering, one kill, field dress, and pack out was all he could manage. He wouldn't waste the bull. He'd picked out a good-sized specimen on previous outings—the one who had recently shed his 5-point rack.

He sighted on him through the 30 mm Swarovski scope. With its extended range capacity, he easily located the chest's heart-lung kill spot just behind the front leg. As he'd been trained to hunt men, so he hunted the elk. He settled, stilled for the kill. Only his finger moved.

There was, suddenly, no wind. The sky was empty, and the sun's weak light continued to patiently call the earth to life as the shot rang out. The bull, head down to the sparse grass, had just moved one foreleg forward, when, as if across an eternity the death begun some seconds before slammed into flesh, the bullet's penetrating force streaking through heavy bone and exploding the bull's heart. The elk's head wavered as if stunned by some unsought visitant, then he dropped mid-stride, dead before he reached the ground. The herd fled mindlessly, their hoofbeats sounding like muffled thunder in the clear, cold day, leaving the bull motionless under a stark sun.

The man stood, re-slung his rifle and backpack, and trudged over the hard-packed terrain. He paused over the bull, bearing witness to his wide-eyed stare into the distance only the dead can see.

He looked to be around 500 pounds, not a mature bull, but certainly enough meat to get the hunter fully back to health. He would gut the bull quickly. Acid leaking into the meat after the kill would spoil what he'd worked to gain. He'd leave that and the massive bones for the wolves to gnaw as a nod to the hierarchy and what he'd come to understand as a reverence for all life.

He skinned the bull, laying it hide side down beside the body. Then he began at the hind leg, working the oiled blade slowly along the gut line, following the edge of the hip, then releasing the ball from the joint. Once separated from the pelvis, he boned it, and placed the meat on the upturned hide to avoid dirt or hair adhering.

Periodically he drank from a water bottle and then from the hot thermos filled with infused turmeric, ginger, cinnamon, and cayenne.

When the hind quarter was finished, he sat in the sun, taking in the sprouting lime-green life, scanning the still-bare trees for signs of predators. They'd be silent, just as he was silent.

It suited him. The deep woods were filled with rot and the earth's burgeoning and the subtle sounds of small lives. But it was the vast silence that he needed. Everything else was superfluous.

He stripped off his thick canvas jacket, now that he was heated by drink and work. He bent to it, taking what he needed—first the forequarters, then methodically removing the backstraps and tenderloins—the strap muscles. Once finished, he turned the bull on its other side, brushed the hide and set to stripping it, harvesting the meat, and saving enough sinew to use as thread over the winter months.

He made short work of it. Once done, he surveyed the still warm, red flesh spread out on the upturned hide, organized for packing. He removed the binoculars from the backpack and scanned the perimeter—there could be an early bear or wolves, coyotes, or the odd mountain lion, but he saw nothing. He made another pass, this time in the trees, scouting for eagles patiently waiting as do all predators. Again nothing.

He rose, leaving it all, jogging down the rise to the mule, and returning to pack the meat in the saddlebags, evenly distributing the weight so she'd make the trip without incident.

They walked slowly back to the gelding, the hunter never glancing behind to the bull's skeletal body. The man had not touched the head or the budding velvet. He'd leave the sacrificial bull that dignity.

Beast in the Bluegrass

1

Cassandra Hutchinson closed her eyes and inhaled deeply, drinking in the sweet smell of early spring and earthy horseflesh as she gently rubbed the big colt's forehead. She opened her eyes and studied the young horse, murmuring "It's all good pretty boy, nothin' but a mess a track out there." The colt's eye softened. "You got this, darlin."

Memphis cocked his back leg and relaxed. He licked and chewed a bit, enjoying Cass' pre-race ministrations. He didn't seem at all perplexed by the commotion building in the gathering crowd, or in the tension palpably present in the other colts and trainers.

Around them, Keeneland Racetrack grounds were alive with early race goers and the scent of dirt, horses, grass, and the rain due in that afternoon. The slight breeze carried a buzz of anticipation—everyone was eager to see how the two-year-olds had matured—they were all hoping to get in on a three-year-old colt who'd blow the field away and head for the Derby come May.

"Lotta commotion for an early race," said Marshall, striding up, tugging on his signature black Stetson. Eden Hill's longtime trainer was nervous as he surveyed the other horses about to hit the track for the first time this year. He turned his attention to

Memphis, the big black colt they hoped would enjoy racing as much as he did training. Eden Hill wasn't hurting, but another super horse wouldn't be something to spit at. They had Deacon, but Memphis, though a different sort of horse altogether, had the makings of a champion. But they'd all agreed, they just wanted to let the colt get his legs under him as the season began in earnest.

Marshall glanced around. He'd never lost his love of Keeneland racetrack's green and cream now shining in the mid-day April sunlight. Marshall took in the budding out trees, the newly planted flowers, the freshly watered grass. The earth, he thought, was coming to life. Keeneland in spring—where everything they'd all worked for would either materialize or go up in smoke. This race marked the beginning.

Marshall sighed. He'd be patient, or try to be—see what the next month brought them. Always best not to get ahead of yourself.

Racing fans milled beneath the towering old sycamore and stood respectfully outside the black wrought-iron rail waiting for the saddled horses to parade past. Men in khakis and blue shirts, ballcaps, and hand-rolled racing forms talked to friends as the women, too, took in the iconic grounds and the racetrack's line of colorful silk jockey statues behind and off to the side.

Cass had donned Eden Hill's pink and orange silks in the large women's jockey quarters but left early to spend a few moments with Memphis before high energy took over. It was his first race, after all, and she wanted to make sure he settled.

As Cass stroked Memphis' neck, Harper Hill walked up and Memphis bent his head around her, his large, luminous eye softening further.

Harper had put Memphis into training after the colt had demonstrated a pronounced desire to run. Several years ago, her husband, detective and former Special Ops commander, JD Cole, had purchased the colt's dam at a mares-in-foal sale and once delivered, he'd presented Memphis to Harper as a wedding present. Despite his incredibly sensitive nature, the colt had the mind, the body, and the drive to run so Harper agreed to give him a try. Why not–she and JD owned two of Lexington's premier Thoroughbred farms, Harper's third generation breeding and racing farm matching JD's broodmare farm perfectly.

Memphis nudged Harper pretty hard then bobbed his head, ready to go. Cass laughed and Marshall shook his head. Jesus, not another Deacon, he thought. Marshall stared into the colt's eye, a practice that always unnerved him with this one. The colt had a mega brain and Marshall swore he could read the trainer's mind. And he'd never seen a colt love his racehorse schooling like this one, rapidly moving through his gate, mind-the-rider cues, get used to mud-in-your-face, and all the skills Marshall had seen other young horses take a whole season to master. And then there was this: Though a sweet colt most of the time, when on the track, Memphis was a competitive monster.

Marshall shook his head, thinking of their badass barnstormer, Deacon. Yeah, he thought, I got another one on my hands. And this one is wicked smart.

Cass, good humored as always, elbowed Marshall in the ribs as he finished saddling the colt. "Get a move on, old man," she laughed. "Just walk him off, and when I jump, throw me aboard."

And that's just what trainer did, then Marshall and Harper walked alongside the colt as Cass settled into the tiny racing saddle. They led the horse around the oval in front of the spectators who appraised the line-up of young horses and jockeys. Then the duo sent Memphis and Cass off down the walkway onto the track, the horses' aluminum plates sending a hollow *clop clop* back to the spectators.

Everyone made their way toward the stands and out into the wide expanse of the racetrack. Marshall and Harper followed and then they, too, took in the track—the green infield with the huge hedge spelling out "Keeneland," set by the large viewing monitor that allowed racegoers to watch the horses as they rounded into the backstretch and turned for home. The two hurried up the stairs to take their seats.

The horses loaded into the starting gate amid gate crew's calls of "three out," "two out," "one back," to the starter. In the starting gate, Cass twined fingers into Memphis' black mane. This was one of her favorite moments of the race, she could feel the colt's heart pounding and it matched her own. She heard a jock down the way call to the starter "Hold on!" while he got his colt under him, others chatted as soft whistles and rustling sounded inside the gates, and quiet laughter drifted her way. Horses' ears twitched at the banter, but Memphis' pointed straight up and forward. His whole being was focused on the track beyond the gate. Cass ran a hand along the top of his mane as other colts snorted and shuffled, picking up the mounting energy. Cass heard a few jocks murmur to their mounts and several of the gate crew settled in and gently held the racehorses' heads so they'd be looking down the track when the gate opened.

Cass glanced down the way to her friend Greg Monroe who was, as usual, aboard the favorite—a huge, dappled gray who generally hugged the rail like he owned it. Cass patted Memphis' coal black neck and touched her helmet, nodding. Among the jocks, Greg's track moniker was "Job" because he could wait forever for a hole to open. He rode clean, got the best mounts, and had befriended Cass early in her stakes race career.

She turned her attention ahead, relishing the smell of the horses, the dirt, the easy banter among jocks and gate crew. The day was warming, and she felt the tension through the line—horse and jockey poised for the start. "Easy boy," she murmured as the horses around her shifted back on their haunches waiting for the gate. The jockeys focused, the crowd rose to its feet, and in a moment, the doors clanged open.

Back in the day, back before Cass had made a name for herself, when she was a green, big-eyed, determined exercise rider, she'd ride anything. You can't win it sitting in the jocks' room, she'd thought. You gotta be in it to win it. She loved riding for the little guys, they were grateful and tossed her extra money—not like the big trainers who thought they were doing her a favor.

She cut her teeth on small tracks, riding gallops and breezes in the mornings, then races in the afternoons and evenings. Even then, the real jocks only came to the track to ride what "big horses" amounted to on the smaller circuit, or they'd drift in late in the morning to shoot the breeze with a trainer. But she kept her focus and learned her craft sitting in the best seat in the house—bent, balanced, and flat-backed, staring down the track between two pricked ears.

She'd hit the gym after morning workouts, built her strength, gained confidence, learned how to handle a sour, lugging-out colt or a tomboy filly.

Most of all, she learned not to take shit off the male jocks.

And yeah, they did dish it out. At first. "Let me by, Cass!" they'd yell coming up on her at the rail. If she had a horse with something left in the tank, she'd shout back, "Hell no! Not today, I got some horse here!" and if she had no horse, track courtesy dictated she let 'em through. She bantered with them on the straight-aways before the second turn and learned patience waiting for the hole to open. She learned to read the other jocks, too, learned who would go, who might wait, who wouldn't give up the rail to his grandma.

And she learned the horses—where the speed horses were, where the closers were. She earned the respect of her peers by riding the right way, the smart way.

And then she started winning.

And that changed everything.

There was Jimmy, he was a dirty rider, and they all knew it. But he'd been winning, so the bad acts stayed in his pocket until Cass beat him. Beat him routinely. Then the knives came out.

It was late summer on a small track in a one turn race. A ride she'd always remember.

Jimmy knew where the cameras were, the son-of-a-bitch, where they were on the turn, where the blind spots were, those two strides. He was going wide, too wide, and he'd come over on her right there, around the turn in the blind spot, not shaving her, he shut her off so she had to check her filly hard, and that was the race. But she caught him at the wire, stood up in the stirrups, whipped him good with her stick. And yes, she got called in by the stewards. "I was tryin' to kill the motherfucker!" she'd screamed and got 10 days for that one. Well, she'd thought at the time, it was worth it.

So she rode, and fought, earned the respect of the jocks at the smaller tracks, then made her way up.

Which was how she was sitting pretty on a big black colt that day in early spring when the gates clanged open. With her fingers in Memphis' mane, she went right with the colt as he made those first two huge jumps, got clear, got under himself, and then they were off to the races.

Around them hooves pounded, the wind flew past, jocks crouched above their mounts, balanced—heel, knee, shoulder—their horses' heads bobbing with each stride, the jocks stealing quick glances to read the field, then arms pumping with the motion of their colt as they picked their spots.

The intensity out of the gate surged through Cass as she felt Memphis coil under her—his energy radiated as she let go and merged with him, guiding him, their minds in sync. Beside them, riders rode still and steady, helping their horses get into an easy, comfortable stride. Jocks called to each other as Cass' hands moved in rhythm. Around them the dirt curled up, and the world outside disappeared.

The track was fast, and the speed horses were already going out. Cass heard their lungs heave like huge bellows, and she felt the earth tremble as over two dozen hooves pounded the track. She stared straight ahead, but out of the corner of her eye she spied Jose already at the rail, nearly standing up in the stirrups, knew he'd go out hard, use up his colt even though he was saving ground.

One jock was picking a fight with the jock just ahead. "Make room, you SOB, I'm gonna ride your ass to the ground, you don't!" To her right, Cleon's colt jumped left but Memphis was already clear, and the bay struggled to find himself as the field left him behind. Luis, as usual, was hanging back. He'd rate his colt, keep him out of trouble. She read the field but the truth was, for Cass, there was nobody else in the world but her and Memphis. She felt herself go deep within, felt the colt, melted into him until the distinction between them disappeared. They raced as one.

Everyone talked about winning, but for Cass, this union with the colt—that's why she rode.

And winning, of course, that wasn't bad either.

They all rounded into the backstretch, Memphis and Greg Monroe's big gray moving easily. Cass felt Memphis coil a bit and softened her hands, letting the colt get into the easy, fluid, effortless stride he had. You never knew how fast you were going on him because he seemed not to exert any effort at all. He just flowed over the track. She'd realized how easily the big colt moved breezing him in the morning. She'd think she was doing a quarter in 25, and Marshal would say, "Nope, 23 and change."

Memphis settled back and the two jocks got to cruising and chatting. Greg seemed waiting to make his move on Seido.

"Nice day for a race," Greg said, genial fellow that he was. They'd carved out a bit of track while in front, the speed horse was expending himself heading for the turn, four others behind him were rating, one horse was gliding up on the rail, and directly behind them, a two-pack struggled to find themselves.

"Yep, likin' it quite a bit," replied Cass. She grinned, feeling the colt beneath her, what he had in the tank—a lot.

Greg glanced behind then scoped out the field around and ahead. "Not too many gonna make the finish, doesn't appear," he commented.

"Nope," she said, noticing the gray was bunching up a little under Greg. She smiled. Greg knew what he was doing, adjusted a tad, and Seido settled back.

"Yeah, got no horse today," he said, glancing over at Cass. "He's the favorite, but he's gonna stop halfway into the stretch." Greg could feel his horse all the way through the race, after the first few jumps out of the gate when the field hit their stride.

He and Cass chatted a bit more under the warm sun, and Greg finally said, "Looks like you got some colt left." He nodded.

Cass smirked and shifted her weight, as the two horses switched leads into the turn. "Yeah, could be . . ." and Greg laughed.

She waited a few seconds more, then nodded her pal's way. "See ya, Greg" she called, and let Memphis pull away. As they rounded the turn, the colt extended his stride, and then, suddenly, they were into the head of the stretch. She looked three or four strides down the field, and as always, saw the race open before her. A light bay and a black horse in front looked to be tiring. She bet they'd lug wide. Beside them two horses were matching each other stride for stride. For the moment, the pack ran four abreast. Then the big bay came up on the left down at the rail. It all registered, but she felt the race more than thought about it.

Memphis cruised easily beneath her, but she could feel him winding up. They were into the middle of the stretch, coming up on the four horses, and she again softened her hands. "Not yet," she said, seeing Memphis' ear twitch back. She moved with the colt by experience turned to instinct, by patiently waiting, by letting go of thought or intention and taking what came to them. Memphis seemed to read her mind as much as her body and again eased back. Cass felt the hole ahead to her left open a split second before it did and sent Memphis a slight knuckle.

He was through the hole in a flash, the two horses fading back, the others drifting right. And then they were out, the bay and the black had drifted wide and now angled toward the center of the track with an eye on the rail, but Memphis had seen it and as the rail opened, the colt easily dropped into the slot. The speed horse had faded.

Cass threw Memphis the reins, turning him loose, silently bid the field "Adieu," and they were gone, the colt lengthening his stride further in the deep stretch, ears pinned, focused. Doing what he was born to do—running, running hard and uncontained in a body Cass felt capable of flight. The crowd roared, but Cass heard nothing. She and Memphis existed in a moment out of time, breathing together, Memphis stretching all the way out, his energy expanding, his power lifting them into a world completely their own.

2

He came under cover of darkness, just before dawn. Harper slept through his arrival, but JD was up, alerted by Wes' text. He was close. JD pulled on a t-shirt and shorts and was up in the kitchen pouring coffee when Wes softly knocked. They'd worked closely in Afghanistan on specially assigned missions, each one coming from their own branch, Wes from the Air Force, JD from the Army. Whatever radar they had going on, Command relished their success and tasked them with several more assignments before each one's service was completed.

They'd remained friends, or what passes for friendship in a combat zone.

JD opened the door and Wes held out a cooler. "Brought some elk." He was broad and strong, but not quite as tall as JD, and wore his shiny black hair in a knot at the back of his head. A slight Asian cast played round his deep gray eyes over a straight nose, his jaw had a square set to it, and he was oddly pale.

Maybe, thought JD, he was still getting over the injury that had sidelined him most of the winter. They'd stayed in touch. He took the cooler, nodded, and headed to the kitchen.

It was still dark, but JD saw the lights on in Grandpa's barn just over the Buck's Creek. John Henry would be feeding soon, then the horses would go out for the day.

"It's good to see you, it's been a while," said JD, his green eyes searching Wes' face for signs of strain. He saw none.

Wes nodded, hefted the duffel off his shoulder and unslung the big pack on his back. He let both fall to the floor, setting his battered old Justin on top of the duffel as the stair lights came on, and Harper descended.

"Hey Wes," she said, cinching her robe and heading around the granite island to the coffee maker. She poured a cup, shooting her husband a silent thank you. She was not coherent prior to caffeine.

Harper gazed out over the creek, wishing Memphis still lived in that barn, the ones housing their personal mounts. She tucked a strand of blond hair behind her ear. He was in the stallion barn, now, with the other racehorses. She sighed. For the foreseeable future, she guessed.

Harper stared at the barn a few more seconds, and then turned to her husband, glancing at Wes. She'd known he was coming, but she couldn't say she was pleased, and it likely showed. JD looked at her—those green eyes always saw everything. Wes was silent most of the time, which was ok with Harper, she wasn't the chatty type, but there was something about him that made her uneasy.

Maybe those eyes. Seemed like they'd seen a version of hell she didn't want any part of. And maybe like they were still looking at it.

She accepted JD's warm hand stroking her hair and closed her blue eyes for a moment, then opened them and smiled at Wes and sipped her coffee.

The silence among them lengthened. It wasn't uncomfortable. They were all shifting into the new dynamic, their routine when Wes showed up. JD and Wes had been through horrors together and had some weird silent communication going on, while JD and Harper had an even deeper connection, but different. The couple was more two sides of one coin, whereas the combat duo seemed the same coin struck twice.

Except that Wes colored outside the lines. He did so without remorse or consideration. If a thing needed doing, he did it, no matter how violent, how unlawful, how unconventional, how inexpedient, how prohibited. Which is why, Harper thought, he lived off the grid. No room for that in the world most everyone else inhabited.

"I'm gonna take Wes over to the station, have him look things over," JD said, not looking at Harper.

Harper took a beat. "Things," she knew, meant cases.

"And Al? What does he say about that?" Al, your boss, Harper thought, but didn't say. JD got away with murder at the precinct, mostly due to Al Walker begging him to come on in the first place. That, and JD's clearance record.

It then occurred to Harper that JD might have ulterior motives. Her husband might be trying to ease Wes into the precinct on a permanent basis.

Not, thought Harper, a wise idea.

JD shrugged, his large shoulders stretched tight against the faded t-shirt. It was the "What Al doesn't know won't hurt him," shrug.

Harper glanced at Wes whose face, per usual, was impassive. He's mystifying, she thought, not for the first time.

JD moved to Harper and put his arm around her shoulders, pulling her close. He loved how she smelled, had loved it since high school. "I got this," he whispered, his lips grazing her hair.

Harper relaxed, glanced again at Wes who hadn't moved. She took another sip of coffee. "Let's get you settled, Wes," she said, and set her cup down in the sink, glancing again at Grandpa's barn. She needed some Memphis time, and vowed she'd get it soon.

Wes picked up his large backpack, hat, and duffel then turned to the door.

"No way, Wes," Harper said, matter-of-factly. "You know the drill. If you're here, you're in a bedroom." She smiled at JD. "Not in the barn."

A few hours later, they were all sitting in the kitchen's breakfast nook eating waffles JD had prepared. Conversation was at a minimum, mostly because Wes took a good long while to settle in anywhere that wasn't out in the deep woods.

JD and Harper knew that and granted him the time he needed.

As Harper and JD were washing up, Harper's phone rang. She glanced at the number.

"It's Cass," she said, drying her hands and answering.

Harper's face went white. "Oh my God, Cass," she said, her left hand flying to her husband. She patted JD's shoulder, so he'd turn around. "Here, I'm putting JD on. Hold on, Cass, slow down!"

JD took the phone, staring into his wife's horrified blue eyes. "We'll be there in a minute, Cass." He stared at the floor a moment as Cass' hysterical voice continued, then said loudly into the phone, "Wes is here, I'll bring him. Do not leave!"

JD turned to his friend. Wes and Cass had an intermittent relationship, begun the first time Wes had visited. "Cass' best friend. She just found him dead in a broodmare stall over at Janero Farms. Maybe stomped to death, maybe something else. We're going," JD said, calling Al Walker to report it. "You're coming, she'll need you," he said to Wes.

They all grabbed their jackets on the way out, Harper nearly tripping over Kelso, their big golden, who'd planted himself just outside the door. The dog watched the trio race to JD's unmarked Ford F-150, jump in and speed off down the long, century-oak lined lane, ducking under the arched "Eden Hill" wrought iron sign. JD flipped on the lights and siren once they turned on Georgetown Road.

Twenty minutes later they turned right off Old Frankfort Pike at the tiny sign: "Janero Broodmares."

The flashing lights appeared just as they came through the iron gates and headed to the closest barn. Apparently other police vehicles had also just arrived on scene. Parking, the three jumped out, and JD ducked under the crime scene tape at the barn's entrance, followed by Harper and Wes.

JD strode forward, past stalls to the right and left loaded with broodmares in various stages of pregnancy or awaiting "in season" confirmation to breed after they'd foaled. The stalls had well-oiled wood half-doors topped with see-through openings covered in spaced wire so the mares could see out and the barn crew could see in. Each stall had clean, sweet-smelling wheat straw shavings, and a few of the mommas, after all the commotion, had decided laying down was a good option.

The barn smelled of warm horses, sweet green hay, and feed. Overhead lights were on and the doors at either end of the barn were open. The early sun drifted in as the barn crew arrived to turn the broodmares and babies out into their various pastures. Later in the season, when it warmed, the moms and babies would be out at night and in for feeding but there was still a chill in the night air.

JD signaled to an officer and nodded toward the crew at the far door. Turnout would have to wait.

The detective continued toward his boss and stood beside two officers as the agitated farm owner talked to Chief Al Walker. To the side, Cass sat against a stall door, her head in her hands, visibly shaking.

"Meat Wagon's on the way," whispered a thin young officer to JD, leaning his way.

JD glanced at Cass and glared at the kid.

"Sorry, boss," the officer said quietly and moved off.

"I have NO idea why Oliver was in here. Or how this could have happened. None!" yelled Janero's owner, Maxwell Sidarus. "What's the stallion manager doing lying dead in a broodmare stall! And that mare is the sweetest, easiest to handle, we have. She wouldn't hurt a fly, for God's sake."

Agitated, he shuffled his boot in the barn aisle dirt, shook his head, and ran a hand through his light brown hair. He glanced down the way and back to the Chief. "This makes no sense at all. Oliver is . . ." He paused, looking stricken. "Oliver was the most competent stallion manager I've had in years." He shook his head again and looked down at the dirt aisle. "This makes absolutely no sense at all," he murmured, then glanced up at Walker. "What in God's name was he doing over here anyway?" he again asked. Of no one.

Walker noted Wes and raised an eyebrow at JD, shook his head, and pointed to a stall down the way. JD walked that way as Harper sank down next to Cass. Walker gave Wes a nod—they'd met previously and if JD had brought him, the captain knew he might as well go with it. There wasn't much he could do about what JD did or did not do, he'd learned that the hard way. He put up with it because . . . well, because JD was JD.

Besides that, Wes was an asset, Walker had seen that right off. He was toying with the idea of offering him a position in the department.

Wes moved silently from broodmare stall to stall, his presence settling the wide-eyed moms-to-be until he arrived at Cass and crouched in front of her. He was quiet, just letting his presence steady her.

15

"I was bringing him breakfast," Cass sobbed, holding up a white bag to Wes, her eyes filled with tears, her brown hair hanging limply to her chin. She looked up as JD passed then back to Wes, her face both grateful and devastated. "After workouts, I came after workouts," she whispered and started crying again, setting the bag down in the dirt aisle, as if that explained anything. "From the track kitchen." She sobbed and stared at the dirt, not comprehending a thing.

Harper glanced at JD's back, her own eyes troubled, then watched Wes move to Cass' side and put his arm around her shoulders. The jockey fell into him, closing her eyes, the tears streaming. Harper laid a light hand along her arm, sighed, and sat as the investigative commotion around them continued.

JD arrived at the stall, pulled on gloves and booties then stepped into what was now the crime scene. The mare had been led out and was being examined. Officers in Tyvek suits moved quietly and efficiently, swabbing material from her hooves, bagging it, photographing, collecting evidence.

JD squatted and gazed at the scene, registering it as if his eyes were a camera. He'd learned to shut down his mind in Afghanistan and simply look. Look and record—that was the first and most important step. Without it, he'd long ago realized he'd lose impressions that time after time later proved significant. Beginning to his right, he did a visual grid, taking in every aspect of the stall, every dent in the wood walls, every stain, every depth shift in the shavings. He made a circuit and came back to where he'd started.

Obviously, Oliver had entered here, thought JD, standing and moving to the stall door, then slightly to the left where the body lay. He bent and studied some churned shavings, then stood and looked to the far corner of the double-sized foaling stall where the

16

mare had stood. The shavings looked normal, the mare hadn't been agitated.

JD glanced to the right and walked a few steps, turned to the door. Odd, he thought, it looked like Oliver had gone to the left, but there were very slight indications of something else, or perhaps someone else. The shavings were barely disturbed but JD noted that they did not indicate a horse had been present. There was also a rather faint straight line toward the body though someone had tried to cover it up. JD followed the path as it led from the stall door, behind him, across the stall entrance, to the body.

Definitely two people. He filed that away and shifted back to Oliver laying on his back, his head cocked to the side. Outside the stall, the farm manager continued to protest. JD heard Walker's subdued voice intermittently attempt to insert some calm. Around them, several mares shifted in their stalls, picking up the tension.

JD went to Oliver's body. He'd known the man slightly, run into him in passing. But having seen his own men, and other soldiers he knew, blown open on Afghanistan battlefields or while on missions, he'd gotten good at switching the human off. He studied Oliver's body dispassionately, saw the slight swelling on his head, but didn't touch or turn him, not wanting the scene disturbed. He looked at the rest of the body. Had the mare done damage, there would be impressions on the man's ribs and hip where bruises and broken bones would likely present beneath the clothing. It didn't appear to JD that the mare had stomped Oliver, but cause of death would be determined later.

JD stood quickly, walked to the stall where the techs were working on the pregnant mare. "Get blood samples, I want to know exactly what's in her bloodstream." Better to cover all the bases.

The white-clad techs nodded. "Already on it," said one, putting a bagged sample into his collection kit.

JD paused there for a moment, crossed his arms, and surveyed the barn's interior. Sidarus' question was a good one—what was the stallion manager doing in the broodmare barn, presumably at night? He slowly did a visual search, raising his eyes to take in the perimeter at height. Completing the circuit confirmed his guess— the broodmare barn had no cameras. JD glanced toward the breakroom.

"And get samples from the coffee." The night worker, on a 7 p.m. to 7 a.m. shift, had been found slumped over a folding table, sound asleep, coffee cup set to the side. She'd already given blood samples and a preliminary statement, but JD wasn't about to overlook a potential drug source. She'd been taken to the hospital to be checked out prior to JD's arrival.

The detective walked back up the dirt aisle, stopping at Cass, Wes, and Harper. He squatted before the jockey, his forearms resting on his thighs. He studied her a moment. Barely five three, Cass was made of muscle, tough as nails inside and out. But today, her deep-set brown eyes were pools of darkness as she gazed at JD, and her chin trembled.

"Cass," JD said gently, "any reason you know of Oliver would be in the broodmare barn?"

The jockey shook her head, looking at the ground. "No, he texted me he'd be over here is all," she said quietly. Then, looking up at JD, "So I came."

"Anything going on in Oliver's life we should know about?" JD continued. He glanced back toward the stall. "Anything that might cause this?"

The jockey stared at the far stall blankly, then gathered herself, glancing at Wes. She turned back to JD, struggled to speak. "Isabelle dumped him," she said finally, leaning on Wes'

18

shoulder. She closed her eyes but after a moment looked at JD. "His girlfriend. They've been rocky for a while." Cass turned her troubled eyes to Harper. "She's a supervisor, works over at the lab."

Harper looked toward JD and their eyes met. The "lab" ran the racehorse samples post-race, checking for banned substances. "I can head over there tomorrow if it would help," she said to him. "I met Isabelle when she worked with Cooley."

Cooley Edison had been Harper's vet before Tim Bradford had come on board. Harper's frown deepened, recalling Edison's bad deeds at Eden Hill a few years ago. Very bad deeds, she recalled, shaking her head. He was serving a hefty term in the slammer at the moment.

JD nodded. Isabelle had not kept very good company. Having Harper along was a good idea, that would help. She could be icy when needed or thaw just about anyone if that was the call.

The detective patted Cass' shoulder and stood. He'd definitely talk to Isabelle, he thought, as he headed back to the stall and Oliver's body. JD knelt beside the dead man, silently asking the body to give up its secrets.

Wes showed up at the stall as JD exited and they both wandered past Al Walker, who was walking with Sidarus toward the far barn exit. Sidarus hurried past the offending stall and Walker jogged a few steps to catch up.

"Stomped," said Wes as the two reached Harper. "Probably. So they say," and JD nodded. The detective held out a hand to his wife and she rose, patting Cass' hair gently. Wes bent and caressed the jockey's wet cheek, holding her gaze a moment. She nodded and looked up at Harper, sadness and resignation in her eyes.

"Thanks, Harper," she whispered and picked up the bag with Oliver's cold breakfast, folding and unfolding the paper top.

Wes stood and looked at JD, his hands in his pockets. A silent communication drifted between them. Wes would stay with Cass, catch up with JD later.

"They see only the obvious," JD said to his wife, as he and Harper headed out to the truck. He'd keep his observations—and his suspicions—to himself for now.

Stomped is what it looked like, given the mare and the victim were in the same stall. But neither of them put much stock in appearances.

3

E arly the next morning, Harper headed to the stallion barn. Memphis wasn't training and Marshall had given her the ok to saddle him up. She had a mind to head over to Hawk Ridge and check on the mares and babies before heading over to the lab. She supposed she needed some normalcy on the mares' side after what she'd seen at Janero.

So it was just as dawn was breaking, that Harper headed into the racing barn, nodding to the grooms and a few exercise riders getting the mounts padded, saddled, and bridled for the workout set conducted under Marshall's watchful eye.

"Hey Sugar," she said, stopping at a finely made chestnut who'd been doing a great job since his recovery a few years ago from a condylar fracture. The colt nodded in his stall as Marcie touched her helmet, acknowledging Harper. Usually, she rode their breakout filly, Meadow, but today she'd be up on a leggy colt who'd held up pretty darned well over the last few seasons— a testament to Marshall, their vet Tim Bradford, and the stallion manager, Lucas, who Harper silently referred to as "The Refrigerator," since that's how the South African was built.

It took a village, that's for sure. And luck.

And then there was Deacon, their big black menace who had thrilled all of Lexington for the past several years. An audacious, mean-as-shit, mega-bodied stallion who was smart and more competitive than the whole barn put together, Deacon did whatever the hell he wanted to whenever he wished. They'd all realized a long time ago that was the only way to treat His Royalty. He liked only two people in the world, his groom, old John Henry, and Harper.

21

As she approached, he gazed down at her with his great amber eyes, arched his neck, and then ever-so-slowly lowered it to lay his muzzle in Harper's open palm.

"My, my, my, I do think he's smitten," said Lucas good naturedly, passing behind her with the feed cart. "How do you do that?" he laughed. Lucas often had to use a pitchfork to get feed into Deacon's trough. He'd already fed the stallion that morning— Deacon must be fed first or there would be hell to pay.

Lucas shook his head and chuckled, watching Deacon. "Sweetness and light, sure enough," he said grinning. Deacon was known to savage other horses in the stretch. No one passed him. Ever.

Harper turned to the stallion manager, her eyes alive with delight. "Hey, he paid for the updated security system and a ton of other stuff around here." She turned back to Deacon. "Didn't you, boy?" she said. "And pretty soon you're gonna make babies that'll do just the same." She placed a soft kiss on Deacon's nose and he turned to his hay.

She went on past the very good-natured Fleet Light. "Mr. Ballast," Lucas called him, meaning he offset Deacon's badass attitude. Next to him, Harper saw her sweet colt Memphis, with his head out of the stall, looking her way.

"I'm coming, I'm coming," she said, lifting the heavy leather halter at his stall, running her thumb over his etched brass nameplate. She entered the black colt's stall carrying the halter and stud lead but took a moment to first lay her hands gently on his withers, closing her eyes and feeling the warmth of his big body, sensing the pulse of energy gently moving beneath her fingers. She listened with her hands and moved her fingers and palms up along his hindquarters, massaging. The colt stretched out his neck, loving the myofascial release and the connection with Harper. He took a deep breath as Harper did, too, and they both settled in for a few quiet moments until she opened her eyes and slipped on the halter, leading him out of the stall and out into the newly rising sun.

Her phone rang.

Harper sighed, looking at the caller ID. JD. She glanced at Memphis, then answered the phone.

"Up to the house," JD said. "We need to get to the lab, talk to Isabelle."

Of course we do, she thought, hanging up. Of course, and it would have to be now. She stroked Memphis' neck, promising him that ride just as soon as she returned.

She handed Memphis over to Lucas and headed up to the house.

The Equine Analytical Testing lab was where all Kentucky run races processed blood and urine samples pre- and post-race to check for violations. Its impressive glass-paned entranceway spoke to the central role the work within played in horse racing. Results from drug tests processed there determined which horse would race, which wouldn't, which horse would be declared the official winner of a race, what trainer would be nabbed and fined, maybe worse, and which trainers skated.

And there were those few, as in any field where a lot of money is involved, who cheated. No matter how many precautions were taken, how many checks, rules, laws, tests, no matter how earnest the oversight was, some people were able to circumvent the testing lab's efforts, the horse race governing bodies' oversight, and the laws put in place to make sure the playing field was level.

Cheaters still cheated and horses were still dying.

Once at the lab, JD flashed his badge and he and Harper were led to an office where Isabelle was waiting. No one questioned why Harper was there or why Isabelle needed to be interviewed. They'd all heard about Oliver. It was a small town when it came to the racing world, so the powers that be had probably put two and two together.

JD thought about his bodycam. Should he switch it on, as he always did? Well, he thought, as he almost always did. Or sometimes did.

Harper gazed his way, her look saying clearly "get in the game." JD flicked the body cam on.

Isabelle stood behind a desk, her white coat draped over the chair back. She was on the shorter side, a bit overweight and had wavy brown hair that hung to her shoulders. Looked like it hadn't been washed in a while. And no make-up to speak of. But there was a haughtiness to her. The narrowed, dismissive look she gave them flashed quickly then faded but JD had seen it.

Interesting, he thought.

The detective gestured toward a trio of chairs in front of the desk, Isabelle strode forward, and they all sat.

"You heard about Oliver," JD began, and Isabelle nodded then looked away. There wasn't a window and her eyes flitted around the room, settling finally on Harper and JD.

"Yeah, I heard," she said roughly, readjusting herself in the chair. Her greasy hair shown under the fluorescent lights. "What do you want with me? I didn't do it."

There was that look again. Challenging.

JD nodded, thinking.

"In fact, I'm not really sure what you're doing here," Isabelle said, picking at a cuticle. "We broke up a while ago."

"Right," said Harper, "that's why we're here. We wondered what happened. It just might be helpful to the investigation."

"You never know," JD chimed in, running a hand through his hair, getting exasperated by the cold shoulder. "He could have been despondent. Wandered into the stall and set off the mare. Any number of things might have occurred, we just don't know at this point."

Harper and JD waited in silence, a trick they'd perfected.

Isabelle looked from one to the other, reached back, plucked a bottle of water from the desk and unscrewed the cap, studying it. She took a drink.

"Well, I can tell you he didn't take it too good," she said, picking at a stain on her dress and refusing to look up. "So maybe you got something there," she murmured.

The pair waited her out, quietly, nodding thoughtfully. Encouraging her to continue.

Isabelle set down the water, tugged at her skirt, picked a strand of hair and began examining it for split ends.

JD and Harper didn't look at each other, their gaze trained Isabelle's way. Non-cooperation wasn't going to fly. They'd wait. They were used to waiting.

The door opened and Isabelle's boss, the lab's director, poked his bald head in, irritated. "Done?" he said, leaning into the room. "She's got work."

JD turned. "Nope. Not yet. We'll send her out."

Isabelle had startled at her boss' voice, being occupied by her greasy split ends, but when he closed the door, a slight smile worked across her mouth though she didn't look up.

"Why don't you tell us exactly what you do here?" JD said. Maybe that was the angle that would crack open something he could use.

Isabelle dropped the hair strand, shook her head in her best ingenue imitation, and flipped it behind her shoulder. She smoothed the rolls on her stomach straining against the dress she wore.

"I don't see how that's relevant," she said.

25

"Humor me," JD said, his green eyes steely.

Isabelle got up and walked around the desk, sat down, moved a pen off some papers, shuffled them around, picking up one then another. Finally, she handed a sheet over the table but far enough away that JD had to get up to retrieve it.

JD looked it over then handed it to Harper.

Test results for a stakes race. The detective looked over the results, noting findings on the post-race winning four-year-old and the "specials"—two horses in the race randomly selected. The blood and urine samples were tested for two types of infractions, levels in excess of substances normally present in horses, such as cobalt and CO_2, and a second group which were substances banned altogether, such as known performance enhancing drugs. JD noted the mare and other horses had come back clean.

"I manage a section of the lab. I also run the tests and do the paperwork when there's a need," Isabelle said flatly. Then: "You know, little vials of blood and urine?" She held her fingers apart to mimic a test tube length, smirking at them. "I play with those." The smirk again.

JD and Harper sat quietly, composed. Not reacting to her.

"And when is there a need?" said JD.

Isabelle shrugged. "Happens. I step in. Somebody's out sick, big races, vacations, sick kids. And times when lot of out-of-competition stuff comes through."

"So it happens pretty often," said JD. It wasn't a question.

Isabelle paused, then shrugged. "Depends on what you mean by 'pretty often.'" Again, the challenging stare. She went on, "Anyway, then it all gets shipped over to the Racing Commission. What they do with 'em is their business." She fiddled with her papers.

JD and Harper had an in-depth understanding of testing, but JD wanted to hear Isabelle talk about it. He wanted to watch her as she did.

Isabelle was acting squirrely. Something about her was off.

"You guys don't need me to give you a lecture," she said finally, dismissively. "And I got work to do." She rose, heading for the door.

"Humor me," JD said again. "Or we can do this at the station." Hardball it is, his look conveyed. Beside him, Harper squinted at Isabelle. JD knew she'd picked up something, too. They'd talk about just what later.

"Fine," Isabelle said, returning to the desk and sitting in the power position behind it. "We test for illegal drugs, therapeutic meds, PEDs, stimulants, depressants, pain killers, tranqs, anabolic steroids . . . things like that." She went through the list, sounding bored. "You do know the drill," she finished, irritated with both of them.

JD nodded. They did.

"So how much testing did you discuss with Oliver about Janero's runners?" JD said. Might as well put it out there, see what happened.

He knew split samples were taken when race day tests were done. If a test came back positive, the trainer could agree to run it again using the split. The Racing Commission and the Lab did great work, given all the pressures and the many ways cheaters always seemed to find new ways to get around the rules. JD and Harper both knew folks at the Commission and the Lab and found them to be dedicated horse people, smart, hard-working, committed, and focused on closing every loophole they found while working hard to find the next latest way to boost the odds of winning in illegal ways.

But someone on the inside, it did happen. Not often, but it happened. Throw enough money in front of people's feet and somebody's bound to bend over and pick it up.

Hence JD's question.

Isabelle blanched.

Ah, JD thought. That's the soft spot.

"I never discussed any test results with Oliver," she replied unsteadily, trying to get herself together. "Never. I wasn't even supposed to have a relationship with him." She paused, appearing confused as if she'd said too much. Then her haughtiness reappeared. "I'm in charge of a lot around here. And Oliver, to tell you the truth, was not that interesting." She resettled herself. "So I called it off. End of story. And I never said a word about anything." She drew herself up and planted her elbows on the table, her palms together. "I've done nothing wrong," she said one too many times, bobbing her fingers at JD for emphasis. "Talk to my boss, he'll tell you the same thing."

JD smiled. Isabelle frowned. It seemed she realized she'd messed up.

Harper put a hand on JD's arm. "Ready?" she said. She understood. They'd gotten what they came for. She rose.

JD sat a moment, letting Isabelle sweat. Then he rose slowly.

"Thanks, Isabelle," he said, "I think we got what we need."

And they left, leaving Isabelle sitting immobilized, staring at their disappearing backs.

4

The next morning, Harper and Marshall arrived at Keeneland a few races before the one they'd come to see. Their star filly, Meadow, was entered in a sprint race due to go off pretty soon, with Cass aboard. Meadow was on the smaller side, but fierce and smart. She'd been the surprise of last season, and now in her three-year-old year Marshall and Harper were anxious to see if the rest of the field had caught up with her. It sometimes happened that way, but they sure hoped not. Meadow was one of the only fillies they had with a chance at the big time.

The pair settled into their Keeneland green folding seats and Harper pulled out her binoculars. There was a race to go off in a few moments, another sprint, so the starting gate was back around the second turn on the backstretch. The field would come around and finish in front of the spectators.

The large screen in front of them showed the starting gate as the last filly was loaded in and in moments, the doors flew open and six fillies leapt out together. They surged forward, each vying for the lead, and as they rounded the turn for home, two fillies extended their stride as their jockeys began urging them forward.

As they were nearing the wire, suddenly, near the back of the pack, a bay filly stumbled and went down. She didn't get up, though she struggled mightily to rise. Her rider had jumped clear and raced back to help her, trying to keep her down until the vet arrived, as around them the lights and sirens sounded, raising the alarm.

"That doesn't look good," Harper murmured, lifting the glasses again. The filly was still down, struggling less but still attempting to get up as was her instinct.

Marshall shook his head. "And so close to home."

The ambulance arrived and the vet jumped out, quickly sedating the filly.

Harper put her glasses down. She didn't want to see the rest. She picked up her phone and typed in "DRF" then checked the daily racing form for the trainer of the downed horse. She was pretty sure, given the silks, but double checked to make sure.

"That's a Janero filly," she said quietly, and Marshall's head whipped around to peer at her phone, his shaggy salt and pepper hair straggling out from beneath his black Stetson.

"Aw, jeez," he said, taking off his hat. "That's tough." He knew all too well how hard a horse going down ate at a trainer. He'd been there. Anytime his horses were injured, ill, off their feed, even in foul temper, it got him right in the heart. They were as much his family as his wife Surrey and Harper were. He'd been that way his whole career, and everyone around him had finally gotten used to the darkness that came over him when his horses were off. He was one of the best in the game, and did it the right way, no cheating.

It had never occurred to him, in fact. Harper glanced at Marshall, concern and worry written all over his face. She patted his arm.

She turned her attention to the track, much as she wished not to. The vet got the filly up so he could attend to her, Harper saw, grateful at least for that. She hoped for the best as the vet wrapped much of her hind limb in a pad, splinted it, and taped it all securely in place. The ambulance was positioned as close as possible to her so she wouldn't have far to walk, and the ramp lowered to as level as possible. She was attended by techs and the vet and carefully loaded into the ambulance, then whisked away for radiographs and, hopefully, a recovery.

But from what Harper saw, she didn't like the odds. The length of time the filly was down, along with the height and structuring of the splint she saw didn't bode well at all for the filly.

Marshall stood, ran a hand over his face, a face full of concern, then caught Harper's attention. He frowned and crooked a thumb toward the track by way of excusing himself, then he hoofed it down to saddle up Meadow, give Cass last instructions, and throw her aboard.

Harper sighed and pocketed her phone. The racing game could make your spirits soar or break your heart. On any given day, it could be either one. She gazed out on the track a moment, hoping for the best for the young filly.

Cass and Meadow entered the track, picked up their pony horse and made their way to the starting gate with the other five fillies in the race. Meadow pranced, her petite frame belying the competitive spirit she had and her amazingly fast turn of foot.

Harper looked around. Not many folks in the stands, the crowd was quite sparce, in fact. She guessed not a lot of racegoers were up for a chilly April race—likely, as the season got underway in earnest the stands would fill.

She picked up her coffee as Marshall arrived back to watch with her. She smiled at him, took a sip as the final filly was loaded in and the gates shot open. Meadow came out blazing as usual, Cass flat-backed over her. The filly needed no urging to take the lead, that was her favorite position, and she often went wire to wire, winning consistently with nice fractions however many furlongs she raced. Versatile, smart, fast, fierce. It was a great winning formula.

And just like that, they were into the middle of the stretch and Meadow's bay head was stretched out, ears pinned, eyes focused. Cass glanced behind to see who was coming up on them. There were two, one on the rail, one just off to the right. Both fillies were closing on Meadow fast, so Cass pumped her arms and raised her stick. She never used it, though, it made Meadow furious. But it was sometimes useful to let her see it, just as a reminder.

It worked. The filly shot forward as the trio entered the deep stretch and Marshall whistled.

"Oh boy!" he cried. "Look at those feet! Look at that! They're a blur!" He jumped up, excited as he always was when one of his youngsters did their thing in spades.

Harper rose, too, grinning, mostly at Marshall.

She raised her cup as Meadow and Cass crossed the finish line. In front of everyone, as usual.

This was one of those days when your spirits soar, she thought, taking Marshall's arm and pulling him down for a peck on the cheek.

At least for them, she thought. Maybe not for Janero.

The pair drove home, Harper at the wheel. She'd head to the office to attend to Eden Hill and Hawk Ridge business before dressing for the permanently disabled jockey fundraiser she and JD would attend that night. She'd been letting work pile up and today was the day she'd set aside to plow through, so she imagined she'd be there the rest of the day.

She and Marshall chatted as they drove under the arched wrought iron Eden Hill sign and headed up the long, curving drive, driving past the house, around Grandpa's barn, and on to the training track, where she dropped off Marshall. Then she headed down the hill to Eden Hill's offices.

Once inside, she hurried past the shiny granite-topped partition separating visitors from Pepper, their majordomo, who never missed a beat running the behind-the-scenes show at two farms. She managed calls in, calls out, stallion inquiries, syndicate inquiries, Hawk Ridge inquiries. There wasn't anything or anyone who didn't funnel through Pepper before arriving at any other aspect of Eden Hill or Hawk Ridge.

Harper and the farms would be lost without her.

And at the moment, as was usually the case, she was holding up a fistful of little yellow callback messages and waving them at Harper.

"Hey, Pepper," Harper said, trying to ignore the fist, sailing by Pepper and into her office, shutting the door behind her.

Before Harper had settled into her chair, the door opened and Pepper stood there grinning.

"As if that ever worked," she said, her short, dark bob gracing her jawline.

"Ha," Harper said.

"Ha, ha," Pepper said, walking in and plunking down a stack of messages. "I'll be back with a sandwich."

Harper looked at her watch. "It's late, I lost track."

Pepper left, glancing back over her shoulder. "You're starving, right?"

Harper smiled at her back. "Well, yeah. Kinda."

Harper sat, flipped through the yellow notes. Then she returned calls, signed checks, looked over vet reports and booked stallion covers for Eden Hill, then mares-in-foal reports from Hawk Ridge, invoices for feed, wheat straw bedding, notes from staff about hayfield plantings, and endless other reports and invoices that daily crossed her desk.

I need to hire a farm manager, she thought, for the umpteenth time. She really did need to do that.

And . . . she didn't.

After her farm manager had been killed back when her sister had died, Harper had taken over the essential duties he'd covered. She'd found she enjoyed it. Surprisingly, she was good with numbers. Well, "for an artist" JD had had said, teasing her. But she'd built solid relationships with other farms, knew how to support the breeding and racing side of the game, and since her marriage to JD, had handled the broodmares with equal devotion. But more than anything, she liked what she did.

She smiled. She'd send some feelers out about a farm manager. But just for today. . . she munched the smoked turkey and cheese sandwich Pepper brought in, sipped her Pepsi, and returned a ton of calls.

Quite late in the day, she got home, ran upstairs, showered, and glanced at her watch. JD better get back or they'd be late.

Again.

The man had no sense of time. He'd get caught up in an interview, a blood spatter report, or a bull session with Al Walker. Who knows when he'd head home.

Harper was finished dressing when she heard the front door slam and JD take the steps two at a time, followed by the thumps of Kelso trailing JD up the stairs.

"Hey," he said, brushing his lips against her hair and heading into the bathroom. "I'll be ready, no worries." He drifted through the bedroom as Harper tucked a strand of hair behind her ear and glared at the bathroom door.

Twenty minutes later, they were sailing down Georgetown Road, Harper in a sleek, light blue dress that matched her eyes, JD in a subdued deep charcoal suit.

Everyone would be at the fundraiser. All the major farm owners, major stake holders in jockey welfare, farm management employees, iconic jockeys, and even Cass. She'd roped Wes into escorting her, and they'd be seated at the same table, along with their vet, Tim Bradford, and of course Marshall and his wife

Surrey. There'd be one more to make eight, but Harper wasn't sure who they had seated with them.

Unlike most of the auctions and stallion season donating or buying fundraisers, this was a dinner. Held in the grand ballroom of a local hotel, it was a thousand-buck-a-plate dinner, which the organizers hoped would work wonders for jockeys with severe brain and physical injuries. Harper and JD had paid for their table and worked with the organizers but had begged off public duties at the dinner itself.

They parked and entered the hotel, searched out the ballroom, and spied their table just off the dais and to the right, a few rows back, as she'd requested. Marshall and Surrey were already seated, and both looked uncomfortable in the fancy setting, as she expected.

Harper and JD made their way under elaborate crystal chandeliers, through the finely dressed crowd, stopping to talk with friends and acquaintances. The tables were draped with soft, hunter green clothes, glittering cut glass goblets, and shining silverware, and each table was graced with flower arrangements and name cards. There was a silent auction display at the back of the ballroom, and Harper knew that after dinner, the ballroom panels would slide back to reveal a large dance floor and band. But that all came later.

The pair arrived at their table just as Wes and Cass were seating themselves, Cass picking up a conversation with Marshall about Meadow's race and what was up next for the filly. Wes sat still as stone as Surrey made a valiant effort to engage him in small talk. She knew Wes, so Harper had no idea why she bothered.

"Where's Tim?" JD asked. Marshall and Cass shook their heads.

Three empty seats. He checked his phone. It was unlike their vet to be late.

Everyone settled in and quieted when the chairman rose and picked up his mic. He spoke to the crowd, thanking them, filling everyone in on the evening's events, and then the waiters began circulating with water, wine, and the first course, a chilled cucumber soup.

Tim and his date, a willowy dark-haired vet tech named Ella, arrived and were seated.

"Sorry," said Tim, "I had some stuff. Over at Janero."

JD's radar went up, and so did Harper's. The table quieted and all eyes turned to Bradford.

"On the racehorse side. Their vet's been out of town so I'm covering," he murmured quietly as around them, table chatter picked up as the chair reseated himself and dinner commenced.

"I had to put a two-year-old down. Anemia, couldn't save him. It just blew up on us."

JD turned to Harper, who appeared as concerned as he was. Anemia. That was unheard of in a young horse. And so severe he was euthanized?

Tim shook out his napkin and smoothed it on his lap, not looking at anyone. Clearly, he was upset. That was also odd. Tim had seen the worse sorts of injuries and maladies. As a racehorse vet you either got used to that or you got out.

"What else," Wes said. Tim's discomfort was apparent to everyone.

Ella reached over and laid a hand on Tim's arm.

"Another horse had severe tendon issues, one dropped dead in training—the necropsy said heart attack. And they lost a filly on the track today, a tibial fracture, shattered nearly."

Harper and Marshall said at once: "As they rounded for home."

"We were there," Harper said.

36

Cass asked who the filly was. On hearing the news from Tim, she said, "I know that filly." She looked at Tim, angry. "Did you see her?"

Tim shook his head. Cass looked from Marshall to Harper.

"They were pretty much right in front of us, so yeah, we saw her go down, but not up close and personal, why?" Marshall said.

Cass sipped her wine. Then she took a gulp. "That filly looked more like Justify than a two-year-old girl. Her body was massive. Massive. Unworldly big." She held up her wine glass, looking for a waiter.

"It's disgusting," she said.

They all knew what Cass was suggesting. The filly had been juiced to build that much muscle.

Harper looked at Tim. "Is that like half their racing barn? All three-year-olds?"

"Two and three-year-olds," Tim said.

Marshall jumped in. "The Racing Commission is on it, right?"

Tim nodded. "They've already been out, I was told. Before today's track incident. Did out-of-competition testing on all the horses, including that filly. Took blood and urine." He paused. "I'm waiting on news from friends on that. And on the necropsy on the horse I put down today. I'll see what they say about the filly."

The mood at the table had plummeted and no one had touched their soup.

JD and Harper looked at each other.

"So the stallion manager is killed and now how many racehorses are dead or in jeopardy?" Harper said.

Wes chimed in, his gray eyes pools of intensity. "We'll head over there in the morning." He looked at JD.

"We'll get some answers," JD said.

"One way or another," Wes said.

5

JD and Wes headed out early the next morning. Wes wanted to take his truck, JD insisted on his unmarked F-150 and they compromised by stopping by the police station for a marked cruiser. It made a point.

The long drive up Janero's entranceway opened out to the left on a large expanse of gently sloping pasture ending in a huge mansion set back on top of the rise—Maxwell Sidarus' place of residence. Two wings, columns, white-washed brick all said "Old Money" loud and clear.

The pair zipped past and headed up toward the racing barns and training tracks, parked in front of A Barn, noted the Janero truck and a few others parked in front of the deep red and slate gray barn. Inside was a short walkway lined by photos of the farm's previous and very successful occupants—horses and jockeys in winner's circles and at Keeneland's sales barn with hefty sales figures noted above the hip number. The photos were stacked one on top of the other from shoulder height on up. On both sides. An impressive array sending a very clear message.

They heard the trainer talking to an exercise rider just to their left down the barn aisle graced on either side with quite a few open stalls housing colts on the training track, and quite a few with youngsters sticking their heads over the Dutch half doors to see what was up with Wes and JD. Most munched contentedly on mouthfuls of green hay.

JD knew of Janero's trainer, but they'd never formally met. He strode up, pulling his ID out with the left hand and holding his right out for a handshake. Might as well start off friendly.

Wes lurked behind, a quiet and lethal presence.

"Gus Pinard?" JD said, his hand lingering in the April chill.

The trainer turned, surprise registering on his long, pock-marked face. Not much of a jaw there, JD noted, and the eyes were hooded.

"Yeah?" he said with a little bit of "What the fuck do you want?" thrown in.

Wes stood beside JD as the three men squared up.

Behind Pinard, the young exercise rider picked up the drift, patted his helmet with his stick, swiveled his colt around and headed for the exit. Around them, the stalled colts found more interesting things to do in the interiors.

"Here to ask you a few questions about the issues you've had lately."

Pinard ignored them, stuck his clipboard under his arm, pulled out his phone and hit speed dial. He turned his back on the pair and mumbled something about the cops being there.

Wes smiled at that. It wasn't a pretty smile.

Pinard turned back around. "I got chores. Heading up to the track. You can talk to Max when he gets here." And he left.

JD let him go, no use chasing after somebody who wasn't about to talk to them anyway.

They waited in silence amid soft chewing sounds, the curious, liquid eyes of bays and grays peering at them, and the smell of sweet alfalfa and orchard grass mixed with dirt.

A couple of minutes later, they heard a car door slam and in walked Sidarus, his full head of wavy brown hair resting on his shoulders, his hands stuck in his black down vest.

He was shorter than both JD and Wes, but walked right up to them looking curious, worried, and forthright. "Any progress on Oliver?" he said.

Not why are you here, in my racing barn. Sidarus was making a point that the murder investigation was stalled.

Dead in the water, more like, thought JD, reading Sidarus' message.

"I heard the Racing Commission was here and did out-of-competition testing on all the horses." JD looked around. This was one barn of three. So they'd lost some, but they were still very much in business on the racing side. Still, the Commission didn't just drop in for no reason.

The murder and whatever was going on at the racing barns had to be connected.

Sidarus scowled. "Yeah, somebody called the tip line. Which is obviously ridiculous."

That was interesting. He filed that away, he'd find out who later. JD had not called anyone at the Commission yet for the test findings, but he would. Two things to check on.

Wes took a step toward Sidarus and Janero's owner stepped back.

The exercise riders with their charges were dribbling back into the barn after their workouts. The colts walked easily, swinging loosely from their shoulder, their heads keeping rhythm with their bodies. Grooms appeared and they got the horses untacked, then they were escorted outside to get sprayed and hot walked.

The stalled horses looked on, hoping to get somebody to take them out for a little new grass.

JD watched it all, well-used to the routine, enjoying the fit, sleek, muscled out bodies. Thinking about what Cass had mentioned at the jockey dinner, he checked out their body structure and mass, looking for any abnormalities that might stand out. He didn't see anything alarming so turned back to Sidarus.

"Why do you think someone reported you?" he asked without accusation. Just curious, his tone said.

Sidarus threw up his hands. "Beats the heck outta me!" He shook his head, looking at the dirt aisle. He looked up. "What business is it of yours, anyhow?" Now his tone was combative.

JD noted that, too. One minute, frustrated—the falsely accused farm owner—and in the next, in-your-face aggressiveness.

Wes chuckled and took another step toward Sidarus.

"Who is this guy?" Sidarus said glaring at JD. "He's no cop. Saw him at the barn, too, when Oliver died." He looked at Wes, then seeing his eyes, turned quickly away, his cheeks suddenly flushed.

JD folded his hands together nicely, let Sidarus see how congenial a policeman he could be, then tapped his Sig Sauer, holstered beneath his jacket, as if to say "It's holstered now. But that can change." He liked the P226, had used it in the service. Its extended barrel and 15 rounds were accurate and deadly, just like he liked his weapons.

Sidarus followed his hand, got the message. Still, his mood was deteriorating, from challenging to foul. "Get off my property. I'm calling my lawyer." And he pulled out his phone.

Wes took one more step, grabbed Sidarus' fancy black, down-filled vest and powered him back to the stall where he slammed him into it, holding him off the ground with one hand.

Sidarus looked terrified.

Wes let him think about that for a moment, then let loose and Sidarus slid down the stall but kept his dignity and didn't fall down.

JD tried not to smile.

Behind him, a big black colt stuck his muzzle in Sidarus' hair and began pulling out strands.

Two-year olds. The babies did like to play.

Sidarus flicked the colt's muzzle and the young horse more or less shrugged, not impressed with the boss, and went back to his haynet.

"Max," JD began, "I'm trying to get to the bottom of Oliver's murder. Why it happened and who did it. The mare in that stall, she had nothing in her system to indicate she had anything to do with it. And, as you know, Oliver's was loaded with opioids. He overdosed. Suicide? Miscalculation? Or someone else administered the drug?"

Sidarus nodded, took a nervous glance at Wes. "Yeah, but you said murder. You're looking for who murdered him. Where'd that come from?"

JD remained impassive, but his green eyes narrowed. "Oliver's head sustained blunt-force trauma. Somebody knocked him out. Somebody dragged his body into the stall and either gave him a hot shot there or did it before he put him in the mare's stall. The coroner said it was highly unlikely that the head trauma was caused by a fall. So, yes, I'm calling it murder."

Sidarus followed, his demeanor a bit more cooperative. "Yeah, man, he was one of the good ones. Real sorry to lose him."

"So we're here because what's going on with your runners. It's concerning. I'm wondering how, not if, it's connected."

Sidarus looked smug. "Well, you're outta luck there, buddy. Every test on every horse came back clean. No PEDs, no excess levels of anything. They found nothing, nada. Zip." He obviously enjoyed delivering the news. "So you get out of my barn, like I said before. There's nothing going on here but good breeding, good training, and some bad luck. Happens, you know it does."

Wes had him by the throat, this time in a blink of an eye. "Maybe you're gonna eat those words, you smug son-of-a-bitch." He threw Sidarus down and this time the man hit the dirt.

From the ground, he hissed at Wes, "I'll sue you from here to kingdom come, don't think I won't, then we'll see who's eating what." He looked down, seeming embarrassed at how little sense his last comment made.

Wes bent over him, let Sidarus take him in. "I'm gonna get you sure enough," he whispered, his eyes flat.

Sidarus wiggled away frantically and got up, dusting himself off. He kept his eyes on Wes and backed all the way to the stall, then stood his ground, glaring at JD.

"You've got no right," he said. "I've done nothing wrong. Get off my property. And don't come back unless you've got a warrant." He turned to Wes, far enough away now to be brave. "And you," he said, stabbing his finger in Wes' direction, "You can just go to hell."

Wes smiled again, like a snake would smile. "Well, that's just pitiful," he said, shook his head, patted his man bun, and walked out of the barn. "Pitiful" he said again, laughing a bit.

The pair jumped in JD's cruiser and burned out.

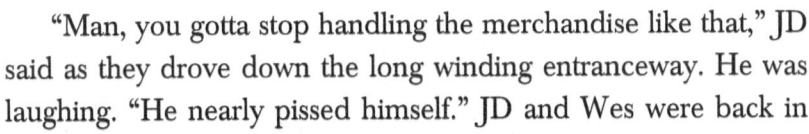

"Man, you gotta stop handling the merchandise like that," JD said as they drove down the long winding entranceway. He was laughing. "He nearly pissed himself." JD and Wes were back in country, fooling around with each other like old times.

Wes squinted at JD. "Sure," he said. "Sure I will."

And they both cackled.

JD sobered. "Naw, man, there's lines we don't cross over here."

Wes stared straight ahead. "You mean you don't cross them." That's all he would say on the subject.

They came to the end of the road and turned right, silent for a while as they headed up toward Versailles.

"I need to talk to Bradford," JD said, as they exited the lovely farms rolling away from the road and entered the business district. Mega groceries, gas stations, feed stores, tack shops, more huge parking lots lined the way.

"Something's going down there, it's bigger than Oliver," JD said, tapping the wheel. "And Isabelle is in it up to her eyeballs." More tapping. "But who else?"

"The trainer."

JD glanced at Wes as he drove. "For sure."

"Sidarus."

"Maybe," JD said. "I gotta talk to Bradford." He punched up Tim on the speed dial and they set up a time later that afternoon. The vet would be at Hawk Ridge just after noon, so agreed to meet him in the first broodmare barn. He needed to talk to JD, anyhow, about the reproductive specialist's findings—Bradford was meeting up with him there. JD filled the vet in on their visit to Janero as he headed home to drop Wes at his truck.

"Yeah, we do need to talk," was all Bradford would say.

6

The Hawk Ridge broodmare barns always brought back memories. Some good, some not so good. JD slammed the car into park, sat back, looked around. In his mind's eye saw his dad muscling a wheelbarrow full of manure, saw 12-year-old Harper and her little sister Paris galloping up, grinning from ear to ear, red-faced and happy. Yeah, he thought, the past held some good times, he'd try not to forget that. He opened the door, slammed it shut against all the bad memories that also welled up, and walked through the deep blue broodmare barn doors.

He waved at Tim Bradford who, at the moment, was conversing with the white clad reproductive specialist they worked with. Around him, a few of the broodmares and babies shuffled in their stalls, awaiting Jake McCann, the moms munching hay, a few babies nursing. A little black nose and two curious eyes peered out of the first stall JD passed, the baby so small she could hardly see over the wood half-door.

Down the aisle McCann was holding up a bag of fluid and the closer JD got, the more troubled he became. Dr. McCann turned to him, smiling, and holding up the bag—fluid he'd just extracted from the mare who his assistant was escorting into her stall, the bay's big back end swaying gently. Her baby stuck his little head out the stall door, ears twitching at the conversation, alert, inquisitive, his big eyes taking in a new world.

"Looks like we got some ocean critters floating around in there," McCann said, handing the rather opaque bag to Bradford and stripping off the plastic from his arm.

McCann saw JD's look and shook his head. "It's not just you all. Dirty mares are on every farm I visit."

JD stuck his hands in his police jacket. "Yeah, I know, but these infections gotta stop. We can't breed them."

"Naw, it won't take," agreed McCann. "And you'll infect the stallion." He tossed the dirty plastic sleeve on the aisle floor as Bradford handed the fluid-filled bag to McCann's assistant just exiting the stall. She slid the door shut and grabbed the bag, all business.

"Which is why we've got the clean test result stipulation in all the breeding contracts," JD said, frowning. He glanced at the mare. This was the second time she'd turned up dirty this season, and it was early. And she was a good mare, everyone wanted her up to the shed.

"We'll get things going," McCann said and started down the aisle for his last few mares-in-foal checks. He turned his sandy head, grinned again, and crooked his finger at his assistant who dutifully wheeled the ultrasound equipment down the aisle after him.

Tim walked toward JD and gave him a grim thumbs up. "We'll get it straightened out," he said. He glanced back at McCann. "He's the best in the business. Just wanted to see what he found today with the mares we wanted to send to the shed. We're good on all but two."

JD nodded, not happy, but if there were only two, they were way ahead of the game, given what some barns were dealing with.

Tim glanced back "He's got a few minutes to talk after the mares' checks." He took a sip of his thermos. "Probably fifteen minutes, he checked some of them before the ones we wanted sent to the shed. We had to hold some in, but glad McCann could fit this in."

"Yeah, Harper wanted to get in on this, I'll get her up here." JD put in a call to Harper and filled her in.

A few minutes later, JD heard a car door slam and Harper walked in. She'd come right over. JD kissed her cheek when she joined the group. She grinned at her romantic husband.

He switched to serious detective and filled the two of them in on his visit to Janero.

Bradford nodded. "I did hear The Racing Commission was over there. They got blood and urine. They were right on it."

JD folded his arms. "Did you hear it all came back clean?"

"I did."

Harper: "They'd check on everything, right?" She looked at Tim.

"Yeah, they'd look for it all, focus on the usual suspects—anabolic steroids, TC02, excess Cobalt, EPOs. As you said, they came up with nothing. The horses came back clean."

Harper looked at her vet. Something was up.

"Yeah, ok, but you have that look," Harper said to Tim. She ran her hand over her blond ponytail sticking out of her Eden Hill ballcap, her eyes worried. "What are they missing? You have something to say, say it."

Bradford glanced down the barn aisle, checking on McCann's progress. He and his assistant had a broodmare out, McCann's plastic-wrapped arm was up her back end, and he was studying his ultrasound. Looked like his last check.

McCann nodded, mumbled some stats on the fetus to the assistant broodmare manager who jotted them down for her boss.

When Bradford was silent, JD squinted at him. "They're missing something because there isn't a test for what Sidarus is using? Or," he corrected himself, "what someone is using over at Janero?"

Tim looked torn as if weighing whether or not to speak.

Harper and JD were quiet, waiting Bradford out.

Tim looked from one to the other. Then he glanced back at McCann again, who was making his way toward them up the long barn aisle, stripping off his plastic sleeve and balling it up.

JD said, "It's not professional to speculate, yeah, yeah, we know."

"But there has been one murder, and clearly horses are dying or, at the very least, put at risk. So spill it, Tim," Harper said as JD glanced behind Tim, waved McCann over, looked back, his intense green eyes trained on Bradford.

The vet nodded, a show of reluctance. "Yeah, ok. Needs to be said." He took a beat. Then: "So they mapped the equine genetic sequence back in 2006. And since then, cheaters, well some cheaters—those with enough money and a chemist in their pocket—have been taking advantage of genes associated with performance."

"Taking advantage how?" Harper said.

Bradford nodded, as McCann joined the group, sticking his hands deep in his stained white coveralls.

From the back of the barn, the young turnout grooms began filing in. They went to their assigned stalls, slid the doors open and entered to halter their moms and get the babies moving. The broodmares nickered, eager to go out, as one-by-one, the young grooms and their charges made their way into the aisle and out the back barn door, hooves quietly clopping, and babies trotting alongside their moms, their tiny manes sticking straight up, their tails like small whisk brooms.

"Hey," Harper said, greeting the reproductive specialist as he arrived. The group moved out of the way so the grooms could maneuver.

McCann had worked with them for several years, so Harper knew him well. The vet had helped Eden Hill out of a few tight jams with their broodmares, but he had in-depth knowledge on several veterinary topics.

The foursome stood to the side as McCann's assistant packed up the vet's equipment and skirted around the grooms and moms.

Tim spoke up. "I'll let Jake take over from here, he's the expert."

McCann nodded his sandy head and got serious. "Tim filled me in on what you all want info on." He held up his hands, palms toward them. "But full disclosure, this stuff is fairly new, so I'm not an expert on it by any stretch, but happy to share what I do know." He shifted his stance and checked on his assistant's progress, then slid his phone out and checked the time. Without looking up, he began, using his "all business" voice.

"You can do what's called enhancing the "expression" of a gene." He looked up, making sure he had everyone's attention. "Manipulate it, modify it so, for example it results in the horse building more muscle mass, or you can increase red blood cell production. There's even a company that's discovered a "motivation" gene, one that's present in horses that want to run."

They all let that sink in. Genes. New territory for sure.

"They've also speculated that the same thing could be done on the stallion side," McCann continued. "If, that is, the right gene is located. The one they'd target to enhance fertility, for instance."

"So what?" Harper said. "Now we're contending with cheaters changing a horse's genes? Would that be permanent?"

McCann nodded. "Right, that's the other problem. They can't really tell right now if or how the germline, the offspring—the horse's foals, for instance—will be altered, too."

Harper took a sip of water and JD stood immobile, deep in thought. She glanced out the back barn door and watched the grooms leading their mares and babies in a line, stopping at each one's assigned pasture. She wondered what the future held for scenes like this one, whether the little ones would be compromised in ways, perhaps dire ones, they couldn't predict. The mares walked quietly, placidly entered their pastures, their babies at their sides, and bent to the new grass—a serene moment amid the darkness closing in around them.

Harper turned back as McCann spoke.

"The problem," the vet continued, "is they've been working on this stuff for some time. Japan is investigating it, certainly Kentucky is. Studies have been done, trying to locate specific genes in equines associated with performance and they've come up with a suite of them. And, of course, everybody's working on tests to detect gene doping—there's been clear headway on that. Everyone's on this, even the Racing Commission has funded research. They're eventually going to build a biological passport, a record on each horse that will contain historical information as well as current. It will follow the Thoroughbred his whole life."

Tim nodded.

JD said: "What about side effects? For gene doping, anything that might be a tip-off?" Tim had mentioned putting down that horse with severe anemia. Unusual.

Tim picked up on JD's comment. "A filly just got put down for a tibial fracture, shattered nearly. And I put down a youngster with anemia so bad, there wasn't anything I could do." His voice trailed off.

"And how about . . . what were the other things?" Harper looked at Tim then JD.

Tim spoke up. "Heart attack, immune deficiencies, ones the colt didn't have earlier. Unusual muscle mass, tendon's compromised, fractures." Tim paused. "I looked into it. Not all at Janero, Lexington—some were at strings in his other locations. But all at the same farm, under the same head trainer. In babies, and pretty young horses."

McCann had nodded as Tim went through his list. "I guess the Racing Commission was on that one."

"Yeah, in Lexington, and found nothing, the horses came back clean," said Tim. "Waiting on a couple of necropsies, but yeah, they looked clean."

"Anemia, that's in the literature," said McCann. "For gene doping. The other stuff, though, could be gene doping, could be EPOs, growth hormones, things we're all too familiar with. The heart attack, for instance, could be cobalt plus Levothyroxine, a hypothyroid drug. Can make the heart race."

JD shook his head. "Sketchy, though. All at the same barn."

"Sounds like something's going on," said McCann, checking the time. He'd most likely heard but was too professional to let on, discretion being a necessary virtue in the tight knit Lexington horse racing world. "But the Commission and the testing labs, they know what they're doing." He paused. "Don't know what to tell you."

JD looked at Harper. "Yeah, we get that. They do, for sure."

McCann checked the time again, looked up. "That's all the time I can spare at the moment. But I'll send Tim some studies if you all want to read up on it." He nodded, his ubiquitous grin fading. "Everybody seems to think this is the "new frontier" the cheaters are about to exploit." He looked at the three of them. "I don't know all there is to know on this, but I hope I've helped."

JD brought himself out of deep thought, his expression bleak. "Yes, thanks." He shook McCann's hand. "Really appreciate the time. I'll take a look at the studies you send."

McCann, his assistant, and their gear all exited the barn and drove off.

7

JD looked at Tim, who nodded as if to say, "Yeah, it's a whole new ballgame. And serious."

"So you think that's why the EPO test on Janero's horses came back clear," Harper said to Tim, putting it together. EPO's stimulate red blood cell production which improves oxygenation to muscle cells and that improves performance. If the gene was being manipulated, that wouldn't show up in a test designed to detect an EPO.

Bradford nodded. "Maybe." He sighed. "But like Jake just said, could be they were dosed with an EPO and the components were messed with so it wouldn't be detected." He paused. "Yet. Not detectable yet. It's always been a catch-up game, you know that."

JD and Harper both nodded. They did know. They'd always run two clean farms. Squeaky clean. But they'd also had more than enough experience with the cheaters. They glanced at each other, and no words were needed.

Harper: "How close are they to a test, that passport thing McCann mentioned?"

"That would be good, but we're not there yet. And, as usual, everyone's trying to catch up to folks who always seem to be one step ahead," said Tim. "So how do we catch them?" JD asked, cutting to the chase.

"If there isn't a test," added Harper. She grabbed JD's hand, glanced out the far door to the pastures filled with small colts and fillies playing in the warming sunlight, racing from one group of mares to another, kicking their tiny hooves and shaking their heads. Joyful, oblivious.

52

"Either catch 'em in the act," Bradford said. "That's if they're doing "in viro"—on site injections right into the cells."

"Ok," Harper said, waiting for the other shoe to fall. Tim had that look again.

"Or?" JD chimed in.

"There's also what's called "ex viro" when they extract a horse's cells, take them to the lab, do the gene manipulation, and reinject them."

"So grab the chemist, and the lab," JD said, and Bradford nodded.

"Yeah, let's hope they're doing 'ex viro,'" Bradford said. "Which I'd bet on. It's easier to control, reduces the risk of an adverse immune response—you can just control things better in a lab."

"So what's the downside?" JD said.

Bradford rubbed his index finger and thumb together in the universal money signal. "What's the usual issue?"

"It's expensive," JD said, putting his hands in his jacket and shaking his head. "Unfortunately, Janero has a shit-ton of money."

He looked up. "Excuse my French."

Everyone was quiet a few moments.

Then Bradford spoke. "I did dig around a little." He smiled slightly at JD.

JD saw his smile and slowly smiled back. He noted Tim's brown eyes were still troubled, but they now held a tiny spark of triumph.

"I got the name of Janero's vet's wife." Bradford nodded to a young groom passing, the mellow, earthy scent of horse drifting over them. "Ex-wife."

JD pulled out his phone. "Shoot, Tim."

"From what I heard, you might do well to talk with her. Name's Gail Williams."

JD handed the phone to Tim. "Give me all you got."
And Tim typed.

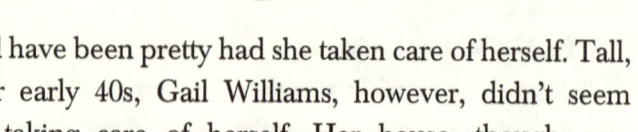

She would have been pretty had she taken care of herself. Tall, stately, in her early 40s, Gail Williams, however, didn't seem interested in taking care of herself. Her house, though, was spotless. She answered the door in green, mid-forearm rubber gloves, which she seemed reluctant to remove.

She looked from JD to Harper and back to JD. Her right eyebrow shot up in question.

Harper spoke. "Mrs. Williams, if you have a few minutes, we'd like to talk to you about your husband."

She looked at JD's navy Hawk Ridge parka. "Jason?" She looked at Harper. "And it's ex-husband. Is he ok? Did something happen to him?"

JD pulled out his ID and introduced them both. "No, he's fine. We're just interested in a brief chat. We're investigating a murder over at the barn he tends to."

Gail's eyes turned serious, and her expression a bit wry. "Yeah, Janero, I heard. Come on in. I'll tell you anything you want to know." She walked on ahead. "Jason's definitely not one of the good guys," she said over her shoulder.

OK, thought JD, here we go.

"Want coffee?" she asked when they got into the kitchen. "I have a whole pot." She gestured for them to sit.

JD looked at the table, then at Harper. They both sat. "Coffee would be great," JD said by way of furthering her cooperation. "Black is fine."

The kitchen around them smelled of coffee, cinnamon, and Pine Sol. Out the kitchen window stood a scraggly tree, a swing set, and a trampoline.

54

Harper nodded, picking up on JD's approach. "Black for me, too, please."

They both settled in while Gail pulled off her gloves, poured, and joined them at the oak-topped table.

In drifted a young couple with a picnic basket. They glanced at the threesome but seemed only to have eyes for each other as they raided the refrigerator, loaded their basket, dropped in a frozen block, and plucked a wine bottle and two glasses off the counter. They left without a further glance.

Gail held up her hands. "Airbnb. Newlyweds." She shrugged, sweeping the non-existent dust off the table. "What are you gonna do?"

Harper looked at JD, then at the door out of which the couple had just scurried. Then back to Gail who sipped in silence.

JD's leg began to bounce.

"So how did you two meet?" Harper said. "You and Jason?"

"We were both track vets. We met there, over at Keeneland on the backside." She thought a minute. "I was there until I couldn't take it anymore. The trainers, mostly. Sometimes the owners."

JD nodded, putting his hand on his thigh beneath the table. Harper did the same, patting it. Down boy, was her message, we'll get there.

Patience was not JD's long suit in these situations.

"We own Eden Hill and Hawk Ridge, so we get it," JD said, finally. More bonding, more cooperation. That's why he'd exchanged his police jacket for his Hawk Ridge parka.

Gail: "I'd say 'That colt has a hairline fracture, don't train him. Let him rest, heal up.' Next thing I know that two-year-old's out on the track, beating that leg. Got so I couldn't see one more baby put down with a needle." She put her hands on the table. "Enough. I had enough."

55

"And Jason?" JD asked, wishing Wes were there with his . . . skillset. He gazed at Gail, considering it. Maybe not, she didn't need to be collateral damage. Wes had a pronounced anti-humanist streak.

Gail looked up. "Oh, he did what he had to do. Went over to the commercial side, started working with the big barns." She sighed. "You see a different side of things. It worked for him."

Gail stared at each of them in turn, then sipped her steaming coffee. "What else do you want to know?"

Harper didn't look at JD. She took the lead: "How did you two split up?" She'd try to get the conversation moving forward toward what they'd come for.

His wife was deft with the maneuvers, thought JD. Usually, nobody saw it coming.

Gail complied, looking suddenly angry. "A few years back, Jason goes to a big equine conference in Paris. Huge, everybody was there. Immunology, orthopedics, genetics, podiatry." She paused, took a gulp of her coffee then winced at how hot it was. She continued: "He's calling me, 'Oh, he went to the Pompidou, the D'Orsay, Musée de Rodin,' on and on about the museums." She cocked her head. "Come to find out, he had an escort. Yeah, a hottie vet he met at the conference. Cecelia something." A flash of darkness flitted over her. "I guess she was, I don't know, new? Something different? I mean, she's Parisian, so she's sophisticated, had that accent."

JD and Harper were quiet.

Gail took another sip of coffee, this time a small one. "So pretty soon, guess who moves to the States? Pretty soon, Jason's flying to New York, San Francisco, all the museums." She laughed scornfully. "Suddenly he has a great interest in art." She put her elbows on the table, her head in her hands. Stayed there a moment. Then a large, deep breath, and her hands dropped to the table, her eyes staying trained on them.

JD's right foot began tattooing the floorboards.

Harper had been in the art world in New York City for years. She'd been to all the museums Gail mentioned, the ones in Paris, and on the east and west coasts. She stretched her hand across the table, touched Gail's arm, and the woman looked up.

"Anyway, he moves in with her, and that was it." Gail paused, turned frank eyes on JD. "To tell you the truth, we'd been over a while. I wasn't surprised, really." She sat back, picked up her coffee, stood and walked to the sink, plunked it down then turned around.

"Sorry. I don't think about that much anymore. You two coming around. I guess it just brought it all back." She crossed her arms and looked into the distance. "I work with small animals now. It's better. I'm out of that world." She looked back at JD and Harper. "And this is what I'm left with. Two kids and a bunch of strangers punching the keypad on my front door all hours of the day and night."

JD let things go for a minute, giving Gail some time. Why not, he thought, his foot on fire, then his patience ran out.

"You said Jason was not one of the good guys. What did you mean by that?"

"Was it the affair?" Harper said, extending sympathy to a woman clearly still in distress.

JD looked at his wife. That's exactly why he'd brought her. Well, one of the reasons. One of the many reasons. She balanced his lack of . . .

"Yeah, sure," she said, breaking into JD's thoughts. "That's part of it. But with the horses, too. I mean, I wouldn't put it past him to be in cahoots over at Keeneland with the trainers dosing their horses." She paused a moment then looked at them with level, clear eyes. "He's capable of that. I hate to say it, but he is."

And there it was. JD looked to Harper, thinking they needed the contact info.

They were all quiet for a few moments. Then: "What else can I tell you? Jason is off somewhere living the dream with his Parisian bombshell and I'm here slogging through one day and the next, bringing up his two boys who, if I'm honest, he doesn't give a hill of beans about."

JD nodded, tried to look supportive. He glanced at Harper, hoping she'd do her thing.

Harper said, gently, "Do you happen to know where they live? Or the woman's full name? We'd like to speak to Jason and to her."

Gail sighed. "Sure. Of course, I do." She looked embarrassed. "I'm sorry, you didn't come to hear my sob story." She thought a moment. "It's Cecelia. Um . . . gosh, hold on, I'll remember. Cecelia Fournier or something like that." She laughed again, self-consciously. "You'd think I'd know the woman's name who took my husband." She looked at them. "Wouldn't you?"

JD again tried to look sympathetic, likely it wasn't working. Sympathy wasn't his best trait in these circumstances. Or his job. "I'm sorry we've taken so much of your time, Mrs. Williams." He gave Harper a quick "We're done here" look. He'd get the address of Janero's vet elsewhere.

"It's Hannigan. I went back to my maiden name."

"Sure," said JD. "I understand. We won't take up more of your day. Thank you for speaking with us so honestly, you've been a great help."

The woman escorted them out, and JD and Harper both made their way rapidly to the car, Harper shaking her head at her husband, a grin on her face.

8

Cass was waiting for her burrito at the microwave, two fingers of straight up Kentucky rye neat in a highball glass. She pulled the robe around her and tapped her slipper, counted down the burrito, heard the ding, and pulled it out. She hadn't heard the door open. It opened quietly, but still she thought later, she might have been more alert.

She was usually sound asleep at this time of night, but something had been keeping her up lately. Maybe it was Oliver, maybe it was just her life, especially now that Wes had come back into it. She sighed and plopped the hot plate down on the cool counter. They couldn't get enough of each other, couldn't get out of each other's way. She was thinking about his clean, hard body and didn't sense the man slide up behind her.

She turned just in time to see his white teeth in the low kitchen lights, his lips pulled back in a sort of sneering smile. He had on a full-headed black mask, so all she saw was that smile and his eyes. Without thinking, she threw the highball glass hard, right at his head, which made him laugh. And then he grabbed and spun her, got behind, got her in a bear hug without effort.

But she'd worked out with Harper for a long time. The two of them had moved from boss/jock to friends some time back and she'd gotten Harper into her self-defense classes. Cass didn't blink when the guy grabbed her. Instinct kicked in, and training. Surprise was her only friend. That and pain. The second she felt his arms wrap, she thrust her hip to the left, brought her arm and her elbow as hard as she could up into his balls, heard him scream and curse, and then exactly the moment he let loose, she twisted out of his grip and raced towards her bedroom to get her gun.

But he sucked in a breath, snorted, and with a few strides was on her, getting her in a very tight bear hug from behind, her kicking and screaming. Cass gathered herself, dropped her weight forward and as she felt him bend over her, she snapped her head back quickly, strongly, trying to catch him in the nose, break it if she could. He grunted, and she was able to get one hand loose. She threw that back, trying to claw his eyes, all the while letting out screams for help and cursing the man to high heaven. Silently he moved his head out of harm's way, got her in an arm lock around the waist, her still kicking and screaming. Then he squeezed his arm like a python, cinching her to his waist. She craned to see him but just caught the stubby growth beneath his chin. His eyes were on the door as he lunged for it, gripping her ever more tightly. Cass squeezed her eyes against the pain, trying to still her mind to think of her next move. If she had one.

He kept moving, paying her no more mind than if she'd been a carpet rolled up under his arm. He was of medium height with ropy arms and legs like tree trunks. And, Cass noted, he wore gloves as well as the mask and smelled like alcohol mixed with cologne. She was no match for him.

At the door, he pulled a wet cloth from his pants pocket and plastered it over her nose, which made her go limp for real. He dropped her, zip-tied her hands, bound her feet, rolled her up in the twine he brought, then the tarp and more twine, slung her over his shoulder like a sack of potatoes. Outside, he loaded her in the back of the SUV, threw a blanket over her, slammed the door shut, slapped it, jumped in the vehicle, and sped off.

Wes was due to pick her up for breakfast, and when he got to Cass' condo, he saw the door was slightly open. He put his glove on his left hand, poked a finger at the door to open it and with his other hand, took out his phone and punched in JD. He knew something was wrong, likely really wrong. He walked in, surveyed the living room, walked down the hall to the kitchen, saw the shattered glass all over the floor and knew she was gone.

JD picked up and he simply said "It's Cass. She's gone." He looked around a few seconds, then flipped on the kitchen light and inspected the room. He saw the burrito sitting on the counter, glanced at the microwave's open door, figured she'd been cooking it, and stuck a finger in the center. It was cold. So she's been taken some time ago, probably sometime in the night.

Maybe a professional. Wes glanced around. Nodded. The place, other than the glass, was clean. Fast and neat. Maybe not the guy's first rodeo.

JD strode in ten minutes later, motioning the crime scene crew in behind him. He'd worked with Wes in country enough to not waste time—when Wes said something was something, JD went with it. He wasn't about to come to the condo without his crew. They fanned out behind him, took their evidence kits out and began their work: quiet, efficient, professional.

JD reminded them: "Grab the electronics. Check the bedroom and bath, look for third party DNA, and fingerprints." Even as he said it, JD knew there would be no fingerprints.

He nodded to Wes, who just said "Yeah, we're making somebody nervous."

JD looked around, nodded. Likely was the middle of the night. No witnesses. Still, he'd make the rounds. Have his people check the surveillance cameras, knock on doors, maybe somebody at least saw the truck or the car. Or the guy, you never knew.

Had to be tied to Janero, thought JD. Wes was right, they were doing something right for someone to make a blatant move like this. They were close to something. JD had some ideas about what that might be. But they were a ways off yet.

61

He just hoped Cass stayed alive long enough for him and Wes to find her. But they needed answers to do that. Not just ideas.

He looked at Wes. Neither of them felt anything—no emotions, no fearful thoughts. Training made sure of that.

And that was Cass' best hope.

9

Half an hour later, JD arrived home and hung up his jacket in the hallway. He walked in, looking for Wes or Harper and spied Wes at the dining table on the other side of the pass-through fireplace.

JD had swung by the precinct, filled Al Walker in, then headed home to link up with Wes. They had work to do. He called Harper's name as he walked around the fireplace but got no answer. He'd texted her about Cass. Brief, to-the-point. They just didn't know much at this stage.

He found Wes at the long table, spread out on a large pad in front of him were an array of weapons. Not all of them, just some. Wes was cleaning them. Preparing. The room smelled of oil and steel. Familiar smells, ones that flipped a switch in JD.

JD surveyed the weapons: the Weatherby, Wes' M-4 semi-auto, and his M-24 sniper rifle. Beside that lay the knives—his butterfly knife, his tactical boot knife, and his Shuriken knives, euphemistically called "Death Stars." JD had seen Wes take a guy's throat out at distance with the razor-sharp stars. The weapons brought back images of the first mission they'd done together, when Wes, as part of the 321 Special Tactics Squadron, had joined him on a JSOAC mission—they'd gone in dark and extracted a high-level U.S operative. They worked together well. It was a fast, efficient extraction. That had proved equally true on subsequent missions.

He looked at Wes, who glanced up briefly. He definitely had his game face on. The operative had come out alive. JD hoped for the same outcome with this mission.

Wes picked up his bayonet knife, fingered it and set it aside. He disassembled his M-9 pistol, the clicks and rachet sounds comforting and familiar to them both—it spoke of control, dominance, lethality. Wes set about silently cleaning it. JD said nothing, watching, knowing he'd be doing the same shortly. Wes picked up his Trijicon scope and set it to his right gently. JD continued to watch Wes settle himself, go deep within—cleaning equipment had that effect on him, too.

He heard the front door slam and his wife's near frantic calls for him.

"In the dining room," he yelled, and in the next moment, she rounded the corner, pulling off her coat and throwing it on the table. She took in the weapons and Wes' focus.

Harper turned to JD, furious. "What do you mean Cass is gone?"

"She's gone" said Wes, flatly, not glancing up. "Somebody took her." He was still in combat mode: The cold burrito, the broken glass. She didn't leave voluntarily. So focus.

Harper looked at JD. She was shaking, her blue eyes stark with disbelief. "Cass is strong. We work out. She knows the moves. She'd put up a fight." Her words came in staccato-like spurts as if that's all she could string together.

JD pulled her to him, wrapped his arms around her and kissed the top of her head.

"What are we doing about it?" she mumbled into his chest.

She pulled back, stepped away. "Surely we're going after her?" Married to JD, Harper well knew the stats on time elapsed in an abduction and the chances of a live recovery.

"You can ditch the "we," said JD. He gave Harper some serious cop eyes.

"Don't even," said Harper, her eyes a steely match. "I'm trained, I can use a gun. I'm going." The feel of her Desert Eagle semi-auto was already itchy in her palm, its silver glint, its jet-black grip. She was good with the 357 mag., its 9 +1 rounds. She kept up her practice. She was good to go.

JD threw his hands in the air and didn't respond to her insistence, knowing it was useless. Instead: "Yeah, of course we're going after her. But we need some clues as to where to look. Any ideas? I'd love to hear them."

The mood in the room was edgy.

Wes looked from Harper to JD, feeling the blowup coming. He stared down JD. Get a grip, his look said. Then he went back to work. "Take it down a notch," was what quietly came out of his mouth.

JD shifted, made an attitude revision. "Seriously, Harper, we need to put something together first."

At that, Wes did look up, "There's too many balls in the air." He took his man bun down, flipped the band over his wrist, popped it a few times. Thinking. The light glinted off his black hair, the high cheekbones, the slant in his gray eyes.

JD and Harper looked at him.

Finally: "We got Isabelle, we got Janero, Oliver." Wes was quiet a moment. "The trainer, the vet, maybe Sidarus."

"And then there's the gene doping," said Harper nodding.

Wes raised an eyebrow. Gene doping? He laid down his sidearm and the cloth, waited for answers.

JD filled him in on the talk with McCann and Bradford. "It's all got to be connected." He stopped. "So let's start at the beginning."

"Oliver's death," said Harper, pulling out her own ponytail. She shook her head as if to get the cobwebs out and stuck her hands in the back pockets of her jeans.

"What did that serve . . . who did it serve?" Wes said.

They were all quiet for a moment. JD spoke up again. "Max said Oliver was one of the best stallion managers he'd had in years. Makes no sense he would try to get rid of him."

"Or else he's covering," said Wes.

JD side-eyed him, nodded. "I'll check on that."

Harper sat in one of the chairs, motioned JD down. "Sit."

Harper looked from JD to Wes. "So who replaced Oliver? As stallion manager."

Wes and JD exchanged a look. "Good question, who did?"

JD said, "I'll check on that, too." He paused. "What else?" He looked at Harper, then at Wes. He'd worked with them both, but separately, and gotten the right results with each. He wondered what they could do if they all worked together. Not for the first time, he dismissed his boss as if he was not a factor—Walker had always given him a lot of rope. Except, recalled JD, when he couldn't. Best to leave his boss out of what he didn't need to know.

He glanced at Harper, hoping she could put her uneasiness around Wes aside.

He considered her. She was deep in thought, serious, intent. She seemed to be doing that, but he knew only time would tell.

"Next up is Janero's vet, seems to me," said Harper. "Jason something." She reached out and stroked Wes' M24, appreciative of solid weapons. Especially ones with scopes.

"Williams," remembered JD. "Jason Williams. I'll set that up—maybe we can get to him this afternoon."

"Good," said Harper, "we need answers, like now, if Cass has any chance at all." She caught the fleeting look that passed from Wes to JD. "What?"

They were both silent.

"We are not going there," she said with force. "We are bringing Cass home." There was not an ounce of back-down in her expression.

They both nodded, but their expressions were skeptical.

After a few more moments, Harper spoke up quietly. "Didn't the vet's ex-wife say Williams was living with an equine vet? The one from Paris? Wonder if she has a specialty. Wonder where she works."

"Yeah, that's good." JD's eyes got very narrow, which is what happened when he picked up the scent. He looked at Wes "We need to drill down on Janero's vet." He looked at Harper. "And his live-in, Cecelia, something, right?"

Harper nodded.

JD looked at his watch, might as well get started.

Harper spoke: "Wasn't Tim talking about some off-site stuff. With the gene doping? He was talking about a lab, right?"

JD spoke up: "'Ex-viro,' that's what he called it." Harper nodded.

Wes spoke up "You mean like Isabelle's lab maybe? Didn't you say she oversaw the testing and did some herself?"

The three of them were quiet a moment. JD nodded.

He looked from one to the other, seeing two slightly more hopeful faces than he'd seen when they began the conversation. "Yeah, exactly." He paused a moment, thinking. "Problem is, we're circling. Feels like we're chasing peripherals but what they all connect to—or who—we don't have that."

"Yet," said Harper.

JD reluctantly nodded. He switched gears. "If I can set it up with Williams, do you want to come with me and Wes?" She'd always been able to pick up on things JD missed. She nodded soberly. He looked at Wes, the "it" factor. This was a complicated, frustrating case and Cass was running out of time.

He wouldn't want anyone else at his side if things got dirty.

No, he corrected himself. When things got dirty.

10

JD headed back to the precinct to make some calls. He needed answers. Once in his office, he dumped his jacket on the chair back and flipped through some reports on the computer. A few moments on the phone made it clear that Oliver had been, in fact, as stellar a stallion manager as Max Sidarus had indicated. A guy named Chad Redfield, originally from northeast Texas then Tulsa, had been Oliver's assistant and had just been appointed manager. He was worth checking into. One more call told him the surveillance cameras and door-to-door at Cass' condo had turned up nothing on the abduction. There was a neighbor next door who heard screaming around one or two o'clock. It wakened her and she thought that might be the hour but didn't actually check. She figured it was the TV and went back to sleep. The neighbor on the other side of Cass' condo was out of town, visiting her daughter. The team still had two condo owners to check on and would report back once they'd contacted them.

He'd told the team to knock on doors in the adjacent neighborhood, check for cameras.

A frustrating case. And they were on the clock.

He made some other calls, trying to set up an appointment to talk with Jason Williams, Janero's vet, over at the farm if possible. He shuffled papers around on his desk, getting more and more agitated as one person after the other in Janero's office gave him the run-around. Finally, he reached Sidarus and asked the owner if the vet was there, his voice clearly expressing his irritation.

"What do you want with Jason?" was Sidarus' response.

"Just want to have a few words, is all," JD said. "I need to cover all the bases in the investigation, I'm sure you understand."

There was a pause on the other end of the phone, "I told you all the tests came back clean. There's no need to bother Jason, he had little or nothing to do with Oliver and certainly not with his death. And besides, Jason's got other clients, we're not the only ones, so he might not even be around."

JD contained himself, with effort. He didn't want to let Sidarus know how serious his interest was in the vet, and his live-in girlfriend, so he decided to go another route. "You're right," JD said, trying to smile. He'd heard that makes your voice sound pleasant. Not like JD actually felt, which was a pronounced desire to reach through the cell phone ether and strangle a major pain in the ass. "I'll check around. If you hear from him, could you let him know I'd like a few words?" He shut up and focused on trying to stop grinding his teeth. "Just a formality," JD finished.

Sidarus let out a slight, exasperated snort. "Sure. Yeah, sure."

JD knew he would not be hearing from Janero's owner anytime soon.

He tried William's private practice office and was told the vet was in surgery. Williams was not performing the surgery, the woman quickly clarified. Evidently Jason's equine bedside manner had failed him, and he'd been cow-kicked attempting to nerve block a lame mare's hock. She got him square in the femur, sent him across the barn aisle—the genial office worker was quite forthcoming with details—so the good vet was, at the moment, getting screws or a plate, the woman on the other end of the phone wasn't sure which.

JD tried not to slam down the phone. He ran two hands through his thick auburn hair, stared out his floor-to-ceiling glass office wall and gazed into the bullpen where uniform-clad men and women worked the phones, made notes on their computers, or read reports. The fluorescent lights didn't flatter any of them.

He'd have to catch up with the vet in a day or so. Depended on how he came out of surgery.

He considered trying to find his live-in, Cecilia Fournier. She'd be at the hospital, no doubt. Something in him wanted them together for the interview. He went with that. Maybe they'd trip up or send each other some signals he wouldn't see if he talked with them separately. He could always bring each of them in if things didn't go as he planned.

JD lowered the blinds and closed himself in, circling back to his desk. Everyone knew not to bother him when his blinds were down. He especially did not want to talk to Al Walker, and he needed to think.

Pretty soon, Wes barged in.

JD rolled his eyes. Of course.

Wes dropped into a seat in front of JD's desk.

"You're not staying."

Wes cocked his head at JD. "Damn right."

"Ok, what?"

"You gotta stop crankin', man."

JD nodded and studied Wes, those gray eyes. "Yeah ok, but Cass."

Wes looked highly annoyed and gestured around the office. "Naw, we're outta here."

JD shook his head.

Wes rose, patted his Justin, motioned for JD, got his jacket from the coat tree, and held it out.

"We're headed to the gun range."

"I know where we're headed," JD muttered, rising. "And it's not the gun range. I need food. Then I gotta get back here and work."

Wes groaned, so as consolation, JD agreed they could head to Wes' favorite low-end restaurant, a seafood place he frequented when he was in town. JD had never been there, it being a chain.

Wes snorted at the comment. "Quite the effete."

JD huffed, then laughed.

They walked into the place, past the graffiti-chalked and scribbled walls and were seated at a beat up, dirty wooden booth in the back by the restrooms, led there by a hostess who took one look at them and made her way to the furthest table.

JD ordered a beer, and Wes ordered a gin and tonic.

"What the hell, Wes," JD said laughing. "Effete my ass."

Wes smiled. "Yeah, man, that's it, lighten it up."

The food came, breaded and greasy everything, and they wolfed it down along with a couple more beers and G&Ts.

"Cass," JD said again

"Don't go there man, I'm telling you, let it come to you."

They were both quiet a minute, and then Wes chuckled.

"Remember that dive in wherever asswipe city in country?"

"We're not going there," JD said.

"The hell we aren't."

JD shot Wes a warning look.

"Jesus, we stunk." Wes shook his head, a rather nostalgic look on his face.

"Ok, well, manly," JD said, smiling, but knowing going back to their exploits would only fire them both up. They didn't need that. Well, JD didn't need that.

"Not like the women noticed," Wes said, toasting JD with his diminishing G&T. He removed the lime and sucked on it.

JD muttered, "I wouldn't know."

"Take my word," Wes smiled and popped a fried okra into his mouth, sipped the last of his G&T through a straw. He set the glass down.

"Ever miss it?"

JD considered that. He was quiet.

"Seriously, man, you ever miss it?"

JD picked up the last of the fried okra, popped it in his mouth, lifted his beer, and said,

"Yeah, I guess. I gotta admit sometimes I do."

"Wes grinned. "And that's how we're gonna get Cass back, we're gonna use some of that in-country shit. We got the chops, all we gotta do is use 'em."

JD squinted at Wes and Wes squinted back.

"Yeah, ok, but stow it for now, Wes, I mean it, stow it until we got the intel."

The waitress passed and JD flicked a finger. She came right over, check already in hand. JD paid, mumbling about expensing it, and they left, heading back to the precinct.

Once there, JD jumped out and glanced back at Wes. "Headed to the range, right?"

"Bet your ass, compadre," Wes said, grinning, and then he sped out, leaving a little rubber in the police parking lot.

JD resumed his seat in the old chair behind his desk, the one he'd brought from home. It was his dad's, so it was well-worn on the armrests, and it squeaked. He looked at each of Harper's photos sitting off to the side of his desk, then fired up the computer and stared at the screen till it went to his screen saver.

The photos shifted from one underwater scene to the next, which annoyed him further. He'd never set up his own set of photos since he spent so little time in his office—until this case, he thought—and even when there, he wasn't a fan of the computer. Usually, he made Cheryl look things up, and sometimes Harper, though that wasn't a well-known fact, it being against regulations.

72

He stopped staring and took a sip of cold coffee. God-awful, he thought, looked at the cup and plunked it down.

He was missing something. Or someone.

Go back to the beginning, he told himself, as he, Wes, and Harper had done earlier. Oliver's murder. He sunk back into the case, a little more focused after his lunch with Wes.

He went over each step he'd taken since discovering the body.

First up: Isabelle. He reviewed his notes on the interview. She was certainly involved. How, he wasn't quite sure of yet. He needed to check on her background—who was she and where did she come from? Where had she worked before? Prior arrests?

He'd get on that today.

He continued reviewing the case. Next up: Chad Redfield, the new stallion manager. He wrote that down. Needed to speak with him, too.

Isabelle and Redfield. He sat with that a while. There was something there, he could feel it. He put a circle around their names. Then he did it again.

What else? He thought, returning to the scene of Oliver's death. The mare in the death stall—her test came back clean. The autopsy report, the blow to the head. Cass' distress. Sidarus' disbelief. JD stopped. Janero's owner actually had seemed genuinely confused, saddened, and agitated. Didn't look feigned. He tucked that away. Sidarus had sure been obstructive and obnoxious when he and Wes had visited the training barn. Maybe he was just as frustrated by the lack of progress as JD was. Or maybe something else was going on.

JD looked at the ceiling, moving into his cold, logical mode. So much was just not clear. In every case, there was always a center, some crime, some person, some secret that all the aspects of a case coalesced around. Where was that here? Or maybe, as he'd asked before, who was it here?

They also hadn't heard anything from anyone about a ransom and that compounded the questions. It was early, but still. Cass seemed an unlikely target for a high-dollar payday.

He rolled down his blue shirt sleeves, then folded them up again over his forearms. What was he overlooking?

He went over the broodmare barn scene again. The techs collecting evidence, the stall with Oliver's body, Walker talking to Sidarus, Wes doing his thing, and Harper seated next to a slumped Cass. He looked at all of it in his mind's eye.

He sat back. Finally, after a few moments, he had it. There you are, he thought, raising his legs and crossing his ankles on his desk. He leaned back and stretched.

The broodmare night shift worker. She'd been drugged, fast asleep when the murder happened.

JD let his legs drop and the chair squeaked as he leaned forward and picked up his office landline.

But what did she see before she'd drunk the laced coffee? What did she know that maybe she didn't know she knew?

He called Harper. She'd be the perfect partner for this trip.

11

C ass huddled in the dimness in the corner of a small, dank, shavings-littered room. She drew her robe tighter around her. The captor had taken the belt, perhaps so she wouldn't hang herself somehow. She supposed that was a good sign. They wanted her alive.

At least for now.

She was freezing, the April chill's humidity sent the cold straight to the bone. She'd spent the night huddled in the robe, her arm crooked as a pillow once she'd busted out of the zip ties and freed her feet. There was not much sleep to be had that way, especially given the circumstances and how she'd had to battle down fear all night.

Where was she? Why was she here? What did they want from her?

She supposed she was in an outbuilding of some sort, maybe a barn or equipment storage structure. It smelled like manure, dead rodents, and dirt. Someplace without heat, that was certain. There was a small, rectangular window set high on the wall across from her. Not much light shown through, and only a bit more when her abductor had opened the door to dump in food, such as it was—stale bread and then some lukewarm slop much later. Both with water, but no utensils. She gauged she'd spent one night, the night she'd been taken, given the light. She'd ridden enough races to know what late afternoon looked like and that's what the slant of the light told her.

This, she figured, was the end of a long 15 hours, so most likely her first full day.

She shuddered. Well, at least they were feeding her something. Whether that was a good sign or not, the verdict was still out.

She'd felt around in the room in the earliest light. She'd been systematic about it, working her way around the base of the structure, looking for rotted wood at the bottom of each board where moisture would have seeped into the plank. She needed only an inch to see out, get a gauge on where she was and maybe figure out how to escape. Once she'd circled the perimeter, she stood and tested each board pressing each one for soft wood, loose boards, screws or nails she might pull out, anything she could use to her advantage. She didn't find anything, but she'd keep trying as long as she was confined. She did find a bucket near the door. She used that as her "facilities" and when her captor had opened the door, in the sliver of dull light she saw him set down a plate and glass next to the bucket. He didn't pick it up.

Maybe she'd heave its contents at him next time he came.

She couldn't tell much about him those brief moments he'd decided to feed her. He still had his face covered and, as in her condo, the low light made it tough to see his eye color. He uttered no words and opened the door only slightly. He was good at concealment.

She stood and stretched. She would not get complacent. Or depressed. She dropped after her stretches and did push-ups, followed by ab work, followed by running in place, followed by more stretches. And so it went.

Who, she wondered, as she worked out, was behind this? What did they want? Money? She had little, and those she knew who had some weren't the sort who were apt to pay. Harper and JD would find her, not pay anyone. And with Wes around . . .

Cass smiled. Whoever it was had no idea what hell they were in for.

That didn't mean she wasn't going to make her break on her own. No sir. She had moves and she'd use them.

She'd keep looking for an exit, a way out, or something she could use to make her escape. She wasn't staying if she could help it and would not be making friends with the mice and spiders, or the snakes she knew were probably around.

She was not that sort of prisoner.

She thought about her captor, reviewing what she'd picked up to see if maybe she knew him. She came up with nothing new— he was of medium height with stubble, a high-class scent, and a bit of muscle. That didn't matter, she knew. She could use his own force against him as she'd been trained, she just needed one, small opportunity.

Warmed enough by her workout, she used her fingernail to scratch a line in the soft wood by her corner.

Day 1.

12

JD headed to pick up Harper a few hours later after looking into Isabelle's background. Interestingly, just prior to arriving in Lexington she had worked for years at a Thoroughbred genetics firm in Ireland, one specializing in identifying and testing for genes predictive of high athletic performance. They worked exclusively with racehorses and the business had a highly successful worldwide clientele.

In other words, Isabelle was an equine genetic specialist.

JD pulled up to the house, shut off his unmarked vehicle and stared out the window. His mind, finally, was clearing. He smiled. He could feel the case starting to shift.

He left the F-150 and hoofed it up the steps, bent and spent a moment scratching behind Kelso's ears, straightened to see Harper at the door throwing on her jacket.

They sped down the oak-lined drive a moment later, JD filling Harper in on what he'd found, especially regarding Isabelle. Clearly there'd be another conversation with her, and soon. JD had also learned that the broodmare night worker wouldn't be available until 7 p.m. when she began her shift. Or he could wait until the next morning, she wouldn't be off until 7 a.m. He'd see how the day went and make that call later.

At the moment, they had bigger fish to fry. Chad Redfield, Janero's new stallion manager. JD wanted Harper's take on him—squirrely or a straight shooter?

~

They arrived at Janero's stallion barns twenty minutes later and parked by the main office. JD went in, introduced himself, flashed his badge, and was directed to the first barn, just down the brick walkway lined with clipped hedges and new, thick green grass. They were, he was told, prepping for the second breeding of three for the day.

Harper joined him as he exited the office and they took stock of the barn off to their left, one of five spread out on the stallion campus. It was gray stone, had a peaked roof, and was topped with a lightning rod. They took no chances with their high-dollar money makers. Off to the left of the barn, a glowing dappled gray stallion was being hosed off, getting ready for breeding duties.

They entered the barn to see a double row of large stallion stalls deeply bedded, several with snoozing stallions nestled into the wheat straw.

JD pulled his badge, flashed it at a woman clad in Janero's colors, complete with the ubiquitous ballcap and logoed red and gray windbreaker. She said Chad was in the breeding shed prepping, noting it was out the back door of the barn down a short walkway to the left. On the way, JD and Harper saw the shed, which was fronted by a large, circular courtyard. Off to the right sat a cinderblock building with a sign that read "Mares' Receiving," where shipped in mares would be teased, cleaned, and then walked to the breeding shed. The place was laid out with care—the stallions would be led out the barn door to the shed and, separately, the mares would walk up from the receiving building.

They found Chad Redfield in the breeding shed's prep and kitchen. He was of medium height, looked to be somewhat muscled out beneath his Janero jacket. He was fiddling with black vests, hanging each one up on the lower cabinet pulls above which were a sink, a microscope, a video monitor, a small refrigerator, and a coffee pot. The large window above that held a scraggly philodendron trying to hang on.

JD and Harper stood in the doorway, but Chad took no notice of them. He was moving fast, his curly red hair bobbing to some tune playing in his ear buds. JD and Harper watched him fidget with a black padded helmet clasp, watched him get exasperated, then throw it in the sink and haul out another one. Then four more. He hung them one-by-one over each of the vests.

Harper and JD glanced at each other. The new stallion manager seemed lost in a world of his own making.

JD stepped forward and Chad abruptly turned his way, his light brown eyes going wide. He plucked out his ear buds, pulled on his ear, a nervous twitch. He glanced behind the pair then back to them, his eyes narrowing.

"You are?" he said, looking from JD to Harper.

JD pulled out his badge, introduced himself and Harper, all the while his eyes studying Redfield as if he were prey.

The badge made an impression. Chad blanched noticeably and ground his teeth. "What's this about?" he said, "I've got work." He moved to the microscope as if to seal the point, fiddled with it, made sure the slides were on hand, and looked back at the silent pair.

"Just a few questions," JD said after a time. "About Oliver." He'd found silence useful. It unsettled even the most unflappable foes.

Interesting, he thought, that he considered Redfield a foe. He'd only just met the man and already didn't like the vibe. JD glanced at Harper. She had her head slightly cocked and was playing with her ponytail in front of her shoulder, studying Redfield, picking up something on the distasteful side, it looked like.

The stallion manager seemed to relax a bit at the mention of Oliver's death. "That was horrible," he said, looking at the sink, a sad pull to his mouth.

JD thought his tone distinctly insincere.

"Sounds like Oliver left some pretty big shoes to fill," Harper said. She glanced out the window, seeing a van pull up to the mares' receiving shed. Then turning back to Redfield, "Which you were then able to step right into."

Chad glared at her, then caught himself. He turned to the refrigerator, removed a small vial, and laid it next to a syringe. He picked up the vial and showed it to JD. "It's a fertility support drug. All legal," he said defensively.

JD and Harper knew Janero had a prominent older stallion, Gisendi, and that shot was likely for him.

"Can you account for your whereabouts the night Oliver died?"

Chad sucked in a breath at that. "Why? Am I a suspect?" He shook his head. "Are you serious?" He seemed highly irritated. "Man, that's why you're here? That's nuts."

"And where were you?"

The stallion manager snorted. "I was either home, asleep. Yeah, alone. Or up getting over here." He waved his hand. "Dunno when he died, but you know. We start early."

JD nodded. "So no one can account for your whereabouts until you arrived here?"

Chad's irritation increased. "Yeah, that would be correct." He sneered at them. "So sue me."

Harper chimed in. "And between midnight and 4:00 a.m. or so on Monday? Where were you then?"

"Why?" Chad demanded, glancing into the shed, then back to Harper. "And who the hell are you to ask me anything?" He glared at her. Then, "Look, this is stupid. I got mares shipping in. I got things to do here." He looked from JD to Harper. "I got nothing to do with any of this."

"Your whereabouts in the early hours of Monday morning?" JD asked. That was when Cass was abducted. Let's see what Chad Redfield would do with that one.

Chad twirled a lock of curly red hair around his finger, a distinctly odd gesture. "Same as I said before, I was at home, sleeping, or heading here." He paused, disgusted. "And yep, alone. I got no life to speak of."

He glanced again to breeding shed, walked into it and toward the open doorway where the mares would enter. He turned back to the pair standing in the prep room doorway and nodded to the mares' receiving building.

"You do see I got work here."

JD smiled. "Just a few more questions. You go about your business, we'll tag along." He let the pressure off Redfield, interested to see what that might expose. Interesting, thought JD, that the stallion manager hadn't questioned what happened on Monday. Maybe because he knew.

Redfield walked back to the prep room, picked up a blue bucket, set it down with some force and poured the stallion rinse into it. He checked the video.

"What can you tell us about Oliver? Any enemies? Any problems you know he was having?" JD said.

Chad picked up his Janero ballcap and settled it on his head, stuck his hands in his pockets.

"Nothing. So far as I know," Chad said. His tone turned sarcastic. "He was well-loved by all."

"So you two didn't get along?" Harper said.

Redfield shrugged. "We were ok. He was a kind of a Boy Scout, if you know what I mean."

"We don't know."

Chad looked out the window to see the big, dappled gray being led back from his wash.

"There's a guy to keep your eye on," Chad said, nodding to the stallion. "Bayone. He's a hellion but gets good babies."

JD noticed Chad's nervousness. His right eye twitched.

"So," said JD turning back to the issue at hand. "Boy Scout?"

"Yeah, well," Chad said, maneuvering. "With Oliver, it was always everything by the book." He suddenly looked exasperated. "You know, right? Sometimes you gotta do what you gotta do."

JD and Harper stared at him. Chad Redfield was getting himself into very warm water. On several fronts.

"Look, we got a lot of stallions here," he said, backpedaling. "Some are perfect gentlemen. Some, they wanna nuzzle and lick, they like the romance." He had a sour look, like he thought that absurd. "Or they prance, and they bite. And kick. And some of 'em scream at the mares." He radiated disgust.

Maybe he didn't like diversity, thought JD. Comes with the territory, dude. JD shifted his stance and checked in with Harper. She was paying rapt attention to Chad, her blue eyes locked on his, hanging on every word that dropped from his lips. JD chuckled. Her superpower—making anyone feel they were the center of the universe while giving nothing away.

"Or they dawdle, they need encouragement," he continued derisively, nodding at Harper as if he'd find agreement there. Seeing none, he continued. "Or they're vicious after they mount. Like Bayone, that guy's always mad about something." He suddenly changed his mojo, no more the forthcoming stallion manager sharing war stories with folks just like him. Now he seemed mad. He glared at JD and Harper, taking stock of their stoic expressions. Now it appeared he was angry he wasn't finding them of like mind.

So he could usually bullshit his way out of a tight squeeze, thought JD. Wasn't working, so what was his next move going to be?

"And this has to do with Oliver, how?" JD said.

Chad picked up a mop, dipped it, wrung it out, and pounded into the shed, abruptly dismissing them both. "Oliver was all about the horses," he said over his shoulder. He turned to them, mop in hand. "You know the game. It isn't all about the horses. It's about money. That's it. That's all it is."

JD and Harper had stepped out into the large square room with shredded rubber flooring. The room had black padded walls with two large, padded blocks and mats for the mares to stand on set on opposite sides of the room. The peaked ceiling, in keeping with the stallion barns' design, was set with an array of lights to illuminate the proceedings.

"Hey, I'm just being honest," Chad said. Just a straight-talking guy, his manner suggested.

Redfield walked across the mare's padded breeding station, made sure the mare's hind feet boots and leather neck shield were in place then he wiped down the padded block.

He turned to the pair. "Oliver didn't want the mares twitched," he said, as an overweight man in a light blue ballcap led a mare toward the shed's open door behind Chad.

"We were always behind schedule because he dallied around with the stallions." He screwed up his face as the handler led the mare in. Chad turned to him and motioned the man to the padded block he'd just cleaned.

"He made little kissing sounds, for Christ's sake," Chad said, motioning in the breeding crew, all now dressed in helmets and vests. "At the stallions. Encouraging them. Ridiculous." He shook his head. "Boy Scout. He wanted the horses to enjoy themselves."

That didn't seem at all odd to JD. They're not robots, he thought, why shouldn't they enjoy themselves?

As the breeding crew secured the mare's leather shield and put the rear boots on her, Redfield walked to the door and motioned the big dappled gray stallion in. He turned to JD and Harper. "We need to breed this guy, so we done here?"

JD shook his head. "Not quite. Just a few more questions."

Redfield huffed, looked like he was about to make a comment, then thought better of it. "Sure, ok," he said. "But you gotta leave now. Wander around if you want. This might take a while." He glanced at Bayone nearing the shed then back to JD and Harper. "You don't wanna be here, believe me. This guy can be dangerous." He nodded at them as if to say he was just looking out for their safety. "And I'm gonna have my hands full."

JD nodded then he and Harper walked out the back toward the mares' receiving building. JD glanced back to see Chad check the video feed in the shed—they recorded all the breedings. "Doesn't seem much could slide by a video."

Harper knew what he was talking about. Thoroughbreds had to be live bred in order to qualify as racehorses—no artificial insemination was allowed, no extra semen injections other than the dismount collection. A recording would pick up any mishandling of the breeding. That's what JD was implying,

She looked at him, grinning. "Seriously?"

"What?"

"For a Special Ops guy, you're kind of a Boy Scout yourself."

JD frowned. The last thing anyone had ever called him was a Boy Scout.

"Ever heard of Hollywood?" Harper shook her head, still smiling. "Anything can be manipulated."

JD laughed. "Yeah, you got me on that one."

It was possible Chad wanted them out of the shed because he was pulling a fast one with Bayone. But that would mean his crew would likely have to be in on it. Well, maybe they were. There were a lot of ways to cheat.

More possibilities. More complications. Well, he thought, they'd have another crack at Redfield after the breeding.

Harper said she'd like to check out the mares' receiving building, see how it compared to their operation at Eden Hill, so they headed that way.

13

JD and Harper entered the smaller building where each mare was presented to the teaser, a stallion used to determine whether the mare was in heat to breed. After her visit to the teaser, she'd be cleaned and led to the shed.

They were greeted by a young woman in dark pigtails just stripping off plastic gloves with sleeves past her elbows. She stood before a brown padded structure configured to hold the mare in place. Behind her was a counter with a sink and other supplies and to her right was a paneled room with a padded floor that faced the teaser's stall inset with a closed window. She was bustling about, getting things ready for the next mare to arrive.

JD introduced himself and Harper and learned her name was Catherine.

"Sure," she said, smiling, stroking one long pigtail. "I know who you two are. You guys are doing real good at the track, even this early."

"Thanks," Harper said, taking the lead. "We appreciate you letting us look around.

Always good to see another operation."

"Oh for sure, you're welcome to look around all you like." She smiled, friendly, as were most doing the behind-the-scenes work.

JD let Harper wander a bit, but he turned his attention to Catherine.

"So Oliver," he began, noting her demeanor suddenly turned south. "What sort of boss was he?"

She looked at JD with palpable sadness. "He pretty much changed everything around here." She looked around then back to JD. "He got it. The horses, you could tell that's where his heart was." She glanced out the door, up toward the breeding shed. "Not like some."

"So Chad's not doing a good job?"

"He's ok," Catherine said quickly. "But Oliver really cared." She looked over at the teaser's window in the next room. "Oliver's the one who got Manfred those barren mares. He's the one wanted Manfred out with them." She looked back at JD. "It did the stallion so much good. He's happy, and he's respectful of the mares." She smiled wanly. "He's got his women," and she glanced out the door again, "and the big guys up there, they've got theirs."

Catherine nodded to the teaser's room. "Go slide the window open if you want to, Manfred's ready to go."

JD nodded. He'd get a bit more from her later if there was time. Harper joined him and they both entered the room where JD slid the stallion's window open. Manfred, a large piebald mustang, stuck his head out, ready for the muzzle. JD smiled at him and looked at Harper. They both appreciated a guy who knew his job. JD slid the teaser's window closed, noting that Manfred didn't object.

Catherine entered and pointed to a trailer just outside where a bay mare was being led off by a young, slim woman in jeans wearing a windbreaker with her farm's logo embroidered on the shoulder.

The woman led the mare into the teasing stall, where she and Catherine talked over the details, Catherine noting them on her clipboard. JD and Harper removed themselves to the room with the padded stand where the bay mare would be washed up after Manfred determined she was ready. They stood watching just outside the wire mesh window.

Catherine opened the window and Manfred stuck his head in the air, teeth pulled back, and scented the mare, then he received his muzzle.

The groom handed the mare to Catherine who led the mare forward a few steps so Manfred could do his job.

She glanced Harper's way, nodding at Manfred. "He's one in a million, for sure. He never complains, always gets the job done, always ready to go." She smiled as she said, "ready to go."

Harper smiled back as Catherine turned the mare's hind end toward Manfred and gently backed her a step closer.

"We've got one just like that," Harper said. "Never aggressive."

Catherine nodded. "Right. Assertive, that's good, but no more." She watched Manfred a minute. "He'll scent, sometimes he'll yell at the mare, sometimes stick his nose in her hindquarters." As she said that, Manfred nuzzled the mare and pretty soon, she spread her back legs, braced, and urinated.

"Ok, she broke down," Catherine said to the mare's groom at the door. "I'll clean her up and you can get her up to the shed." The woman nodded.

Catherine led the mare into the room where JD and Harper stood, placed her in the padded brace as her groom came in the door and stood at the mare's head, holding the lead rope loosely.

Catherine washed her hands at the sink, pulled on new plastic gloves, went to the mare and wrapped her tail in vet wrap. Then she picked up her sponge from the bucket and began prepping the mare so she'd be clean to present to the stallion.

She continued her praise. "Manfred's never bit anyone, never tried to jump through the window. He's great," she said, swabbing the mare. "Really professional and quick to finish his business."

JD nodded. "You're right. A good teaser's worth his weight." He smiled, watched Catherine a minute then said: "Probably best

89

if we get back to the shed—we need a few more words with your boss."

Harper paused and put a hand on JD's arm. "So what's your take on what happened? With Oliver?" she said to Catherine. She evidently hadn't heard JD's earlier conversation.

The woman again sobered. She patted the mare softly, thinking.

"I can't tell you what a loss that was, him dying." She glanced at Manfred's closed window. "Oliver was the one worth his weight in gold," she said quietly. She thought another minute. "Not someone you can really replace," she finally said, glancing out the doorway to the shed. "Not by any stretch." She nodded and smiled sadly to them.

On the way back to the breeding shed, Harper mentioned that Catherine hadn't seemed all that impressed with Chad as Oliver's replacement.

"No, she looked like she'd sucked a lemon when his name came up."

They discussed it. From Chad's own mouth and now from Catherine, Oliver's focus was the horses, and Chad's was all about the money.

And that, JD thought, was a good summary of the racing game.

They entered the breeding shed's prep room where they found Redfield fiddling with the video screen.

"Got a minute? I'd like to wrap this up," said JD to Chad's back.

The stallion manager jumped, then turned, his eyes wide. "You creep up on everybody like that?" he said with some defensiveness.

Harper looked at JD, then back to Chad. "Whenever he can," she said.

"I got another mare coming up, so make it quick," Chad said, clearly unhappy with their presence.

"So Oliver. No enemies you can think of?" JD said, picking up where they'd left off.

Redfield leaned on the counter. "Naw, none I can think of. Like I said, Oliver was a Boy Scout."

He looked at Harper and a nasty sneer appeared. "And as for me stepping into his shoes, conveniently, I think was your point." He leered at Harper. "I paid my dues. I been in the horse business a long, long time and I earned this, earned this the hard way. So you can just set yourself straight on that one."

JD studied the stallion manager. Not so much what he said, but his attitude, his demeanor. Redfield had the same whiff of superiority hiding beneath an agitated surface that he'd picked up from Isabelle. Again, JD went back to the feeling that they were connected, somehow. Isabelle. Interesting.

JD pushed that button. "So what dealings do you have with the testing lab? We heard the Racing Commission was over here, took samples." JD focused on Redfield intently, wanting to see his reaction to the lab and the recent testing. He continued. "And we spoke to one of the supervisors, Isabelle. I think she was Oliver's girlfriend shortly before he died. Any light you can shed there?"

Chad's coloring was doing him no favors. His fair complexion flushed red. He'd done ok at the mention of the lab and the Commission, but JD noticed that Isabelle's name brought on the nerves.

"What?" was all Redfield could muster. He seemed rooted in place.

Harper jumped in. "We wondered if you knew anything about the recent drug testing over on the racing side. Or if you'd met Isabelle and might fill us in on her relationship with Oliver."

Chad was quiet a moment, seeming to think about it. When he spoke, he'd regained some composure, but not much.

"Well, I'm not all that clued in on the racing side of things," he said. "We get the colts and stallions when they're done. The good ones, anyhow." He paused. When JD and Harper were quiet, he said: "So I don't know about any of that . . . I mean," he corrected himself, blushing again, "of course I heard the Racing Commission was over there, of course I heard."

He fiddled with the video settings a moment. Not looking at JD and Harper, he finished: "And sure, I saw Oliver's girlfriend." He looked at them. "Once or twice." Redfield glanced out the prep room door, watching for the mare. "They weren't a thing for very long."

"Oh, so you were aware of their relationship?" Harper said, smiling.

Chad's eyes snapped back to Harper at that. "Not any more or less than anyone else," Chad replied, the defensiveness surfacing again. "Listen, we got another mare coming up here pretty quick," he said, "and I got things to do. We done here?" His face had the set of challenge, his pale brown eyes hard.

When JD and Harper were quiet and didn't move to exit, he said: "Look, I don't know what else I can tell you. I'm not gonna pretend me and Oliver were best friends. Or that I double dated with him and his girlfriend. We weren't and we didn't." Chad ran his hands through his curly red hair. He again had that defiant set to his jaw.

Harper nodded.

"But he taught me this side of the game, and like I said, I earned my spot. What happened to Oliver? I'm just as much in

92

the dark as everybody else. But I'll take what I earned and that's all I got."

Squirrely, thought JD. He glanced at Harper. Her mouth was in that hard little line that said "bullshit."

JD turned back to Redfield. "Sure, we're done. For now." He paused, noting Redfield didn't like the "for now" at all. "You've been more help than you know," JD finished, handing Redfield his card, and smiling inwardly. He did enjoy toying with the bad guys a little too much.

And Chad was definitely one of those. He motioned to Harper and said they'd see themselves out.

They left Chad standing at the video monitor, one minute looking arrogant and the next worried.

14

Harper woke up and looked at the clock: 4 a.m. She was agitated. Cass, she knew, was running out of time. She glanced over at JD, snoring softly.

They'd not made much more progress after their visit with Chad Redfield the previous day. Harper had farm business to attend to and JD had a meeting in the evening foisted on him by Al Walker, so he had to speak to the broodmare night shift worker in the morning.

That would be this morning. She glanced over at her husband. Let him get a few more hours, she thought, lifting the covers gently from her body.

Harper was not handling what seemed like unending delays in the case well. Walker knew the chances for Cass decreased with every passing hour, so last night's unscheduled meeting infuriated her. Every second Cass was missing spelled less and less chance of her survival.

Harper needed something. Something physical. Something fast and physical. Memphis was set to run in an upcoming weekend race, so he'd be doing a breeze, maybe a blowout, sometime this week. Might as well be today. She texted Marshall. "I'm up on Memphis. Be at the training track before dawn and go prior to the first set. Don't even say it. I'm up on him."

Marshall immediately texted back, he was awake, too. "Yeah. Heard about Cass." There was nothing for another few moments, then, "Breeze him. He's due."

She dressed and padded downstairs. She made coffee and leaned on the counter, gazing out into the dark, the moon fading yet still sending its eerie light over Buck's Creek and Grandpa's barn.

She grabbed her work gear—helmet, padded vest, and stick—pulled on riding boots and a thermal jacket then headed over to the barn just as the faintest pinks and purples shown over the horizon.

Lucas was cutting twine off some square bales when she arrived, so Harper told him to she was taking Memphis out to the training track and got his gear. The colt turned a soft, wise eye Harper's way as she approached, eager as she lifted the tiny saddle on his back, fitted his bridle and padded noseband, and led him out to the track. The horses they passed paid no attention, Lucas being the main event. He had the hay.

Marshall had his hands deep in his pockets and was leaning on the white rail when they approached. He heard Memphis and turned, concern showing in his eyes under the lights that would flicker off once dawn came on fully.

Eden Hill's trainer pulled on his Stetson as he always did when he was excited, agitated, or worried. He clicked his stopwatch on and off nervously as the pair approached, then reached up and stroked the colt's black head.

"You take care of her out there, hear?" he said softly.

Harper stroked Marshall's arm affectionately, reassuringly. The last time she'd done morning work was over at Keeneland's small track when one of the riders had tried to run the colt she rode into the rail.

"Didn't happen then, Marshall," she said, reading his mind. "Not then, not now." She looked at her colt, ran her hand along his muscled-out neck.

"Best get to it," she said, smiling, knowing the first set would be out shortly.

Memphis nodded under Marshall's fingers stroking his head, loving the scratch he got.

Harper looked at her colt, thinking he was agreeing with her, not taking care of an itch. The colt swung his head toward her, his ears pricked her way. Then he looked out over the track and when Harper moved the reins he looked back.

She noticed his soft eye had disappeared and in its place was eagerness. He snorted and stomped, impatient to go.

"Pick it up at each pole, let's see what he's got," said Marshall, getting his timer out. Then, after a moment. "Within reason. Do not blow him out." He waited another second. "I said do not blow him out, you hear me?"

The dawn was now coming on and the lights flickered and went out. Harper had turned Memphis, and Marshall threw her up.

"You hear me?" He said again, dawn's pink and blue colors filtering over the serious look on his face.

Harper nodded, having plans of her own. She knew Marshall didn't want her to turn the colt loose because he was worried about her, not because it would mess up Memphis' training.

She'd do whatever Memphis felt like doing. Neither of them needed permission from anyone.

She settled into the tiny, shiny black saddle, bent and checked her stirrups, straightened and patted her helmet, then withdrew her stick from her back where she'd stuck it into her breeches.

She inhaled deeply, leaned forward and caressed Memphis' neck, loving the scent of horse as familiar to her as her husband's. This was where she grew up, where she felt safe and most herself— on the back of a horse.

She moved Memphis from a walk to a trot, rising smoothly over him, sinking her heels, bending her body into the flat-backed position that would allow her hands to communicate to her colt and help keep them both balanced.

She felt Memphis coil beneath her, pulling a little, eager to eat up the track. His huge lungs expanded and contracted quickly as they moved into a gallop, Harper feeling the colt grow larger under her as the great bellows took in air and exhaled, a rhythm as effortless and natural as the quickening hooves sounding in the cool breeze that stung her cheeks in the meager light.

She stayed still above him, joining his eagerness, her own heart beating faster, looking up the track between his pricked black ears, all thought left far behind. Ahead was the first pole where she'd pick up his pace. Both the colt and rider had eyes only for the dirt unspooling before them. Memphis needed no encouragement, no cue other than Harper's thought. Before the pole, she felt him surge and stayed with him, rating him with her hands so he wouldn't go stratospheric.

Memphis' head bobbed and Harper let him out a bit as the next few poles flew by along the backstretch, and felt his neck extend. His body flowed over the track, his motion fluid.

She loosed the reins, giving him his head and the colt leapt forward, all four feet off the ground, his stride lengthening, his body fully stretched out. For that one moment there on the backstretch, she gave Memphis back to himself completely, closing her eyes, experiencing his freedom as her own.

In the next instant, Harper's eyes flew open, feeling what before had been a breeze turn into wind biting her face. She gathered the reins, shifted her weight into the turn, helping Memphis switch leads, and then they were out, Memphis accelerating, his neck flat, ears pinned, Harper hovering above him. Moments later, they flew past Marshall, Harper standing in the stirrups, her cold cheeks wet in the wind.

She let Memphis ease back, wind down to a gallop then canter then trot, then she turned him and walked him back toward her trainer.

She saw the exercise riders approaching in their black vests and helmets, a few saluting her with their sticks. She bent and lay on Memphis' neck, feeling his great muscles, his heat and heart, his sleek gracefulness, then she sat up and walked on feeling a bit restored.

As she approached Marshall, she noticed that there was someone standing beside him. She didn't know the person, but Marshall was showing him the stopwatch, and the guy let out a soft whistle.

She and Memphis stopped to let the other riders, colts, and fillies enter the track and take up their positions. They followed Keeneland track protocols, so a few lined up perpendicular to the track to await their turn, while some moved right into the work, the low banter beginning among those waiting. Harper was happy when her crew was happy. She looked at Marshall. They were a family, and Marshall made sure each person working the horses knew that.

She dismounted outside the gate, holding Memphis for a moment to hear what Marshall had to say. The instant the colt noticed the man standing next to Marshall, he shied and sidestepped, clearly uncomfortable.

"Hey buddy," she said, turning to her big, black colt, who was staring a hole through the man. And then Memphis reared and snorted and pawed the air, which set off the young horses on the training track. Harper walked toward her colt as he reared and got him under control. She needed to get him to his cool down, but he had to settle first.

Her curiosity had been piqued by his response to the stranger. Keeping her eye on the colt for a moment, she turned to Marshall as Memphis quieted now that he wasn't close to the man. Harper raised an eyebrow at Marshall, who nodded. The fellow next to her had a long face and eyes sunk back in his head. Harper felt uneasy, as uneasy as Memphis.

She considered the colt. He had an uncanny way of reading a situation accurately. His radar picked up things it sometimes took her a bit longer to discern.

She smiled. In some ways, Memphis was to her what she was to JD. At least when it came to radar.

Memphis turned his intelligent eye her way and backed up a few more steps.

Got it, she thought, waving a hand to Marshall and heading back to the barn. No use getting the colt any more riled up. She'd catch up with Marshall once she got Memphis handed off to the hot walker. The minute she turned the colt toward the barn, he relaxed into a loose, easy walk, but she kept her eye on him.

After she got Memphis unsaddled, she handed him over to Simon. She went back down to the training track, noticing that whoever it was had left. He sure wasn't there very long.

Marshall was fiddling with his black Stetson, lifting it off his head and settling it back on, keeping his eyes trained on the track as the young colts and fillies moved into their training, at first warming up, just as Harper had done, and then moving into jogs or gallops or funneling down to the far rail in twos for a faster work out.

She stayed quiet a moment beside Marshall, looking out over the runners. Then, in a soft voice she asked, "So who was that guy?"

Marshall glanced at his stopwatch. "I have a better question." He turned and glared at her, fingering his binoculars then held them up, letting Harper know he'd watched her. "What was that stunt you pulled out there?"

"What?"

"The reins? The eyes?" Marshall threw his arms wide. He had the look a concerned father has when their kid goes off grid.

"Yeah," was what came out of Harper's mouth. She looked down, scuffed a boot. She knew what was coming.

"That was stupid."

"Yeah," she said, her head still down.

"Full out on a loose rein? Hell of a thing if he stumbled—the reins could've gone over his head, along with you—gotten caught in his legs."

"But they didn't." Harper looked out over the track.

"But they could have." Marshall paused, stuck his hands back in his pockets. "You could have hurt yourself bad and that colt, maybe killed him."

She thought: I don't live in that universe.

"Stupid. Not to mention you—you could've . . ." He trailed off, glaring at her again.

Harper looked at him, realizing what he was really saying. He'd raised her and her sister Paris, after the car accident. Now Paris was dead, too. Harper was all he had left. She softened, laced her arm through his.

He stared out at the track, still peeved.

"But I didn't," she said. "Nobody died, Marshall." She pulled him close. "And nobody's gonna die," she finished quietly and with conviction. She thought about Cass as Marshall wrapped his arm around her shoulder.

He took out his watch, changed the subject. "That work on your colt out there was something," he said, showing her the time.

She smiled. She'd never have guessed they were going that fast. She and Cass had talked about that. She wiped her face as if to clear the last of her tears.

Cass. She'd lost her agitation out on the track, but now, thinking of her friend . . .

"You have to watch it with Memphis," Marshall was saying. "He's a tricky one." The trainer glanced at the track. "Fluid and wicked smart." He shook his head and pocketed his watch. He nodded to his assistant down the way who'd come up with the set and had his clipboard in hand and his stopwatch already working.

Marshall turned to Harper, smoothed his hand along the top rail as they both heard the horses breathing and their hooves pounding. The sun was up enough to cast a bit of warmth over them now. Marshall bent and picked up a coffee from the dirt and handed it to Harper. She warmed her hands while she waited for Marshall to speak.

"That guy you saw, that was Gus Pinard," he said. He looked both serious and a little confused. "Janero's trainer."

"Really." A red flag went up for Harper.

"Yeah, weird, right?" said Marshall, and he turned back to watch the training, but continued. "I mean, he and I use to talk back in the day. Before he moved over to Janero. But I haven't seen him in a couple of years. Since he's been there, he just kind of dropped off my radar."

"What did he want?"

Marshall thought a moment. "Well, at first he asked about what races I thought one of his fillies set up for. Why he asked me that, I have no idea. And he scoped out Memphis, of course."

"Well, he didn't come to see the colt," said Harper. "Nobody knew I'd work him before the first set."

Marshall nodded. "Hey Marcie," he called to Meadow's rider. "Let's change it up, maybe no breeze today." He turned to

Harper. "She did a bullet before that last race. Need to give her a breather."

Marcie saluted and eased Meadow into a trot, moving to her position on the track.

Marshall resumed the conversation. "I had the distinct feeling Gus was pumping me for information."

"Pumping you for information about the runners?"

"No, that's the weird part. He wanted to know about the investigation into Oliver's death. He wanted to know how JD was coming along with it."

He looked Harper square in the face as she turned to him. "Like I know," he said. He turned back to the track, perplexed. "I don't know, it was just a really strange conversation."

"So what did you tell him?"

"I told him he'd have to ask JD. I didn't know nothing from nothing." He paused. And then, "Which is actually the truth." He turned to Harper. "You guys never tell me anything." He looked hurt.

Harper knew that wasn't at all true. She patted his forearm. "So sensitive," she said, smiling. Then, "So he left?"

"Yeah, right after that. Very strange." The trainer's voice trailed off.

Harper nodded. She thanked Marshall for the work on Memphis, hugged him hard, and told him she'd catch up on the horses later.

Strange about Pinard. She thought it over on the way up to the barn to check on Memphis. She pulled out her carrots and took Memphis from the groom who was caring for him after his cool down, and escorted him back to his stall, feeding him one carrot round at a time as they went, ending with a peppermint. She nodded to Lucas who gave her a thumbs up on the colt going out to graze; he'd wait a bit then hand him off to a groom. The stallion manager waved a hand to Harper and turned into the feed room.

She'd have to let JD know about Pinard's visit, and about Marshall's reaction. She stroked Memphis' sleek, black neck, kissed his soft muzzle, and took the heavy leather halter off. She'd keep Memphis' reaction to Pinard to herself. She ran her hand along the colt's back just as Lucas appeared and topped off one of the colt's two water buckets. Unlike most in the barn, Memphis waited for Harper's goodbye before sucking up half his bucket.

She silently wished him well on his upcoming race and whispered "Safe trip" as she always did.

Once back home, she parked the car, and instead of going in, she made her way down to Grandpa's barn, just over Bucks Creek, where they housed all their personal horses. John Henry had grained the horses and was topping off the water, throwing some square bales into each stall. He'd do turnout just after they'd eaten. She walked past the stalls, pausing to talk to and caress each one, noticing one empty stall.

She turned in time to see a big bay named Odin walking into the barn, wearing a western saddle upon which sat Wes. He'd obviously needed some horse time just as much as she had. She glanced at the time. Early. It was still cold out, as her ride on Memphis had proved. She wondered if Wes was as frustrated as she was about the stalled investigation and as worried about Cass as she was. As frustrated and worried as they all were.

She looked around as Wes and Odin entered, taking in the first barn her Grandpa had built. Built with trees he'd felled himself on the property. Visions of childhood flooded in—she and her sister Paris had grown up in this barn, helping her grandfather muck out the stalls, the girls throwing bits of manure at each other and laughing, her Grandpa looking on in mock sternness. None of them would have traded where they were for any place on earth. The barn held memories of JD too, in his lanky, gawky teenage years, always coming over, saying he wanted to help her grandpa, but everybody knew he was there for Harper.

She smiled. Nothing had changed on that score.

15

C ass hadn't found anything to work with on her travels around the small room—no loose or rotted boards soft enough to matter, no nails she could pry out.

But another plan had taken shape in her mind. She sat in the corner, fingering the black horsehair bracelet. Then she slipped it off. It was braided, it was Deacon's hair. Cass resisted the emotions trying to well up. Wes had made it for her after hearing of Deacon's stunning win over Aviragus in the Maker's Mark Mile last year. Almost a year exactly. She stared at the small window, remembering. Deacon, a colt for the ages, the commentators had said.

Momentarily, she felt the weight of it all, wondering if she'd ever see him again. Or Meadow, the little filly with the fiercest heart, or Memphis, whose intelligence and spirit matched a body that might rival Deacon's. She had a ride on Memphis coming up. Right there's a reason to get outta here, she thought. Deacon, Meadow, Memphis. Harper and JD had given her the best rides of her life, as well as their friendship. They'd made her part of their family. No one had ever done that before. She knew JD and Harper wouldn't stop until they found her.

She raised the woven hair to her nostrils, closed her eyes, and inhaled. Then she gently set it down, clearing some shavings so its presence was apparent.

Wes would come. Wes, Harper, and JD. Wes would find it. He'd know she'd been there. If her plan worked, she'd still be alive. If not, well, at least he'd know.

She leaned back on the room's wooden wall, picked at the shavings, and thought through her plan again. When he opened the door to give her food, her captor didn't enter the room. He wasn't stupid. He stayed safely in the doorway, then bent and placed her plate just inside the door, reached back and grabbed the water he'd set down and placed that in the room, as well. And he'd worn the black head mask each time, so she still had no visual.

The door opened inward. And she'd heard him approach, his boots shuffled enough to make his presence apparent.

She smiled in the pre-dawn darkness. Next time would be the last time, buddy, she promised. She bent one knee and then the other, got up and began her workout.

She measured her cardiac work. Though this was only the second day of her capture, she knew the signs of dehydration, and she was not getting enough water. Not enough food, either, but she needed water more. She'd been lucky in her riding career. Most jocks knew the pangs of hunger and dehydration. It was a jock's life, keeping the weight off. But she'd never had to watch her weight like some or sweat out fluids to make weight.

She'd been fortunate. But now, she knew she had to watch her exertion. No telling how long she'd be there. She needed to be smart if she hoped to survive.

Unlike her captor.

He wasn't that smart, she thought. He hadn't rebound her hands and feet.

She'd wondered about that. On one hand, it didn't make sense. Why allow her any freedom? But then, she mused, maybe she knew him. Maybe he'd not wanted to give her opportunities to identify him, so had kept his distance. That would make some sort of sense. But the truth was, whatever the reason, him not tying her up was a mistake.

And that would cost him.

16

JD rolled over, hearing the door shut and the car fire up. Long years in the service had made him a light sleeper, so he was up when Harper had stirred out of bed. He knew she needed space, knew she was worried about Cass, but once he heard the front door, he was up, in the shower, then dressed, and coffee in hand, he was out the door not far behind her.

He headed to the precinct just as dawn broke, its soft pinks and blues at odds with how he felt.

He knew Wes was ready to go, too. Neither of them was very good at inaction.

He intended to head over to Janero's broodmare barn to speak with the night worker and then head straight to the lab to grill Isabelle. Maybe Wes would be good to bring along. He'd give him a call. He also needed to check with the hospital, see if Janero's vet, Jason Williams, was alert enough for an interview.

But first he would stop by the precinct. He wanted to look into Chad Redfield a bit more, see what his past held prior to coming to Kentucky.

He grabbed another coffee once at the police station, headed to his office, and turned on the computer. There were a few police officers at their desks, but he mostly had the place to himself. He was toying with the idea of calling in the FBI on Cass. If she'd been taken across state lines, they'd be good to have in on the hunt, and that was their jurisdiction anyway. JD paused. He was used to doing things on his own and resisted outside interference, which is how he thought of it. Interference, not help. He and Wes were alike in that. He knew it wasn't always the wiser course. But they'd gotten results and the quickest outcomes with that MO. So he'd go with it.

He sat back. But Wes was right, he'd never get results pressing this hard. He rolled his shoulders, cracked his neck, and settled. Let the game come to you, he reminded himself. That wasn't easy when it got personal.

He nosed around on the computer, reviewed a couple of databases, and eventually found out some interesting things about Mr. Redfield from his days in and around Tulsa. Not much before then, but once in the Sooner state he'd done some work with quarter horses and also with bulls. He'd been present when questionable practices went on with them both. Bulls headed to the PBR had been given anabolic steroids and other illegal drugs during Chad's work with a bull stock contractor. Then there were the clenbuterol test results when he shifted to quarter horses. Labs tested hair samples on the breed because clenbuterol is illegal no matter when it's administered to racing quarter horses and with hair, you can't clearly pin down when the infraction took place. That's why the Kentucky Racing Commission didn't routinely use it.

JD shook himself, he was getting off track.

Chad was present in each situation, and in positions where he could have had a hand in both. He was never arrested, or even implicated, but JD wondered if his move to Kentucky happened to get out from under some heavy heat in Oklahoma before it reached the boiling point. Redfield's connections to both bull and quarter horse drugging might mean he had pharma connections.

His cell phone rang. It was Cheryl, one of the officers who'd been tracking down the two last people living in Cass' condo. JD answered it, figuring she had some news or she'd have waited a bit to call. He glanced at the time—6:30.

He'd have to get a move on to get to Janero's broodmare barn before the night shift worker left at 7 a.m. He got on his jacket and headed to his unmarked F-150, all the while listening to Cheryl's report.

One of the condo dwellers had come home about twelve thirty or a bit after the night Cass was taken. She'd seen a man she didn't recognize by an SUV, looking at the row of condos Cass lived in. She thought it odd, given the hour. But then, she said, people visited frequently and even she was just getting home. At the time, she thought the guy might have had a dog. She hadn't been close enough to see for sure, and wasn't concerned enough to check. She hadn't gotten a license plate number, but she did say she thought the vehicle was dark-colored and fairly old. That's all she had, but at least it was something. Nothing so far had shown up in the wider door-to-door, but they were still checking.

JD thought about the guy with the SUV. Right time, generally, and certainly the right place.

He started the truck and asked Cheryl to get the team on all surveillance cameras they could find. Let's see if they could figure out where he went after he took Cass.

If, JD reminded himself, he was the one who'd taken her.

Well, thought JD, giving Wes a call, it was the only lead he had. And if they found she had crossed state lines—Ohio, after all, was just up the road—he'd for sure call in the Feds.

He called Harper, too, but the phone went to voicemail. He left a message.

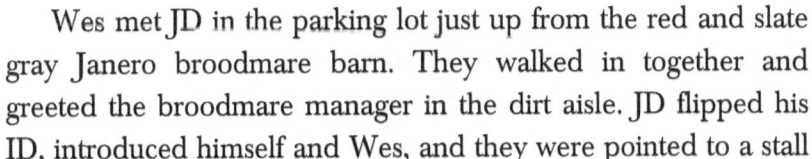

Wes met JD in the parking lot just up from the red and slate gray Janero broodmare barn. They walked in together and greeted the broodmare manager in the dirt aisle. JD flipped his ID, introduced himself and Wes, and they were pointed to a stall two from the end. They walked up among broodmare grooms filing in, heading to their assigned moms and babies.

Through the wire stall mesh, JD saw a very pregnant bay mare and her attendant who was allowing the expectant mom to sniff a wet towel. JD introduced himself and Wes again, and learned the wide, Slavic-faced woman's name was Molly. She'd been foaling for thirty years, she told them, her crinkly eyes soft with obvious affection for her work.

"This momma's gonna go here pretty soon, see those veins around the halter there? How enlarged they are? Pulsing?" She turned to them. "That's the adrenaline kicking in." She nodded as the mare curled around Molly, her luminous eyes going soft. The affection was mutual.

Molly held up the towel. "Baby magic, that's what I call it. Got this amniotic fluid from that new mom down the way last night. Gets the hormones up," she said, stroking the mare's neck.

JD was patient. He knew all about foaling, had been attending to it all his life at Hawk Ridge. But he let Molly talk. Good to establish a connection. He glanced at Wes, saw the impatience. Ok, he thought, he's right. Best get to it.

"Molly," JD began gently, trying to turn her attention to the issue they'd come for. "The night Oliver died, can we go back to that night?"

Molly's eyes turned to them, shining with emotion. "Oh yes," she said, her gaze turning to the stall's floor shavings. "That was . . ." her voice faltered. She looked stricken. "He was such a nice man," she said.

"Do you remember anything about that night?" Wes asked.

Around them, the scent of hay and horse rose and drifted. The sound of grooms softly talking to their mares and babies filtered through the cool April morning.

"Not really," Molly said, stroking her mare's cheek. The horse broke off and began to circle the stall, so Molly exited to stand with them in the aisle. "I need to get her out in the pasture," she said. "Odd to drop the baby in the day, but she's about to."

"We'll only be a minute more," JD said. "Anything you can remember would be helpful. Even if it seems unrelated."

Molly's brow knit. She didn't say anything for a few moments. Then: "Well, ok, this is going to sound, well, stupid probably." She glanced at JD then Wes. JD nodded his encouragement. Wes didn't change his expression.

"I know I was knocked out, so this was surely a dream," she began. "But you said 'anything,' right?"

JD nodded, staying quiet so she'd continue.

"I do remember. . ." She stopped, her expression uncertain. "You sure? This is, well . . . Ok, anyway, I had a dream that I heard something." She shook her head as if she thought herself ridiculous for saying it.

JD said, "Good, that's good. What happened in the dream?" She was likely not completely unconscious so what she "dreamed" could well have been the murder.

"Two guys talking," she said, encouraged by JD. "Then one guy started screaming." She stopped to think. "The horses were upset, I remember that. And I wanted to go to them, but for some reason, I didn't." She looked at them, her brow deeply furrowed. She seemed troubled. "I kept wanting to go to the mares, but I don't know, I just couldn't." She looked confused.

Wes said: "The guy screaming. What did he say?"

JD's cell phone vibrated. He glanced at the number, didn't recognize it and let it go to voicemail.

She shook her head. "I honestly don't know. I just remember really loud screaming." She thought another minute, her broad face and small eyes looking down at the barn aisle dirt. "Yeah, that's all I remember." She looked up. "A dream, right? I mean I was knocked out."

JD touched her shoulder. "Right, it was likely a dream. But we really appreciate you taking the time." He handed her his card. "If you remember anything else, anything at all, please call me right away."

Molly nodded, picked up a lead rope from outside the mare's stall, and slid the door open. "Is that all you need?" she said. "Can I get this mare out so she can have her baby?"

JD nodded, smiling, and Molly got the mare hooked up and brought her into the aisle, her dark brown belly swollen with a new baby racehorse about to make an appearance.

Outside the barn, JD said: "So that's pretty clear—there was somebody with Oliver. Likely gave him that tap on the skull and the hot shot." He filled Wes in on what Cheryl had reported about the man and the SUV outside Cass' condo plus what he'd found out about Chad Redfield's Oklahoma activities.

Wes nodded. "I'm gonna go sight in the long guns."

JD watched him get in his truck. Wes was right, they were close.

But they'd been close for a while. They needed to get on top of it.

17

JD headed over to the testing lab to talk with Isabelle. The equine genetic expert, mused JD, a small item of interest she hadn't disclosed in their first interview. He called Harper again, but the phone again went to voicemail.

At the lab, he was escorted through a narrow walkway lined on one side with computers and white-clad lab workers peering at data and on the other by fluid-filled tubes situated in plastic holders before various sorts of testing apparatus.

Isabelle sat in her office looking at the computer screen then jotting down something on a legal-sized notepad.

JD knocked at the open doorway and surveyed the crammed office. Isabelle looked up, her eyes instantly narrowing. She pulled her lab coat tighter around her, her girth not allowing the closure.

"You again," she said. She turned back to her computer.

JD walked in, moved a pile of papers off a chair, glanced at the overflowing bookcases and folded his hands.

"You neglected to mention you are an expert in genetics," he said to her profile.

She turned to him. "What of it?" The challenge was back in her eyes and in the set of her jaw. She stroked a greasy lock of hair. "What does that possibly have to do with me dating Oliver?" she huffed.

"He was murdered," JD said. "So everything is relevant."

"Murdered?" she stammered. "Hey, I didn't hear that," she said nervously.

JD ignored it. He leaned his elbows on his knees and stared her in the eyes. "I'm pretty sure somebody's messing with the genes of the horses over at Janero." Truthfully, he wasn't all that sure since there was no hard evidence. But he'd bet on it.

Her eyes went wide.

"And you're the only one connected to the murder victim who also has gene expertise and testing information about Janero's runners."

She stood up, pulled her phone out.

"Ok, we're done," she said coldly, punching in a number and staring down at JD. "I'm calling my lawyer." She turned to the side and mumbled her lawyer's name into the phone.

JD smiled. So she had a lawyer. "I'd say that was a good idea."

He got up and walked out.

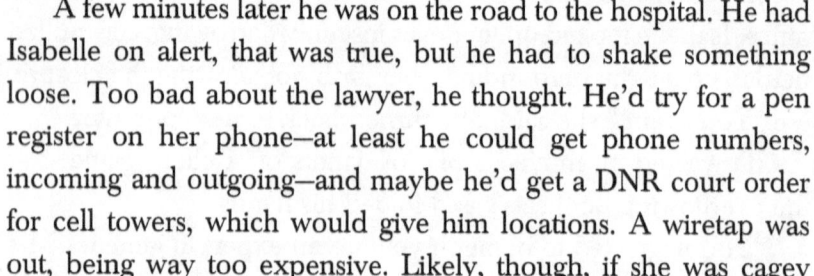

A few minutes later he was on the road to the hospital. He had Isabelle on alert, that was true, but he had to shake something loose. Too bad about the lawyer, he thought. He'd try for a pen register on her phone—at least he could get phone numbers, incoming and outgoing—and maybe he'd get a DNR court order for cell towers, which would give him locations. A wiretap was out, being way too expensive. Likely, though, if she was cagey enough to call her lawyer, JD realized, it was unlikely he'd find anything on the phone.

Jason Williams, Janero's vet, had been cleared for an interview after the operation. On the way to the hospital Harper called, and JD filled her in on the developments. She mentioned that Janero's trainer had showed up at workouts pumping Marshall for information on the investigation.

JD considered that. Interesting. He filed that away to think about after his interview with Jason Williams. He was about to ask her what she was doing at workouts, when Harper mentioned she had farm business, so JD was on his own with Williams. But they both agreed a meet-up among her, Wes, and JD needed to happen soon. The case was fast moving, and they needed to pool information. And ideas. And next steps. Harper reminded him that he did have a boss, asking him if he was only filling in her and Wes, or had he found any time at all for Al Walker?

"Humorous, babe," JD said, knowing she was right. His boss was generally the last to know. Maybe he'd put in a call to him. Yeah, he thought, right after he talked to Jason Williams and his live-in. Right after that.

Harper smiled at JD's moments of silence, thinking that maybe she needed to make a few calls herself. She'd call Marshall and Tim Bradford, the more minds on this the better. Harper told JD she'd put in a call to Wes and set a meeting up. JD hung up and stared at the phone a second, then turned his eyes back to the road.

Volunteering to call Wes? That was odd. Likely more a measure of how concerned she was about Cass, he decided, than that she was warming to Wes.

He parked and jogged into the hospital, rode the elevator up, flashed his badge and was directed to a room down the shiny hallway lined with gurneys and blue-clad hospital workers—the doctors with stethoscopes around their necks, the nurses carrying the rest of the load.

Jason Williams was eating Jell-O as he entered, his left leg hoisted in the air, maybe for swelling, thought JD, but what did he know. A small, brown-haired woman sat off to the side flipping through a fashion magazine.

JD introduced himself to Williams, and asked if the woman was Cecelia Fournier, Jason's live-in French equine vet. They both looked startled at the last question, and the vet nodded.

Jason Williams was a white-blond, hazel-eyed, square jawed, handsome guy from what JD could see. He put his Jell-O on the tray to the side and focused on JD.

"What's this about?" Williams asked, glancing at Cecelia then back to JD. "I suppose Oliver, right?"

JD nodded.

"How can I help?" he said, sitting back against his pillows. "Oliver was a stand-up guy," he said, shaking his head. "Didn't know him well, of course, but anytime I was over on the stallion side, he was professional and clearly knew his stuff."

"Was that often?" JD said.

Williams scratched an itch on his arm. "Not really. They've got an older stallion, Gissendi, and they had a few infections in a couple of others." He looked up at JD, the epitome of concern. "Those infections are hitting everybody these days."

Cecelia nodded, concern registering on her face, too.

JD turned to her. "And where is it you work?"

The pair exchanged glances. Cecelia looked slightly uncomfortable but answered. "I work with Jason, in the practice." She shrugged. "I go where he send me." She hadn't lost her French accent.

"And your area of interest?" JD said, drilling down on who she was a bit more.

"How is this relevant?" Williams broke in, sitting up a bit against his pillows, a frown on his beach boy face.

JD didn't smile. "Just routine," he said and turned back to Cecelia. "Do you focus on anything in particular? Reproduction? The racing side?"

She reluctantly responded. "Yes, when I was in France, I work with the group. We deal with the racehorses."

JD nodded. "Lots less injuries there. Better enforcement of laws. Less drugs. Why come to the States?" He'd get to her expertise in a moment.

The nurse came in with Jason's meds, and she proffered them with a cup of water. She looked at JD as Jason downed the pills without taking his eyes off the detective. The nurse left in a hurry, taking the cart with the vet's unfinished Jell-O.

"This is obvious, no?" Cecelia said, reaching for Williams' hand. He grasped hers and they were both quiet, staring at JD.

They both adopted an innocent "we're deeply in love" look and awaited JD's response.

He turned to Williams, giving the vet a hefty cop stare. "What can you tell me about your work at Janero? Specifically with the racehorses, the younger ones."

The vet turned solemn. "They've sure had some issues." He nodded sadly then looked up. "I did what I could." He pointed to his leg. "As soon as this heals up enough, I'll continue to do that." He looked at Cecelia. "We both will."

Cecelia spoke up. "I am focusing on nutrition. For the young ones. I maybe make the suggestions when their Mr. Pinard asks."

Gus Pinard, thought JD. Janero's trainer. "So your focus is nutrition?" JD said, and Cecelia nodded.

JD studied them. They certainly presented a guileless front. They'd been forthcoming, if a little reluctant. But then, most people are nervous being interviewed by a cop.

He mulled it over. The vet, in situations like this, was generally involved, especially if drugs are present. But maybe with gene modification, they'd also need a different sort of expertise. A chemist? He stared at them. The truth was, he just didn't know enough at this point to understand exactly what was going on at Janero.

JD took another tack. "So the youngsters over there. The one Bradford put down with anemia. The other issues they've had."

"I know the Commission was out there. No harm, no foul, we heard," Williams said.

JD nodded. "True, the horses were clean. But I'm interested in what you think about gene modification. Think that might be at play over there?"

They both seemed confused. Cecelia spoke up first. "I hear this in Europe. Hear about it." She paused. "But here, no. I hear nothing about this here."

Williams was looking at Cecelia intently as she spoke. When she was finished, he turned to JD. "I have been reading up on that." He spread his arms. "We all have." He considered the question a moment more. "But like Cecelia said. I haven't heard about that going on here." He looked frankly at JD. "Yet. I guess that's the truth. It will get here. And I know Kentucky is funding research. I know the gene sequence has been mapped." He looked at Cecelia. "But I just don't have enough information to answer you."

JD nodded and stared at them both a moment, considering each one's demeanor. At least for the moment, he decided, he'd accept that they were both telling the truth. Why the vet's ex-wife felt he was capable of drugging racehorses? Well, he figured, that could be her bitterness talking. He'd go with that for now. At least until things came to light to prove otherwise.

He left Cecelia his card and exited.

In the truck, JD briefly wondered if he was reading the case wrong. Was Oliver's death a simple murder having nothing to do with the horses at Janero? Was Cass' abduction related to one but not the other? Was he going down a blind alley altogether investigating the runners at Janero? The Racing Commission had found all the horses clean. Janero's vet seemed kind of a Boy

Scout, to use Chad's words. And he had nothing, really, on Chad. He was crass, certainly, but weren't so many involved in racing? And Isabelle. Maybe she was simply an unpleasant person doing her job and being her obnoxious self.

Maybe. He leaned back in the car seat, frustrated. Then he heard his stomach growl and glanced at the phone. One thirty, no wonder. He might as well head home, grab some lunch, link up with Harper, and see what she'd set up with Wes. He could use everyone's help on this. They needed to get all the information they'd gathered out on the table.

Then JD noticed the voicemail. In the interviews after he'd left the broodmare barn, it had slipped his mind. He punched it up, starting the car as he did.

The message was brief: "Back off. What'll happen if you don't is pretty fucking simple. You'll never see that little spitfire jock you got again. I won't warn you twice." And he hung up.

The voice was cool and composed. There was no hype, no agitation. He meant what he said. The voice was disguised but the message was clear.

And that voicemail changed everything.

18

JD sat in Harper's office and wolfed down a roast beef sandwich, alternating with chips, and gulping a Pepsi. He'd filled Harper in on everything he knew and let her listen to the voicemail.

With a mouthful, he said: "So we know he—it's a "he" for sure. Or that's my guess. He knows about the case."

"Clearly," said Harper, her face very worried.

JD nodded, glancing at Pepper in the doorway. She lifted an eyebrow, JD shook his head, indicating he didn't need anything. She left and he turned back to Harper.

"And Cass being taken was to send a message."

"One we didn't pick up on," Harper said. She grabbed up a pen and rapidly tapped it on her desk. "Well," she corrected herself, her blue eyes focused, "we did pick up on it. We just chose to ignore that and find her."

Marshall walked in, glanced at them both, removed his Stetson and quietly sat down next to JD, putting his hat on the table between them.

Harper said: "JD got a threat." She looked at Marshall. "About Cass."

With that, Marshall swiveled and looked at the detective, pulled on his walrus mustache. JD wiped his mouth, gulped his Pepsi. "Whoever it was knows the racing business, he used the word "jock" not "jockey" and he knows Cass rides for us." He let Marshall hear the voicemail.

Marshall was quiet after, looked at Harper.

"And probably knows her personal connection to us, too," Harper said. "But we knew all that before." Her eyes glanced at her computer screen then back to them both.

"We gotta find her quick," said Marshall. They nodded.

Wes strode in, his M24 sniper rifle slung around his back. He saw their faces, and leaned on the wall, knee cocked and braced against it. He moved the rifle to his left shoulder, barrel down. He seemed casually menacing.

JD's phone rang. He looked at the number and answered it. "Yeah." Then he was quiet for a time. "Ok, thanks. Yeah, I know. We'll talk later."

He looked up. "Tim. He's over at Janero. That old stallion over there? Gissendi? Just dropped dead. Heart attack they're saying."

They were all quiet a moment.

Marshall patted the arms on his chair. "Happens," he said sadly. And yes, they all knew it did. Some said the amount of covers the stallions were increasingly asked to do shortened their lives. Two hemispheres, the U.S. season and then abroad. And the Jockey Club had been unable to limit the U.S. covers.

Harper: "Yeah, but it also "happens" when genes are messed with."

"Or due to any number of other substances," JD chimed in. They'd all heard the stories.

Wes had been quiet but now had a question. "Why is your vet over there? They have a vet."

JD nodded, looking at Wes. Good point. "Right. In fact, their vet—Jason Williams—the one who's in the hospital. He has a whole practice." He looked at Harper. "Doesn't need Tim at all."

Everybody was quiet. The office noise drifted in—phones ringing, people chatting as they passed the doorway, doors closing, the microwave ding. Wes reached over and quietly closed it.

Finally Harper spoke up, looking at JD. "I wonder if your take on Williams and his live-in was right. Maybe he actually is innocent but has suspicions."

"Ones he didn't share with me."

"Yeah, but," Harper continued, "if he didn't want his practice involved, he'd get somebody outside to cover for him."

Marshall jumped in. "And Tim's as straight-arrow as they come."

"Plus he's our vet, Williams has to know that." This from JD. His green eyes narrowed, as he thought it through.

"So he's doing what he can under the radar," Marshall said.

"Playing both sides," Wes said. "Keep his client in the event Janero's clean. But help take them down, if not."

Harper spoke up. "I'd lay odds he doesn't go back to Janero when he's out of the hospital. Too many question marks, he wouldn't want his name associated with the place one way or the other." She paused and they all considered that a minute. Then: "I set a meeting for all of us, including Tim." She looked at her phone. "About now. It's 2:30." She looked at JD. "What do you want to do, wait on Tim?"

JD thought a moment then stood, ran a hand through his hair. "I'll head over to the precinct." He looked at Wes. "Come." He looked at the M24. "But leave that somewhere." To Harper: "I'm gonna check in with Cheryl on any surveillance they may have on that SUV. Also see what came up with Isabelle's phone, if anything. And what else I can find on her—somebody has to know something. She can't be doing this all on her own."

Harper nodded. "Redfield, right? You think he's in on it with her? You said he'd been involved some stuff in Oklahoma."

JD looked dubious. "Maybe. No proof. But the guy's got that vibe."

Marshall spoke up. "Could somebody please fill me in here?" He was clearly frustrated.

Harper nodded to JD. "You two go on. I'll get Marshall up to speed, and Tim if he doesn't get stuck at Janero."

JD walked behind Harper's desk and kissed her blond hair, tipped her face to his and lightly brushed his lips against hers. She didn't smile. "I know," he said into her eyes, "we'll find her in time."

19

S he had nodded off, but something woke her. Alert, she sat up and listened.

Yes, she heard his boots. He was coming.

Late afternoon, Cass judged, by the light coming in the far window. She patted around, laid her fingers on the braided bracelet. She thought about Deacon and the other horses. And Wes. It fueled her determination.

Her abductor continued to approach. So this was likely what passed for "dinner," she thought, glancing again at the window. Lukewarm slop, if yesterday was any indication.

She got up quietly. She'd gone over several scenarios of how she could make her escape. In fact, she'd gone over them a multitude of times in her mind, envisioning them just as she envisioned races she was set to ride.

She tucked her rubber-soled slippers into her waistband, and moved to the door, positioning herself at a right angle to it with her right hand, chest high, resting softly on the door so she'd feel the second it began to open. She placed her left palm at hip-level on the door. She moved her legs into position, shoulder-wide, then she settled herself, ready for the instant he turned the knob and opened the door.

She heard him grunt softly as he set the water bottle down, stood, grabbed the knob and slowly opened the door just enough to bend and set down the plate of food in his left hand.

He didn't get the chance.

Cass felt no fear as she gripped the door with her right hand and, using that as leverage, stepped forward with her left foot, bent

124

her right knee and whipped around the door, snapping her leg straight, striking his left leg hard just above the knee.

He cried out as the knee buckled and, dropping the plate, he fell to his side gripping the injured knee with both hands.

Taking out his knee would slow him a lot. She wished she'd had her boots—she would have broken his leg.

Cass leaped over him the second he dropped, her head up, running headlong for the shaft of light ahead and to the left—she hoped that meant a doorway. She didn't look back, she didn't look around, she didn't think. She ran as an animal would, on instinct. She ran with focus, staying within herself as she did on a full-out colt, her eyes on the door at the far end of the building.

That door meant freedom.

And then she was out, still running hard, breathing more quickly now, sending every ounce of energy to her churning legs. She spied woods on the other side of the scraggly dirt lot housing a rusted tractor, a burned SUV, a shiny pick-up, and beyond it to the right, a dingy double-wide. She made hard for the woods, hearing him behind her now, cursing her as he ran.

Shots rang out behind her, but they went wide. She heard a dull *thwack* as one hit the tree trunk to her left, then another as the next bullet went wide and the grazed bark of an old elm.

She chanced a glance back and saw he was attempting to run, but with the injury, he was limping, and not making much headway.

He was a harrowing sight with that mask, even slowed as he was—all she could make out were his eyes, but she was too far away to see them clearly. She'd bet, though, they were hard little marbles of pain.

Good, you son-of-a-bitch, she thought.

She turned back to the woods, somehow found a higher gear, and plunged forward into them, her robe billowing out behind

125

her. She pulled it around her so as not to be a larger target, dodged budded out elms, oaks, and a few sycamore trees, leapt logs, and prayed her legs wouldn't tangle in the dense, cool, dank undergrowth. Her arms pumped, her breathing again quickened, her stride lengthened. The light shimmered and dappled the understory as the late afternoon sun sank toward the horizon.

More shots, but they sounded farther away. She ran harder.

As much as any filly or colt she'd ridden, Cass was in full flight.

She didn't feel the cold, though its damp chill seeped through her robe now. She heard no birds or scurrying ground creatures, she didn't dare stop, though the trees grew more dense the deeper into the woods she ran. She dodged and zig-zagged, kept moving, not thinking about him, only what lay directly ahead. She thought momentarily about her slippers, still tucked in her waistband. Still she ran on, trusting her stamina and fitness, if not the forest floor.

The leaf fall was getting deeper now, slowing her. She hadn't heard the gun since she'd made for the denser forest. Maybe out of amo, she thought. The light grew more faint. She had no idea how long or far she'd run, but felt the toll her capture had taken creeping in. She glanced back again, not seeing her pursuer but knowing he had to be following. She refused to give in to fatigue or fear. He'd taken her for a reason so he wouldn't stop until he found her again. She ran on as fast as the deep, fragrantly rotting leaves would allow.

Cass finally chanced stopping behind a big-trunked oak. She inhaled the decomposing leaves, the air cooling even more around her. She panted, her heart racing, not knowing how much further she could go. She pulled her slippers out and bent to put them on. Her feet were bleeding, but she didn't feel it. The adrenaline would wear off eventually, she knew. She had to get as far ahead of him as possible before that happened.

Feet shod, she paused a moment more to survey the woods, pulling her robe tighter around her to fend off the ever-seeping chill. Peering around the tree, she saw no one, heard no one.

She turned back. Which way led to the nearest road? Or house? She couldn't tell. On every side there was only deep, darkening woods. Except, of course, behind her. But she wasn't heading that way any time soon.

She plunged ahead, choosing to veer left, for no other reason than that's the direction her feet took her.

20

JD set up what he could at the precinct, Wes sitting silently beside him, his gray eyes flat. He drew a lot of quick, somewhat nervous, side glances. JD wasn't hoping to get much from Isabelle's phone. She didn't strike him as dumb, but you never knew. He'd asked for her financials, too, and was waiting to hear on that.

Cheryl had nothing to report on the surveillance, but they continued to work that angle—it had only been a few hours, she reminded JD. Frustrated, the pair left after about twenty minutes, having found out nothing new on any front.

Wes headed to get a workout in, then said he'd "wander around," which was Wes speak for head to the woods. He needed some time alone. Too many people, he wasn't used to that. JD got that and was a little envious. He could use a little "get out of Dodge" time himself but couldn't afford it. He nodded to Wes, said he'd see him when he saw him, but asked him to keep his phone on just in case. Wes nodded and took off, his black weapons gear bag stowed on the back seat of his truck.

JD and Harper had a quiet night, but not a restful one. The detective made a fire, it was unusually chilly for April, and as Harper watched the flames, she wondered about Cass—where she was, if she warm, if she was still alive.

JD eased back on the leather couch before the fire, pulled her to him. They stayed that way, watching the fire, his left hand stroking his wife's arm. The only way to survive combat, he'd realized early on, was to turn the part that made you human off.

Shut it down but retain the animal side and the intellect. And it had to be that—not *your* animal nature or *your* mind, simply an embodied, functioning, disassociated set of operative parts. He rested his lips on Harper's hair.

When he'd returned to the States, he hadn't been able to turn the human back on. It was Harper who made that happen, though that process had scared him more than combat. Over the few years since, he'd consciously practiced turning himself off and then back on. He had made some headway, but only, he knew, because he stayed connected to his wife.

Without her, he'd be in the woods with Wes.

And yet, like Wes, he knew he was still capable of anything. Because sometimes "anything" is exactly what's needed.

He turned his eyes to the fire. In some ways, Harper had more courage than he and Wes put together. She'd survived the death of her entire family, including the murder of her sister. She'd been relentless in finding out who'd killed her. She'd almost lost her own life in the process. And through all that and in the ensuing years, she'd kept her family's legacy alive, no matter the toll that took.

She had more metal than anyone knew. Anyone, perhaps, other than Marshall, who'd watched over Harper and her sister Paris all those years.

Now it was JD's turn. He had no intention of abandoning that duty. He felt Harper's warmth and settled into the evening.

They'd survive this, too, he knew that. Whatever happened, they'd survive it.

Harper finally stirred, picking up on his thoughts. She looked at him, her eyes full of understanding. And hope. After all she'd lost, still she wouldn't allow herself to lose hope.

Cheryl called the next morning. JD listened, nodding, then hung up. He set his coffee cup down gently on the kitchen's granite island countertop. He held Harper's eyes a few seconds, then said: "The case is breaking. Surveillance came up with the SUV."

Harper smiled. "Go," she said forcefully. "Go now." She ran around the island and grabbed her husband, kissing him full on the lips. "I'll get my gear ready. You call."

And JD was out the door, alerting Wes on the way.

He passed Cheryl on the way to his office and crooked a finger. She followed, closing the door behind her and leaning on it, coffee in one hand, some notes in the other. She was brief, to the point. They'd picked up an old SUV, dark-colored, heading west several miles from Cass' condo. Right night, right time. No highway, but they'd picked up the same SUV intermittently and it looked like it was steadily heading south then west. Only a partial license plate and no view through the front windshield, so no ID.

JD nodded, his eyes glued to her, seeing she had more. "And?" he said, impatient.

"Out that way," the officer said, "there's not much in the way of development. Lots of woods, sparse population." She consulted her notes. "With the partial, we picked up one man who owns a run-down piece of property in the vicinity that backs up to the Daniel Boone National Forest. No telling if it's him, but it looked the most promising." She handed her notes to JD. "His name and address, home and work, are at the bottom," she said, pointing.

JD glanced at the notes. "Will Mindak," he read, and looked up.

"Right," Cheryl said. "He's got some priors. Ag assault, B&E, like that."

JD glanced out the glass wall of his office. "You fill Walker in?" he asked.

"I didn't, but I can," she replied, and JD nodded.

130

He thanked Cheryl, told her great work, and headed to the F-150. He'd head home, gear up, wait on Wes, and then the three of them were heading west.

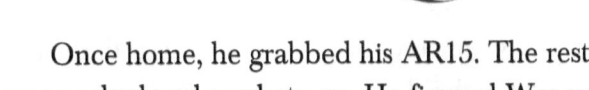

Once home, he grabbed his AR15. The rest of the equipment was packed and ready to go. He figured Wes would favor his M4 semi-auto and the M9 pistol, but he had his other toys along with the sniper rifle on hand, so they'd scope out the situation and use what they needed. JD already had his Sig Sauer holstered and ready to go.

Harper was geared up, standing in the hallway waiting on him. She fingered the Desert Eagle fondly. She was lethal with that thing, and she knew it.

Wes arrived shortly and they hopped in Harper's Range Rover, stowing the gear in the cargo space behind the rear seats. They discussed calling in SWAT and decided against it. That would limit their options.

They wound through the city in the mid-morning light traffic, headed south on 75 toward Berea, then veered slightly west just after Mt. Vernon, weaving through back roads following the GPS until sometime later, they made their way into a very poor area where, JD knew, the underground drug trade flourished. After passing more woods and finding fewer and fewer shacks, they veered toward a gravel two-track as the lane narrowed. Up ahead, they could see it dead-ended in Mindak's property.

"Need to go in on foot," mumbled Wes, and JD pulled over, secreting the Range Rover in a stand of trees surrounded by dense bushes that would screen the vehicle from the property. Not, however, from the entranceway. Hopefully they could take care of business quickly and not chance someone coming home that way.

Wes said he'd go on ahead, scout the property and be back. JD nodded and munched a protein bar. When Wes left, he glanced up, glad for the cloud cover. Harper reached over, wordless, and grabbed the bar, alternately sipping her water and munching what passed for lunch.

Wes was back pretty quickly, noting there was a dark, old burned-out SUV parked in the dirt lot outside a run-down double wide. He detected no movement inside the trailer. To the right of the double-wide was a small old, dull gray pole barn, its roof in disrepair with one corner caved in. To the left of the trailer was a rusted tractor and beyond that, woods. It didn't look as if anyone was home, but they guy could be sleeping or watching TV. There was a dish attached to the trailer.

JD nodded at Wes' report and pulled out his body cam. They all had on vests. JD nodded to Wes and said: "Do your thing. I'll stay out of your way."

Harper, Wes, and JD exited the vehicle, each with their firearm at the ready. JD and Wes had their long guns slung over their shoulders, and Harper held her Desert Eagle at her side, muzzle pointed to the ground. Wes led, with JD and Harper following. Harper knew how to walk silently, knew their hand signals and would be right behind them, awaiting instructions.

They moved forward quickly in a straight line, JD's hand on Wes' shoulder once they got closer to the property's dirt dooryard. Wes raised a hand and they halted, listening for a dog or anything stirring. Hearing nothing, Wes signaled JD to head to the right side of the double-wide, while Harper stayed secluded in the adjacent woods as back-up.

Wes lifted his gun to shoulder height as did JD, and they went forward in a slight crouch, JD moving quickly to the right of the trailer, Wes moving to the door. Once there, he quietly tried the doorknob, looked over at JD quizzically, turned the knob and raced in, JD coming up right behind him. Each one moved quietly, rifles up, clearing the kitchen, then small living room, and moving down the hall.

In a moment, JD heard Wes. "Clear," he signaled, striding back down the hall toward JD. "Nobody home."

They looked around. A few roaches scurried over the dirty floor and wall above the sink, searching for any scrap of food. There appeared none, though the counter and sink were littered with crusted dishes and empty longnecks. The waste can, though, roiled with bugs.

"Been gone a while," said Wes.

The place smelled musty and closed-up, mixed with an assortment of grime, grease, smoke, decomposing garbage, and rancid food.

"Barn next," said JD, and they headed out, signaling Harper. She came out of the woods and joined the pair. They headed to the barn's open doorway and slotted through silently, Wes in the lead, JD behind, his eyes sweeping the perimeter on either side. Harper brought up the rear, her Desert Eagle raised, her arms straight, her head slightly cocked, walking at an angle to the men, checking behind them, watching their backs.

The barn also appeared deserted, with four empty stalls along the left and a long, poured concrete storage pad to the right. They headed down the dirt aisle, the light getting dimmer, and arrived at the far end of the barn to find a door standing ajar. Wes pointed overhead and circled a finger then he and JD moved forward into an empty room, Wes going straight ahead, JD heading right.

JD bent down and fingered the pale amber shavings, holding them up for Wes to see. They were new. Wes nodded, making his way around the edges of the small room in the scant light afforded by the far rectangular window.

"Anything?" asked Harper, standing guard at the door.

"Nothing," said JD, glancing over the room, his eyes focused.

In the corner, Wes stooped, stood, and turned to JD. "She was here," he said, holding out a circle of horsehair.

Harper slumped against the door, her eyes tearing up. Wes looked from JD to her and said: "Stop it." Then he strode past her, eyes on the dirt, heading outside, JD and Harper following.

"We screwed up the barn and out here a ways," Wes said once outside, studying the dirt and sparse grass in the dooryard. "I can't see any tracks with ours all over the place." He walked forward making a grid pattern, his eyes on the ground. "Stay there, don't move," he ordered them.

He was tracking, JD realized, something Wes was very good at. He switched off his bodycam and looked at Harper. They stayed put, guns down.

Wes turned around, glanced at the barn behind Harper and JD, then turned back to the scraggly lot, then his eyes lifted to the far stand of trees. He stepped to his right, bent, gently moved something aside, stood, took three steps forward, glanced back and walked forward again slowly, all the while his eyes on the dirt and struggling vegetation.

Harper watched him, a tiny glimmer of hope rising in her.

Wes continued forward, bending and walking a few steps, crouching and glancing backward and forward. He bent down once more, nudged a bit of small rock, stood and turned to her. "Got it," he said, pointing to the ground and gazing toward the woods.

Everyone breathed.

JD and Harper approached Wes, standing to his right.

"Two sets of tracks," he said. "One is certainly Cass." He looked at them. "Look at the stride, that's her. No shoes, either." He walked back toward the barn. "The second is this set." He pointed to the ground and made a line toward the barn. Harper and JD walked back and saw what he pointed at. They also saw where their own tracks made clarity impossible.

Wes pointed to the left then on down the entranceway. "Looks like there might be some tread marks over there. Not much, but worth a look later." JD made a note to make sure the team got a cast, if possible.

"This one's injured," continued Wes, pointing to the second set of tracks. "You've got a shallower, scuffed print here from the left leg." He glanced up at JD.

Harper smiled. "I told you she'd fight." She turned to JD. "She did that." She shook her head, still smiling. "She got away." There were tears in her eyes. This time she let them come.

"She's alive."

21

They followed Wes into the woods, still with their guns, Wes' and JD's slung, Harper's Desert Eagle, as before, at her side.

Eventually Wes tracked Cass' prints to the big oak, noting errant bullets in a few trunks along the way. At the oak, he studied the ground and several feet beyond, noting she'd donned some sort of footgear, and then run on to the left.

Around them, the leaf mold deepened, the sun's rays glittered like confetti on the forest floor. The day grew warmer as the sun reached its zenith, but increasingly, not much penetrated the deeper into the woods they trekked.

Harper called out to Cass, hoping they were close, hoping Cass could hear them, but they received no answer.

Wes kept moving forward, stopped short and then moved on. He began nosing around for the pursuer's tracks and on up ahead saw he'd turned back. Maybe because it got dark, maybe because he hurt too bad to continue. Wes returned to Cass' trail, both JD and Harper following, staying way out of Wes' way.

He was better than a dog, thought JD. He could see a grain of sand rolled off a rock—he'd done that in country. Eyesight like a hawk and focus like a laser. JD took Harper's hand and made sure they stayed off to the side of the tracks.

The trio moved on for another hour through the dense understory and a myriad of evergreens, oaks, and elms. All at once, Wes stopped. Light dappled his black hair and dark gray jacket. It was cool in the forest, cooler than out in the open. JD and Harper stayed a yard or so back, quietly watching Wes, waiting for his next move.

He turned to his right, seemed to scent the air as a wolf might, and took two long strides to a slight ravine. He bent and yelled "I got her! Cass! Cass!," and he began pawing at the wet leaves. JD and Harper raced up, saw Cass' face and then her body come into view. Wes lifted her quickly out of the mire, her hair and robe streaked with mud.

She appeared unconscious. Harper cried out and rushed forward, as Wes stripped off his coat, then his chamois shirt, handed it to JD without taking his eyes off Cass. He then set her down gently and ripped off the robe and her pajama top, lifted her, pressing her bare skin to his own.

Harper stood next to them, her eyes steely. "Is she . . ."

"She's hypothermic," Wes said. He reached back for his shirt and jacket, wrapped those around Cass' small, limp figure, took her up in his arms, turned and began running, holding Cass tightly, sharing his rising body heat.

JD gathered Cass' strewn wet clothes and called in for a chopper. It would take them over an hour to get back to the trailer, enough time for a chopper to arrive. Landing the aircraft might compromise the scene, but air-lifting Cass was her best chance.

JD knew running with Cass was dangerous. Jostling her increased the risk of heart damage, especially if she was severely hypothermic, and that could be fatal. But so could hypothermia and who knew what other injuries she'd sustained. They needed to get her to the hospital—fast.

"Is she breathing?" yelled Harper, racing after Wes, dodging trees, and stumbling in the dense understory. "Is she ok?" she called again. Harper ran blindly, focusing only on Wes' back.

JD caught her and together they ran after Wes whose long years living in the woods suited him for the task. He ran easily, gracefully, weaving through the trees, running as if on top of the rotting leaf mold. Even JD's long stride was no match for Wes,

137

who had nothing to say—his sole intent was getting Cass out of the woods.

Harper quieted, settling in for the long run back to the dooryard. JD ran silently at her side. There was nothing for either of them to say, they just needed to keep moving.

The day was warming, thought JD, and that would help warm Cass' body as they continued. The trees would thin the closer they got to the clearing, letting more sunlight through. He glanced at Harper, whose face was set in serious determination. If will could save Cass, Harper's intensity would do it.

The time wore on, yet the three continued their pace. No one spoke. Harper and JD trailed Wes, following the path he cut, trusting he'd find the most direct route back. Above them, birds sang and flitted from tree to tree. The air was now saturated, heavy, and close. Still they ran on, now needing water, but no one heeded thirst or weariness. After another forty minutes, the trees began to thin, and ahead the clearing appeared. Wes was still well in the lead.

As they approached the dooryard, they heard the slow *thwop thwop* of a helicopter's blades, recalling the Blackhawks so familiar to the men. Then Wes burst from the woods followed by JD and Harper who bent over, her hands on her knees.

The chopper medics, standing at the ready outside the craft, ran toward them, a bag of warmed liquid in one medic's hand, a stretcher and warmed blankets carried by the other two.

Wes carefully laid Cass on the stretcher and mopped his streaming face. She was groggy but coming to consciousness, looking at Wes but unable to speak. Harper rushed up, her hair a mess, sweat in her eyes, and bent over Cass, but the medics pushed her away, covering the small jockey with blankets, lifting her, getting the warm fluids started, taking her vitals, and getting her quickly into the chopper. In a moment they lifted off.

Harper watched the takeoff, then turned toward Wes. After a moment, she walked slowly toward him. He was taller than her, but she looked at him eye to eye.

"Thank you," she said with emotion held in check. She wiped sweat from her dirty face. "Thank you. We couldn't have found Cass without you."

Wes held her eyes. "I take care of my own," he said, glancing at JD, then nodding at her.

JD watched them both, seeing something shift between them.

The aircraft turned northeast and accelerated, tilting forward, gaining speed. The chopper was nearly out of sight after only moments. It and the precious cargo were a small speck in the cloudless sky.

After the hours of exertion, Harper was exhausted. She sank to the dirt, head down and sat there, staring at the meager weeds and rubble. JD ran back to the Range Rover, deposited Cass' clothes, and got bottles of water. In a minute he was back, handing them out, everyone drinking in silence. JD and Wes nodded to each other, and Wes set off to gather what evidence and information he could. JD squatted next to Harper.

"I have to go," she said flatly, setting her water down. "I need to see her."

JD knew Harper was dealing with Cass, but also the memory of her sister. That's what she meant. She had to see Cass alive, something she wasn't afforded with Paris. He stroked her blond hair, picked a twig and a leaf from it. "I know," he said softly. "Let me and Wes take a look around, find out who this guy is." He looked up, saw the trailer door standing open. "Then we'll go." He kissed Harper's cheek gently. "Just stay put. I'll be right back." He stood, took off his body cam, left it and his water bottle with Harper, patted his Sig Sauer and made for the trailer.

Inside, he was hit by the rotting, putrid stench. He hadn't noticed it as much the first time, being intent on finding Will Mindak and Cass.

Who was this guy, and how was he connected to the case, and to them?

JD saw Wes shuffling through some papers. He held out a few bills and pay stubs in the dim light of the interior. "Christ, get a window open," Wes said, and wiped the sweat from his face.

JD reviewed the paperwork, the pay stubs confirming the note Cheryl had made about Mindak's employment at a lumber yard not far from there. There were some unopened bills, the dates suggesting the owner had not picked up his mail for a few weeks. He looked around. His crew would gather the rest of the evidence—fingerprints, any devices, hair, blood, clothing samples. The usual. He'd send Cass' clothes to the lab, too—they might yield something.

They made a brief inspection of the torched SUV and the barn, skirting the human tracks and meager tire tread, but neither yielded any obvious additional information. JD thought the perp had torched the vehicle to get rid of any DNA. Not stupid.

They left shortly after, speeding toward Lexington and the hospital, no one saying much on the way.

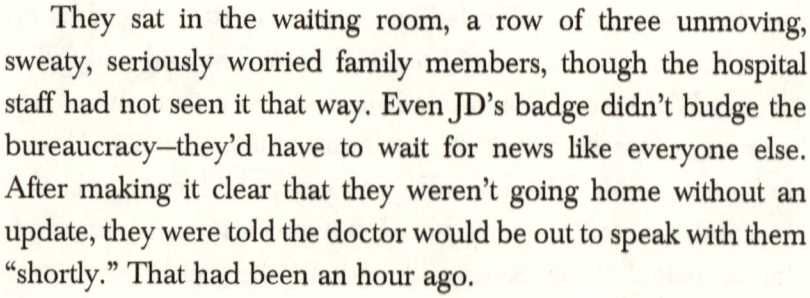

They sat in the waiting room, a row of three unmoving, sweaty, seriously worried family members, though the hospital staff had not seen it that way. Even JD's badge didn't budge the bureaucracy—they'd have to wait for news like everyone else. After making it clear that they weren't going home without an update, they were told the doctor would be out to speak with them "shortly." That had been an hour ago.

Harper went to the restroom and splashed water on her face, then straightened. In the mirror her blue eyes were stark, filled with familiar dread. She ran her fingers through her tangled hair and tucked it behind both ears. A mom and two young boys, twins, entered the restroom and headed for a stall. Worry seemed etched on everyone's face.

Heading back to the waiting room, she saw the doctor with Wes and JD and hurried forward. JD turned to Harper and reached an arm out, his auburn hair gray with dirt, his face streaked.

"She'll be fine," the doc was saying. He'd obviously had long practice at dealing with family members, he got the biggest concern out of the way first. "It might take a bit," he said looking at Wes, "but you were right to get her here as fast as you could. Hypothermia is nothing to fool around with. We need to keep her here at least overnight, monitor her glucose levels, electrolytes, make sure there's no renal or cardiac involvement. But I'm optimistic. She's in good shape, she's bouncing back well."

"How long before we can see her?" Harper said, and the doctor smiled.

"Let's give her some time to rest." He turned to go, then turned back. "She's got some pretty good cuts on her feet. Running, that's what you told the nurse? We just need to treat those, make sure no infection occurs. But all in all, she's in remarkably good shape, considering."

JD and Wes nodded. Harper's shoulder's slumped, the anxiety draining a bit.

"You can see her tomorrow, barring unforeseen developments. We'll discharge her if all goes as planned," the doctor finished. "Go home, you look like you could use some rest yourselves." He patted Harper's shoulder reassuringly and left.

22

The next morning, JD and Wes headed to the precinct to strategize. JD leaned his chair back on two legs behind his desk, twirling a pen around each finger, a trick he'd learned in high school.

"Such talent," Wes said, amused. Everyone had felt relief hearing the doc's words the afternoon before and their spirits had lifted a bit at the prospect of Cass' recovery. Harper had headed to the hospital first thing to await getting in to see her or her discharge.

JD glanced around his spare office, noting there was not much in the way of "decorations." Two photos, that was about it. He hadn't spent this much time at the precinct since he'd started there.

JD plunked his chair down. Back to business.

"Not sure I need to drive all the way down there just to check on Mindak's work. The supervisor told Cheryl he'd not been around for weeks. Seems a dead end."

"Who is this guy?" Wes said. "And where the hell is he?"

JD cranked his neck to the right then the left. They thought about that a moment. Then JD spied the Chief heading his way. Al Walker opened the door, peered at Wes, walked in, and shut it.

"So?" Walker said, rubbing his forehead and sliding a hand through his hair. He looked a little exasperated and more than a little harried.

JD filled Walker in on the most recent developments in the case, the Chief nodding at each significant finding. "Yeah, good," he said, glancing at Wes. "That was great work on tracking." He turned to JD: "Sounds like you're making progress." He looked back at Wes, his focus seemingly torn between being impressed with Wes' obvious skills and irritation with his detective. "I'd like a few minutes," he said to Wes, "whenever you have time."

Wes seemed less than pleased but agreed.

Walker asked a few more questions, then requested that JD please keep him updated. He pointed at JD to emphasize the point. As he opened the door, he mentioned how much he did not appreciate having to search out his detective to know how the case was going. Then he smiled, shook his head, and left.

JD put his hand up before Wes could speak. "He just wants to ask if you'd be interested in coming on board."

Wes scowled.

"Just hear him out." JD stared at Wes. "There are worse ways to spend a life."

"I like my life just fine," Wes said, his eyes sliding into unreadable territory.

"Damn sphynx," JD said, grinning.

"Inscrutable," Wes said, sardonically. Then he, too, smiled.

They got back to the case.

They agreed Will Mindak was key, so JD figured he'd drive back down—not sure he'd learn anything new at the lumber yard, but who knows—and check in with the tech crew at the scene. Wes said he'd come with, but JD asked him to make sure Cass got settled in at home in the event she was, in fact, discharged.

Wes shook his head, but in the end, JD prevailed, and they both set off to their respective duties.

The lumber yard was surprisingly busy. Huge wood planks were stacked neatly to the right of the parking lot next to logs needing processing. Ahead were metal buildings with wide open doors showing more finished lumber waiting for builders and construction crews. Bobcats, cranes, and front loaders seemed well-handled by the lumber yard crew. JD made his way to the supervisor's trailer and entered to find an electric heater humming and a heavyset man with sparse brown hair dressed in a sweat-stained, short-sleeved khaki shirt on the phone. He was seated behind a desk strewn with paperwork and glanced up, poked his black glasses up on his nose, and mumbled "I needed to go" into the receiver.

"You're the police officer?" he asked, folding his hands on the dirty desk, nodding at JD's official jacket. He pointed to a chair and JD sat.

"As I mentioned, just wanting some information on an employee—Will Mindak."

"Not sure I can tell you much," the supervisor muttered, rummaging through the papers. "Hasn't been around in weeks."

"No explanation?"

"Nope."

JD considered the man. Then: "Did you look into that? He have any friends here?"

The man was quiet, rubbed his grizzled cheek. "Around here, you got your drug addicts, you got your drug dealers. And none of 'em got friends." He snorted. "Guys go MIA all the time—cops, ODs, know what I mean?" He nodded at JD. "But yeah, I tried his cell a few times. No answer." He looked at JD frankly. "Not unusual, like I said."

JD: "Write down the phone number, please." He waited, received a yellow sticky pad with Mindak's number, thanked the supervisor and left.

OK, a lead. Something. On the way to the crime scene, JD called the number and got nothing. He called Wes who simply said: "Get the dogs out there."

144

JD considered that, weaving through the rural backroads. Maybe. He'd see what was going on at the crime scene first.

The techs were packing up when he arrived in the dooryard. The van and one car were closing up as JD walked over, looking for the woman in charge.

"Doesn't look like we got much," she said, standing at the van's driver-side door. She nodded toward the torched SUV and stripped off her gloves, pocketing them. "But we'll run it. I'll let you know."

JD nodded and as the vehicles pulled out, he gave Mindak's phone another try. No answer. He walked to the trailer, trying again. Nothing. Then to the barn, but again, nothing.

Ok, he thought, the canine unit it is. He made the call.

He headed out, called Harper, and learned Cass had been discharged and was now securely snuggled down on the couch, her feet propped up on the coffee table.

"She's insisting they're fine," Harper said, meaning her feet. "She keeps hobbling around. I told her she was gonna stay put or I was driving her back to the hospital."

"A lot of good that likely did," JD said, smiling. Cass had her fight all the way back, a good sign.

"Yeah, and get this. She's riding the colt. So she says."

Cass was due up on Memphis on Saturday for a big race. It was Thursday, so she'd only have a few days to recover.

"Marshall was going to scratch him."

JD adjusted his ear buds. "Scratch him. Sounds like a good idea or you know Cass will be all over him."

"I'll talk to him."

"Maybe let her ride," JD said, reconsidering. "Let's just see, might be the best thing for her.

"JD, she can't walk!"

The detective smiled. He'd debrief her when he got home. "Yeah, but you know she can ride."

He stopped by the precinct and put in a call to Tim Bradford. The old Janero stallion's necropsy listed heart attack as the cause of death, so the insurance would kick in. Again, the questions loomed. Was Janero involved in drugging Gissendi or dabbling in gene modification? Both could result in heart attacks, and there were drugs that wouldn't register on a necropsy. But older stallions also died in and out of breeding season from natural causes. The situation was still not at all clear.

Cheryl reported there was nothing on the tap on Isabelle's phone, but they had found an offshore account in Morocco, a country where Isabelle would have jumped through a lot of hoops to open a bank account—each institution could create its own regulations about opening one. It was also a jurisdictional CRS reporting member, but JD had heard that getting financial information out of there had proved iffy. The case was proving full of "yes, buts" and an increasingly impenetrable fog.

He'd see if Cheryl could work her "friends in high places" magic on that account in Morocco.

So, considered JD: Will Mindak. He fired up the computer and again looked into him but found little more than Cheryl had reported earlier—a few assaults, a minor drug charge, two B&Es of little consequence. His parole officer was JD's next call, but he didn't have much to say. The parolee was nondescript, the officer reported, one of those people who vanished from thought once out of sight.

Mindak had no family and no obvious connection to Janero, Chad Redfield, Isabelle, or Oliver. No connection to horse racing. He was a mystery, and an absent one. JD had put out feelers on bus tickets or other possible exits he might have taken out of Lexington. But with no family, no friends, and no obvious destination to check on, finding the guy seemed unlikely. Maybe Wes' instincts were right, JD thought—the dogs. He'd wait on them, see if they turned up anything.

23

Once home, JD found Harper and Cass in a heated argument, both seated on the couch in the living room, facing each other, yelling. Cass' face was red. Wes leaned against the granite island, arms crossed, a slight smile on his face.

Off to Harper's side, Kelso sat, a worried look on his golden face, his tail swishing slowly.

"Hey," JD said. He made no dent in their vociferous back and forth. They were arguing, predictably, about Cass riding Memphis in Saturday's race.

JD strode forward, his presence silencing them. "I need to talk to Cass," he said quietly. "We'll deal with the race later."

Harper threw a dirty look Cass' way, got up without a word, stroked Kelso's head, made for the coat rack and was out the door a moment later, Kelso trailing her.

Whatever, JD thought, and not for the first time. He turned to Cass, saw the rigid set of her jaw, and glanced at Wes who shrugged, still smiling.

"We can talk about the colt in a minute," JD began, turning back to Cass. "I need all you've got on the guy who took you."

Cass leaned back on the couch, her small frame tense. A moment of fear crossed her face then her eyes went hard. She took a beat and then related most of what JD and Wes already knew, which was not much. The guy always wore a mask, was strong, never came into the room he'd confined her in. But there were two new points that JD thought might eventually make a difference. First, Cass said, the guy wore some high-end cologne, or at least that's how it had registered with her—high-end, expensive. And yes, she was pretty sure she'd recognize it.

Secondly, after three run-throughs, she finally recalled another vehicle in the dirt dooryard as she'd made her escape. JD knew taking her through her race to the woods wasn't easy. Her face whitened, her lips drew together in a taut line, reimagining her flight. But finally, she recalled a pick-up, a big one, she thought maybe a Ford, parked next to the burned-out SUV. She didn't recall the color, just said it seemed "shiny," which could mean well-cared for as in washed, or new.

JD filed both bits of information away. He'd figure out how to get Cass in the presence of Max Sidarus, Gus Pinard, Chad Redfield, and perhaps their vet, Jason Williams. Maybe one of them would carry the scent she'd recognize, though he knew that wouldn't be a definitive ID. He'd follow up on the truck with the tech team—he'd asked them to look for the treads Wes had noticed—and ask Cheryl to check on the vehicles owned by each person involved.

They all agreed Cass' captor was not stupid. He'd kept his distance, planned the abduction and where to hold her in advance. So, thought JD, he must be someone connected to Janero to have followed JD's progress enough to know when applying leverage was needed. It hadn't worked, but JD gave the guy credit. It had been a pretty good plan.

In the end, though, not a brilliant one. JD now had more, not less, information about the abductor, who was in all probability, also Oliver's killer.

"If you get the doc's ok," JD finished, "I'm good with you riding Saturday."

Cass' brown eyes flashed, and she pulled out her phone.

"If not," he finished, "you're grounded."

From the island, JD heard Wes laugh. It was an odd sound, not often heard. The detective looked his way. "Yeah, ok," JD said, smirking at him. "Fine. You're babysitting if she can't ride."

149

Saturday morning came and, not surprisingly, Cass had prevailed. She'd be up on Memphis for Keeneland's 1:30 race. Two turns, so it would be a test for all the 3-year-olds.

Cass liked the longer races, you could overcome a lot of mistakes though she didn't make many. And she'd breezed Memphis at distance, so she and Marshall felt he'd do fine, but the other colts wouldn't necessarily have two turns under their belts yet. She'd see.

Her feet bothered her, but she'd ridden in worse shape. She'd squeezed an ok out of the doc with some effort, she was good to go.

Cass adjusted her stirrups, bent, and patted the colt's neck as she always did as the jockeys headed to pick up their ponies in the post parade, and go on to the starting gate. The stands were crowded, a sea of folks in frocks and khakis stood or sat or milled about the green and cream stands, most all in good spirits, enjoying the afternoon's welcome warming rays.

Cass surveyed the field, considering her mount. Memphis reminded her of a filly she'd ridden long ago—smart, competitive, and versatile. The filly could run short distances, long distances—5/8th of a mile up to a mile and an eighth—she'd run on turf, on dirt, hell, thought Cass, she'd run on gravel. Brilliant filly. She stroked Memphis and rose up and down softly as they moved into a trot, their big paint pony turning them loose as they neared the gate. Brilliant filly, she thought again, just like this guy. She ran her hand along the crest of Memphis' black mane.

She checked out the riders. Up ahead was a macho jock—always jacking his horse in the starting gate, getting him rattled. Two years ago, that guy had his horse so riled up, the colt charged the gate thinking it was opening, fell back down on his haunches.

He could have flipped in the gate, it did happen. He'd use up his colt early, thought Cass, too much ego, dismissing him as a threat.

She spied Hector loading his steel gray colt, a jock she'd gotten the best of a while back, before she rode for Harper and JD. She'd been riding exercise on a talented filly. She wanted the mount in the filly's next race, but the trainer gave her to Hector. Cass grinned, remembering. She'd had a little conversation with that trainer, asked him who'd be stronger on the filly—her or Hector? The trainer had looked at her funny, like the question was a no-brainer. Hector, of course, the guy.

So, she said, ok, how about this? He goes to the jock's room, sits in the hotbox for four hours, pulls 6 pounds of sweat, doesn't eat, sucks on an ice cube to make weight. Probably hasn't eaten since the day before, probably dehydrated, maybe did some Lasix. She, on the other hand, would have a BLT, a glass of milk, and a Twinkie.

She got the filly. And won the race. And made an enemy of Hector.

Memphis' biggest competitor, though, was a huge, deep red bay who'd pulled post position 5, two down from Memphis. Off the track, Shelly Banks, his jock, was as mild-mannered as his colt, Kaiyre. But in a race, they were both monsters. Cass watched the colt as he approached the gate, bowing his neck, jigging, prancing. During races, he'd grab the bit, pull like hell, try to run off. He needed a strong guy like Shelly—together they'd won a lot of races. This would be a test for Memphis.

They all loaded into the gate, the crowd settled, then suddenly the gates swung open and eight colts dropped down, pushed off on their toes, surged forward, and the world fell away.

Cass went with Memphis, staying right over him, holding him straight and steady as around them jocks vied for position. To the right, a colt who'd broken left had missed those first few jumps and was out of the race before it began. The other horses were gone.

Hector had dropped to the rail, as usual, and was saving ground into the first turn. Shelly was up ahead to the right, letting Kaiyre get under himself, while ahead of them the two speed horses pulled away. They all went along that way, most of the jocks rating their mounts, picking their spots, letting the colts get into an easy rhythm. After they rounded the first turn and hit the backstretch, the jocks with the speed colts attempted to get them to relax, take a breather for a quarter. Cass and Memphis were running comfortably off the pace behind three horses bunched just ahead. They were in last place, but Cass knew Memphis had enough in the tank, so she wasn't worried.

Most jocks rode fashionably high, though Cass stayed in her flat-backed, quiet crouch. The only sound was the rushing wind and hooves pounding the dirt. Cass glanced left to see Hector still hugging the rail. He looked her way and scowled.

The pace picked up and Cass gave Memphis a knuckle. He shot through the hole that opened among the three horses ahead of them. To her left, Hector let his mount out a little, staying with her, though off to the left. Beneath her, Memphis coiled as the turn for home came into view. She let him out a tad, and they came up next to Shelly and Kaiyre, the big bay looking like he could run to Del Mar and not miss a beat. The two speed horses faded and labored ahead to the left, as Memphis and Kaiyre took the measure of each other. On the rail, Hector kept right up with them as the two speed horses faded back further, out of the race.

Cass glanced at Shelly, a big guy for a jock, and in a race, focused and terse.

"How you gonna do, you think?" Cass said out of the corner of her mouth, Memphis' head bobbing, the colt pulling, wanting to go. She softened her hands, and he stayed with Kaiyre, though Cass felt his body wound tight as a spring.

"Gonna have it all by the stretch," Shelly said.

"Lemme know when you're going," Cass said, still sending "Not yet" signals to Memphis.

Kaiyre looked as ready to explode as Memphis, but they ran, rating, approaching the final turn.

Cass put an eye on Hector, you never knew what he might pull.

No sooner had she thought that, then Hector's gray colt surged ahead, going into the turn, a dumb macho move. Cass shifted weight as Memphis changed leads, while beside them on the outside Shelly stayed right with them, both colts on the bit, beginning to pull harder.

Out of nowhere came one of the two speed horses, getting a second wind. The black colt squeezed inside Cass, a discourteous move in the turn, but Cass kept her cool and coming out of the turn, heard Shelly call "See ya'll!" and Kaiyre moved effortlessly forward, his stride lengthening, his motion easy and fluid. Memphis flicked an ear and Cass didn't have to do anything but think "Go Time," and the colt flattened both ears, dug in, and was off like a bolt.

The pair dropped into the center of the track, the jocks arms now pumping, the two colts extending their stride, tails flaring back, manes whipping in the wind. They dropped a bit closer to the rail saving any ground they could, Cass on the inside, Shelly and Kaiyre just to their right, Hector and his big gray behind them on the rail but coming on fast.

They were two abreast into the deep stretch, Hector dropping in behind, another stupid move, the sound of hooves and lungs heaving loud in their ears, the wind howling past and the crowd screaming.

Hector moved forward, pushing them from behind—he'd clip a heel if he kept on, send them all to the dirt with broken bones or worse. Cass focused more intensely ahead, pumped her arms and Memphis moved out of danger, Kaiyre's huge body going right with them.

Memphis rolled his eye at Kaiyre, nosed ahead, his ears pinned, his turn of foot even faster. Shelly rode Kaiyre steady and strong, and the big colt got a nose and then a neck ahead. Cass felt Memphis bear down, coiling deep inside himself. And then he let go, his huge hind end launching him forward, floating it seemed, above the track, pure, primitive power surging from him, at one with Cass as they crossed the wire.

Those few seconds . . . the finish line matter not at all.

And then the roar began, but to Cass, it meant nothing. She slowed Memphis to a canter, then a trot, then a walk. She bent over him, felt his great heart pound, closed her eyes and inhaled. If she had her way, she'd stay there forever.

To hell with her bleeding feet.

24

JD had skipped the race, wanting to stay focused on the case. Harper called, ebullient, put Marshall on, who was elated. Harper grabbed the phone back and told him Wes was taking Cass out for a celebration dinner, get her mind off things. Memphis had pranced off the track, she said, had his beer, nuzzled John Henry non-stop, and was transporting home. Before they hung up, Harper reported that she and Marshall had spent a few minutes with Kaiyre's trainer, congratulating him on a fine race. They'd all agreed, Memphis and Kaiyre were well-matched and would be seeing each other again, soon—their rivalry was just getting started.

JD sat back and took a moment, letting it sink in. He'd never been happier about giving the colt to Harper at their wedding than at the moment. They all needed a lift and, with Deacon retiring to stud, it seemed they had a colt who just might follow in his footsteps.

He ran a hand through his thick hair and rolled his sleeves up to the elbow, habits that, had anyone been watching, would convey his frustration. He was glad Cass was back and safe, but he couldn't let up on the case.

The investigation was filled with dead ends, and though he had leads and would follow each one, so far the track record had not been great. Cheryl had come up with nothing on Isabelle's phone, as JD thought would be the case. And even with her connections, nothing on Isabelle's offshore account in Morocco, either. But, JD thought, just that she had an account was significant. That and the fact that she'd lawyer'd up convinced him that she was into something.

The lab had found nothing useful on Cass' clothing. The tech teams also came up empty—they couldn't do a thing with the tread marks Wes had seen in the double-wide's dooryard. The three of them had sashayed around the yard and the chopper put the finishing touches on obscuring whatever might have been there. Even given that, JD knew he'd make the same decision again.

He put in some calls, and finally hooked into Max Sidarus at Janero. JD asked about any large pickup, possibly a Ford, maybe relatively new, driven by anyone at the farm. It was a ridiculous question, JD knew that. Thoroughbred farms had pickups all over the place. But Sidarus surprised him, said sure, Janero issued a big Ford to all the managers. Ford F-450s, in signature slate gray with deep red trim. They got new ones every so often, and yeah, Sidarus reported, this was one of those years.

So the trainer and Chad would both be driving them, shiny and new. Maybe Sidarus, too, but he was physically too small to fit the abductor's profile. So the pick-up issue wasn't going to give him any useful information, either. It could be either of his two suspects—Gus Pinard, the trainer, or Chad Redfield, the stallion manager. On different sides of the farm, but both were big enough to have carried off Cass.

And though JD's instincts told him Isabelle was messing with their horses, likely giving Janero drug testing info on their runners as well as well as modifying genes, that's all he had on her. Instincts. Was, in fact, whatever Isabelle was up to completely separate from Oliver's death? Were the horse injuries and deaths at Janero simply bad luck, as Sidarus had said? Or was Gus Pinard, acting alone, drugging their racehorses and flying just under the testing radar, resulting in the injuries and breakdowns? It happened. And Chad Redfield. JD wondered if he, like Isabelle, was simply obnoxious but not up to anything nefarious. He had nothing on either of them so he had to consider they might not be involved—with each other or with anything going on at Janero.

He scowled. He knew they were knee deep in it. He just didn't have proof.

Yet.

The phone rang and he banged on the receiver bottom, catching the phone as it shot off the landline's base unit. Generally, no one called him on it, but it did give him a chance to vent, if only a little.

"Yeah," he said. He listened to Cheryl, nodded, made a few doodles with a pen. "Ok, yeah, thanks. I'll wait on the coroner."

He sat back and folded his arms over his stomach, propped his feet up, squinted, and thought about the news.

Will Mindak was dead. Cheryl had run the prints already. The canine handler said his head "had seen better days" having evidently handled a bullet between the eyes. They'd found the grave without much trouble. Nobody'd gone to any lengths to disguise the burial site, though Mindak was deep enough to deter predators. Where Cass had gone left racing through the woods, the dog had gone right. The body was up a short way. They were searching the area for more graves. You never knew, was Cheryl's feeling, and better to be thorough the first time around. JD agreed.

Mindak, dead. JD had that feeling after visiting the trailer and lumber yard. Now it was confirmed. Another death to add to Oliver's. And the horses'. But how Mindak was connected to the perpetrator—if he was connected, JD corrected himself—was an open question. JD thought it through. Mindak's location might have proved out of the way enough, in a low-income, drug-ridden area still easily reached from Lexington, that whoever was behind all this might simply have offed Mindak as a matter of convenience. Nobody was going looking for him, as JD had learned when looking into his background and speaking with his parole officer. So did the bad guy know something about Mindak that made him a good target? Or was it just luck that the victim was a non-descript nobody that no one missed?

Good luck for the perp, bad luck for Mindak.

JD fooled around in the office a while longer, then left to meet up with Wes before his dinner with Cass. Target practice always settled him. He picked up Wes at Impact Armory where he'd made an appointment to talk guns, then they headed over to Hawk Ridge, intending to set up in the old cabin on the property to get their pistols in order and chamber their amo.

Wes settled back in the F-150 as they made their way to JD's family farm, crossed his arms, lifted his boots onto the console, and pulled his old Justin cowboy hat over his eyes.

"Late night, bud?" JD said, seeing Wes' eyes close.

"Yeah." He squinted an eye open. "Late and, uh, active."

JD recalled Cass' room was connected to Wes', so that made sense. Strange, though, since Cass had a race the next morning. Late nights weren't her usual way of operating.

"So you two are . . ."

"It is what it is," Wes said, tugging the brim with two fingers. "Don't bring up the job offer."

"I'm just sayin'," JD said.

Wes was silent.

"Ain't comin' back from this one," JD said, smiling, and they drove on.

That evening, JD and Harper mulled over the case. They mulled it over with drinks, which is what they did when a case went like this one. Dead ends, one after another. Harper, though, was in good spirits since they'd at least gotten Cass back.

JD hauled out his laptop as they leaned over the kitchen island and reviewed his notes. He read what he had out loud, and after he was done, they were both quiet.

He leaned back on the kitchen counter in front of the window and sipped his Blue Run rye whiskey, neat. Harper picked up her merlot and sipped along with him. Neither said a word for a several minutes, then JD turned around and gazed out the window toward Grandpa's barn. He fingered the short glass, deep in thought.

Behind him, Harper spoke: "You've got, essentially, nothing." JD's back was turned, but he nodded. And sipped. "Well, yeah, thanks for stating the obvious," he muttered. He turned to Harper. "I'm gonna come up with something, though, I'm not letting this case go."

They were quiet a while longer.

"You don't have enough for a warrant—on Redfield, obviously not on Pinard, or on Isabelle?"

JD shook his head. "Nope." He stared into his drink.

Harper suddenly stood up straight and put her wine glass on the counter. "What about the broodmare woman?"

"Holly?" JD looked up, a question in his green eyes. "The one on night duty, who was drugged when Oliver bought it?"

Harper nodded. "Yeah, what if she could recognize the voice in her dream?" She put air quotes around "dream."

JD stared at her, thought about it, then nodded, his furrowed eyebrows creating two vertical lines between them. Then his eyes went sharp, which happened when something in a case clicked into place.

"Yep, that's it. That's our next step." He walked around the island and grabbed his wife, wrapped her gently in his arms, leaning his head on her hair. They stayed that way a moment, then he kissed her hair softly. She snuggled in, and he whispered, "Gotta go, babe."

Then he was out the door.

"What are you gonna do at . . ." Harper called to her disappearing husband and looked at her watch. "Nine-thirty . . .?" She headed for the stairs with her wine. JD was, well, . . . she smiled slightly. Might as well read her book.

25

JD headed over to Chad's house for an impromptu "interview" complete with recording. Nine-thirty, he thought, was perfect. He needed a recording so he could then drive over to Janero's barn and see if Holly, on night duty, could identify the voice. He needed more than one recording, so he'd have to figure that out after his little visit with Redfield.

He pulled into the stallion manager's street, a tree-lined, mid-price-range group of homes only a segment of the horse set could afford. Chad was one of that subset. Neither mega-wealthy owner nor dirt poor worker bee, he could afford the mini-mansion JD spied, modeled, it seemed to him, on the house in *Gone With the Wind*—a ridiculous Greek Revival throwback wanna-be that anyone with an ounce of political correctness would run from as if his pants were on fire.

Surrounding the house was a head-high "hand-laid" stone wall mimicking Lexington's real ones, laid long ago first by Scots-Irish immigrants then in the 1800s by slaves. JD hated pretension—either lay the stones right or don't do it at all, he muttered.

The porch lights were blazing as JD walked through the wrought iron gate, up the steps, passing the white, uplit columns and rang the doorbell.

No one answered, so JD began clanging the brass horse door knocker and banging on the pristine white door, his fist clenched, his cell phone in his other hand.

Still no one answered. JD was about to deduce that Mr. Redfield was out for the evening, when Chad opened the door wearing an ankle-length gray robe, holding a glass of rose in his hand, and sporting a good case of curly red bed head.

"Oh what the fuck," Redfield said, seeing JD standing on his lit porch. His pale brown eyes held both resignation and anger. He peered behind the detective and to either side then, seeing no one else in attendance, began to shut the door.

JD's foot prevented that. The detective clicked on the audio recorder and pried the screen door open while shoving his right foot further into the doorway.

"A few words," JD said, stepping into the high-ceilinged hallway.

"We already had a few words," Chad said caustically. "I'm all outta words."

"A few more," JD said. He held out his hand, gesturing at the open doorway to the right where sat an oddly out-of-place contemporary sofa in Kelly green in front of a steel and glass coffee table. "Let's sit."

Redfield looked over his shoulder briefly, presumably, JD thought, toward the bedroom up the staircase, slumped a bit, and limped into the front room, depositing himself in the club chair in front of the couch, his left leg straight out, flaring his robe around him. "Let's get this over with." He looked at his watch, scowling. "At 9-fucking-fifty-five on a Saturday night."

JD ignored it and set his phone on the coffee table between them.

"So looks like you got an injured leg there."

"Got kicked in the shed," Chad said. "Occupational hazard."

Yeah, thought JD, kicked by a pint-sized jockey more like, thinking about Cass' escape, initiated by her well-placed kick. She got him good, made him fall over, in fact. JD mulled it over a minute. He'd like to get a look at that leg. He'd bet on a darned good bruise above the knee.

He changed course, knowing hell would freeze over before Chad would show him the leg. "About your alibis for the night

162

Oliver was killed and the jockey, Cass Hutchinson, was abducted."

Redfield squirmed a bit and sipped his wine. "I told you, I was home, here, I was here sleeping."

"But there is no way to verify that, is there?" JD said.

Redfield again looked at his watch. "This could not have waited until morning?" He went from miffed to seriously put out in a matter of seconds.

From the balcony, JD heard a plaintive male voice. "Chad, whatever is *taking* you so long? Who was at the door?"

Redfield looked to the ceiling momentarily, mumbling "Jesus" then into the hallway. "Neighbor, no worries. Be there in a minute," he called up the stairs as if nothing was amiss, his face flushing a deep red.

JD nodded, smiling. "So, he's your . . ."

Redfield nodded, furious. "Yes," Chad spat. "As well as somebody's . . . husband."

JD was silent, enjoying watching him squirm.

"You see how it is, surely," he said morosely, gulping his drink.

JD had enough recorded but wanted one more thing—Chad with his voice raised. Holly had said one of the voices was screaming. He pulled out a notebook and pen, turned it slowly to a new, blank page. "I'll need his name, address, the works." He passed the notebook over. "And of course, we'll need an interview. At the station, preferably."

"The hell you will!" Chad yelled. "I've had enough of this. God-damnit." He glanced out into the hallway. "Edward knows nothing. Abso-fucking-lutely nothing. You leave him out of this."

JD stared at Redfield, thinking he was not the brightest bulb in the chandelier. He should get a lawyer on the phone, but instead he was too non-plussed at being outed, and outed with a married man, to realize it.

JD stood, smoothing his pants. "Well, I'll give you until Monday noon to get Edward in. After that, he doesn't show, all bets are off." JD turned to go. "Tell him to speak to Cheryl, or me if I'm there." He took a few steps toward the hallway, turned back and said, "I'll see myself out."

On the way to Janero's broodmare barn to meet up with Holly, JD put a call into Max Sidarus, explained only that he wanted to speak to Holly again but didn't say why. Janero's owner sleepily asked JD if he was serious, given the hour, pressing the point about why, but got nowhere. Disgusted, he said he'd clear JD through the gates with the night watch and to the barn, but only the broodmare barn. This, he said, would not be a fishing expedition, but he'd call Holly and alert her to expect him. JD disconnected and ran a hand over his late-night stubble. He didn't tell Max Sidarus the reason for the interview—he didn't want anyone to know what he was up to in the event Holly identified Redfield.

Next JD listened to the tape recording, noting some phrases. He stopped to get gas, paid at the pump, walked into the Stop N Go, got a rather drunk guy buying smokes to yell into the phone, then got the clerk to utter a few of Chad's phrases, and left. One more stop at a bar, and JD got two more volunteers, one a guy about Chad's age, the other an older man, both inebriated. JD made sure they spoke coherently and clearly to avoid the drunk factor when Holly listened. It was easier to con a soused guy than a sober one into recording something for a cop, so there it was. Four men plus Chad. Done. JD glanced at the time: 11:02. Perfect. He was off to the broodmare barn and hopefully, to more than a stab in the dark with Holly.

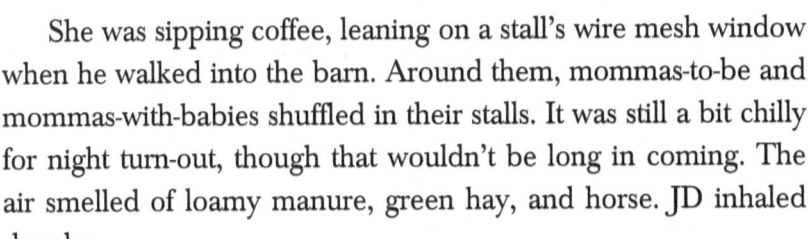

She was sipping coffee, leaning on a stall's wire mesh window when he walked into the barn. Around them, mommas-to-be and mommas-with-babies shuffled in their stalls. It was still a bit chilly for night turn-out, though that wouldn't be long in coming. The air smelled of loamy manure, green hay, and horse. JD inhaled deeply.

Holly turned and toasted him with her Styrofoam cup. "Evening," she said and turned back to her mare who came up and touched a soft muzzle to the black wire, her eyes luminous. "Mr. Sidarus called," Holly said, her eyes on the mare. She planted a kiss on the horse's nose. "We can talk in the break room," and she headed that way, JD trailing.

She stood at the folding table, cup in hand. "We got a couple mares gonna go tonight, maybe, so I don't have a lot of time. But ask away." Her broad face held a look both curious and wary.

JD explained what he wanted to do.

"You know I said I must have been dreaming." Holly said. "I'll listen, but I'm not sure how much good it will do." She seemed perplexed by the prospect.

JD pulled out his phone. Neither of them sat. "This won't take long," he said. "Just see if any of these voices seem like one of the people you heard in your dream."

"You mean you think I wasn't dreaming," she said, catching on. Her hands fidgeted with her coffee cup.

JD looked up from his phone. "It's possible."

She nodded and JD played the first voice—the young man from the bar. Holly listened intently and shook her head no. JD hit the second recording—the drunk at the gas station. Again, Holly's eyes narrowed, and she concentrated on the voice. She shook her head again. Then she looked up at JD. The detective

165

smiled slightly. "You're doing great. Just a few more," and he clicked on Chad's recording. The moment Chad began speaking, Holly grabbed the table edge with her free hand and looked up at JD with alarm.

"That's him," she said with conviction. "That's the guy I heard."

JD let her listen a bit more. "You're sure?"

Holly nodded vigorously. "I'm pretty darned sure."

JD forwarded the recording a bit to get Chad yelling and played that. He watched Holly's short intake of breath.

"That's him, that's the guy who was screaming," she said, now confused and fearful. "He's the one killed Oliver, you think?"

JD nodded. "We're looking into that." JD patted her shoulder. "But listen." He stopped to make sure she was paying attention. "This is important. Do not tell anyone what happened here tonight. Not Max Sidarus, not the broodmare manager, not your best friend, not your boyfriend."

"I don't have one," Holly mumbled, looking at the table.

"Not anyone," JD said. "I mean it. We've had two murders and an abduction."

At that, Holly flared with fear. "Two?"

JD nodded. "If Max asks you what we talked about, just tell him I followed up on a few things, like what time you think you fell asleep. Had you seen anyone lurking around the breakroom before you drank the coffee, things like that. Not this, got it?"

Holly nodded, her eyes fearful. "You think I'd be in danger, that's it, isn't it?"

"You just go about your work as usual. If no one's aware of our conversation, you'll be fine."

Holly looked dubious but shrugged. "Can't wind back time, I guess," she said. "I can't not hear what I heard."

From the aisle came a nicker, then shortly after a snort, then a very loud groan.

"Somebody's rolling," said Holly, referring to the groan, "or could be a birth about to happen. I'll need to see in a minute."

JD patted her shoulder again. "You've been a great help, Holly. Go on, attend to your mares. Just don't say anything and you'll be safe."

26

The next morning, JD called in a request for a search warrant based on Holly's ID. He left out Chad's obvious limp, that being less than conclusive. After quizzing JD on the case, the magistrate denied the warrant, noting that the broodmare night worker had been drugged and was found out cold, so her identification of the suspect's voice did not hold water. In his opinion.

JD's next call was to Al Walker, who didn't pick up his phone. JD then called the Chief's home and was told Walker had gone to the precinct for a few hours. On a Sunday, his wife complained. JD hung up and headed over.

The precinct was at a low hum, only a few folks moseying around unhurriedly, it being a slow Sunday, it seemed. The desk sergeant and those pulling duty were there, but the place wasn't buzzing by a long shot.

JD stomped through and headed to the Chief's office, didn't knock, and barged in. He filled Walker in on the latest non-development.

"It makes no sense," JD said, pacing. "I've got a witness, there at the scene, can identify Chad Redfield's voice. What the hell else do they need for a warrant?" The detective stuffed his hands in his pockets and glared at the Chief.

Walker shrugged, and looked at his computer screen, avoiding his detective's eyes. The sparks were flying.

"Don't get your pants in a wad," Walker murmured, and straightened three pens on his desk. He glanced up. "This is not rocket science, JD. You have to get more evidence. Hard evidence. Not some woman who'd been drugged." He shrugged.

"Yeah, yeah," JD said, running his hand through his hair.

"And you could use a haircut," the Chief added.

"Whatever."

"Becoming your favorite phrase," Walker said, and stared at his detective frankly.

JD turned his back on the boss and opened the door. Before him was a dark room chock full of computers and desks.

"What are you going to do?" Walker asked JD's back, noting the muscles bunched along his upper back.

"You don't wanna know," JD said and walked out without turning around.

"Yeah, yeah,'" Walker muttered, "whatever," and went back to his computer.

That night, JD and Wes set up a block up from Redfield's house. They had on dark clothes, and both had gloves and black ski masks at the ready. They'd determined Chad was out for the evening–JD had Cheryl in plain clothes trail the suspect to report where he was and when he headed home. Cheryl was cool, they'd worked some under-the-table maneuvers together. She was JD's go-to, said she liked doing spy shit.

"I can go in," Wes said, smoothing his black hair back and slipping a covered rubber band around it. He pulled out his lock picks and a little device he'd gotten on the dark web–it ran codes on electronics and had bypassed all the alarm systems he'd encountered thus far. He'd road tested it more than a few times, not being one to get caught with faulty equipment. He slipped on his gloves.

"I need to go in," JD said, pulling his own gloves on, "you know that." He understood Wes was protecting him. If anything went wrong, Wes wanted to be the one inside, not JD.

Wes nodded, not pressing the point. "I'll get you in," he said, "and reset when you're done."

JD nodded, and they walked the block, staying close to the trees lining the road, in deep shadow. Nobody was out and about at 10 p.m., presumably the residents were early to bed, early to rise types. If they were in the racehorse game, that made sense.

Once at the property, JD, still in deep shadow, ran a gloved hand lightly along the wall's top, checking for deterrents of the painful sort though there was a front gate, but you never knew until you knew, and he didn't want to find out the hard way. He nodded to Wes and they jumped, got footholds, and scaled the wall easily.

They sidled up the property's left side, close to the bushes still in deep darkness, and darted onto the porch in a crouch, Wes pulling out his equipment. The lights were bright on the exterior as in his first visit, a risk JD was willing to take. He glanced at the wall they'd just gone over and stayed low. He needed evidence and wasn't going to get it doing business as usual.

JD entered when his partner finished working on the pad, handing the code breaker to JD. Wes had schooled the detective in its use, but if Wes was around, JD would hand that duty off to the pro. Wes took off back to the street to surveille, tapping his ear to remind JD to let him know when he was needed for the alarm reset.

The interior was dimly lit by lofty chandeliers along a hallway lined by a frameless mirror and a few horse race paintings. JD walked ahead, stopping to listen every now and then, his Sig Saur held in two hands as he cleared the first floor. He quickly mounted the stairs, pistol still drawn, and found himself on the landing in darkness. Ahead were a series of doors, all closed.

He pulled out his flashlight, turned on the beam, stuck it in his mouth and continued through the hallway. He turned off the flashlight as he opened each door, ascertaining whether the heavy curtains were drawn or not. Those rooms that were secure allowed him to use his light and he proceeded this way, door to door, clearing the floor.

Finding Chad's very large bedroom, he entered, noted the Plantation blinds were down and closed so he turned on the flashlight, holding it in his hand, scanning the room. Not much of interest in the room itself—an extra-large king, a mirror above it, a dresser, some family photos, a recliner next to a table by the window.

The master bath was to the right. JD checked it out, snagging a bit of hair from a brush, and swabbing Chad's toothbrush, depositing the sample in a sealed bag. He couldn't use it officially, but, he figured, who knows what's going to come in handy. He returned to the bedroom, and across the way, saw an open doorway and walked through to a large dressing room.

After entering, he closed the door to the bedroom and shown the light around until he found the switch, flipped on the overhead light to illuminate the room, and took it in. The room was lined in oak paneling and to his right was a long row of hanging work clothes—vests, down parkas, lighter jackets, and so on, all logoed and in Janero's slate gray and deep red colors. Above was a shelf lined with Janero ballcaps, and below was an assortment of boots.

There was a large square bureau in the middle, with drawers on all four sides. The top was clear. To JD's left was a long rack of civilian clothes—suits, shirts, ironed blue jeans, khakis bent over padded hangers, a leather coat. The man was a clothes horse, thought JD, opening a few of the bureau drawers to find rolled ties on the civilian side, socks, what appeared to be ironed underwear, etc., while on the Janero side, there were polos and other work clothes not fit for hanging. Either end of the bureau held sweaters, and JD also found a junk drawer of sorts with leather wallets, old pocket watches, some bracelets, and boxes of cufflinks.

On the far side were mirrors—a central pair, then two on either side that were hinged so as to give a more complete view of the dressed stallion manager. A clothes horse with a streak of vanity, JD thought. To the right of the mirror was solid paneling with a framed photo of Bayone hung at eye-height. JD removed it, and began tapping on the panels, pressing here and there, until lo and behold, a door swung open. JD laughed out loud—how disappointingly predictable.

He stared at the interior steel door inset with a pad and pulled out Wes' device. After fumbling around, he finally got the thing to work, and the door clicked. JD used his gloved finger to push it open and peered into the darkness, then stepping forward, he flipped the light switch on the room's wall.

There was a chair on rollers sitting on a piece of large plastic straight ahead, an array of mounted guns and knives on the left wall, and a horizontal flat shelf that circled the room on which lay a phone and a computer to the right of the chair. The shelf held an array of empty test tubes in holders as well as rows of neatly arranged pill bottles, syringes, smaller vials of liquids with foil tops. Drugs, JD found on closer inspection, lots and lots of equine drugs.

He examined a few and noted handwritten labels but no prescribing vet. They were clearly illegally procured. JD pulled out his phone and took shots of everything. Then he tapped the computer, a bit clumsy even with the form-fitting gloves, but, as he knew already, it needed a passcode so that was a dead end.

Below the shelf to the left side of the chair were a set of drawers, many of them empty, but one containing a few more burners and another containing clean plastic plates. JD wanted to take those, run them, see if they contained any DNA from Cass, anything that might link Chad to her abduction. Tempting as that was, he left everything in place.

He glanced at the test tubes and boxes, thinking he'd seen enough to nail Redfield on illegal drugging and, given the test tubes, likely gene modification of Janero racehorses. And if the plastic plates panned out, maybe on the abduction. He'd have to seriously ponder how to legally grab some evidence.

But for now, he could certainly get all the EMEI numbers off the Sim card trays on each of the burner phones. He set about photographing the number on each one—on the desktop and in the drawer. If he could get one small, usable bit of legal evidence against Redfield, he might be able to get clearance to trace the stallion manager's calls.

Or . . . He smiled to himself. Or, he could be in the vicinity when an "exigent circumstance" presented itself in Mr. Redfield's abode. Then he could go in without a warrant.

And he would definitely be putting some pressure on Edward Planck, the name Chad had written down in JD's notebook. He glanced around. With what he'd found, Redfield was not getting another ounce of wiggle room.

Satisfied somewhat—the case had taken a major step forward—he set everything in order, shut off the light in the secret room, reset the door, rehung the stallion photo, and glanced around making sure the dressing room was as he'd found it. If the guy ironed his freaking underwear, he'd sure as hell pick up on the least little thing out of place.

He tapped his phone, sending a signal to Wes who would meet him at the front door in a few. Then he made his way quickly through the hallway, checking it all as he went, headed downstairs, and out the door. He handed the electronic device to Wes who set the alarm, and they were soon back on the street in the shadows, heading to the car.

No one had seen them. Redfield, Cheryl reported, was perhaps having the time of his life at a private party at one of Nicholasville's horse farms. He may or may not have ditched Edward along the way. At any rate, thought JD, he didn't stray far from Thoroughbred country, that was clear.

27

The next morning, JD was standing in front of the glass walls of Meyers, Clark, and Beyerston law offices when they opened at 10 a.m. The receptionist unlocked the door and stood back so he could enter. He flashed his badge and asked to speak with Edward Planck. The receptionist stifled a knowing smile—evidently Edward had a reputation—and motioned JD to a bank of deep indigo couches and chairs, asking if he'd like coffee, tea, or water. After he declined, she rounded to her desk and summoned the good lawyer.

Edward Planck, dressed in a dark charcoal pin-striped suit with a brilliant white shirt and loosened tie, nearly ran into the reception area, distress written all over him. "I'm Mr. Planck, what can I do for you?" He paused and, in a moment, a lawyer smile got plastered on in place of the distress.

"A few words," JD said, rising. "If we could speak in your office, that would be best."

The receptionist looked on with unabashed interest, which drew a glare from Edward.

The tall, lithe Edward held the door with his arm, and JD strode through behind him.

Once seated—JD in front of a high-gloss black desk, Edward behind with his hands folded on top—the lawyer said: "This is about Chad, isn't it? He told me it was you the other night."

JD nodded, pulled out his small notebook and pen, which always made folks nervous.

"That was harassment," Planck said. "Pure and simple."

JD didn't miss a beat. "I need to verify Mr. Redfield's alibi for two nights." He consulted his notebook as if he needed to recall the dates, then looked up, mentioning them. "He said he was home both evenings, and if those included your presence, which he did not say was the case, then I could check those boxes off."

Edward worked up a look of serious concern, a look of sincerity and deep concern. "Well, hmmmmm," he said, obviously thinking about how to get out of this one, "as you might surmise, disclosing our relationship is not something I am able to, um . . . Well." He spread his hands, not, evidently, able to think of what else to add.

Behind his desk hung a photo of him and his wife in profile on their wedding day, blissfully gazing into each other's eyes. Another hung to its side—a family outing, three small girls perched on huge rocks, while daddy, squatting in khaki cargo shorts, a safari shirt, and hat, looked lovingly in their direction. Several other family photos adorned the wall below those two, which were the largest and most prominently displayed. He made sure his clients would have no clue about Edward Planck's actual proclivities.

JD gave the lawyer a few moments to stew.

"Well, here's the deal," JD finally said, "If you can't verify Chad's whereabouts on these dates, then I can't clear him. And, to be frank, he's looking better and better for the murder of his boss and an abduction." Let's see if he could get them both to squirm.

Edward sat back in his high-backed, padded black chair. JD liked the looks of it, maybe he'd ask about the brand.

"Huh," Edward said, in a very un-lawyer-like manner. He folded his hands in his lap, gazing past JD's right shoulder, lost in deep thought.

"Lying to a police officer," JD began, and Edward's eyes ratcheted to the detective's.

"You do not have to advise me on the law," he said curtly.

Edward then caved in. JD saw it before Edward likely felt it.

"Ok, yes," he began. "I was with Chad on that second date you mentioned. I remember it because it was it was, well, an anniversary of sorts." He looked a bit sickly. A bit green, as if he'd eaten bad oysters. But he rallied, quickly pulling himself together.

"But the first date, no." He looked sad. "On that night, I was with my family." He gestured over his shoulder to the photos, keeping his eyes down, gazing at his reflection in the highly polished desk.

JD had kept quiet, nodding along with Edward's stuttering recollections. So Planck had not substantiated Chad's alibi for Oliver's murder, but he had verified being with him the night Cass was abducted.

JD finished up taking notes he didn't really need to take, stood, closed the notebook, pocketed it, and thanked Edward who stood awkwardly, and stuck out his hand.

Maybe he thinks I'm a client? thought JD. He simply nodded at the hand, which then fell like lead at the lawyer's side. JD said he'd see himself out.

He turned back once in the hallway to see Edward Planck's agitated face through his plate glass windowed office, speaking vehemently into his phone.

I wonder who he's talking to, smirked JD to himself as he walked down the hall, tipped his finger to the receptionist once in the waiting room, and headed to the elevator.

JD was about fifteen minutes out from Planck's office, heading home, when Al Walker called, reading him the riot act the moment JD answered. His boss reported having just received a call from Chad Redfield's lawyer alerting him to JD's actions, which he described as "harassment," a reportable offence, the lawyer had insisted.

"Let me guess," JD said, interrupting his boss. "Edward Planck." He grinned, thinking that was fast. He explained the Planck/Redfield relationship, and assured Walker that he was not stepping outside his authority.

"So interviewing a suspect in the late evening hours is what?" yelled Walker into the phone. "That's what Planck said—that you'd banged on Redfield's door at some ungodly hour and harassed him without provocation." He was silent only a second. "We do not need any bad publicity on this, JD. We do not need that. Take a step back. Take a big God-damned step back."

JD was silent, there being nothing to say. Al Walker knew him, knew he wouldn't do anything of the sort. The boss just needed to vent. So JD let him vent.

"I mean it, JD," the Chief stressed. "You and that beast from the forest. You gotta watch it on this one. Everything by the book. Right? You hear me?"

"I hear you," JD said.

They hung up and JD continued toward home to tell Harper and Wes about the latest developments.

And to think about exigent circumstances.

Soon after, though, he pulled to the side of the road and stopped. So Chad's upset about harassment, JD mused. I'll show him harassment.

He turned the vehicle back onto the road, whipped a U-turn at the cops-only turnaround, and headed back toward Janero. He'd tail Redfield until he had something on him. Not normally patient, JD could muster some up when there was something to be gained. In this case, he could care less about how long it took to get what he needed to nail the stallion manager.

The rest of the morning was spent parked on the side of the road, around the corner from the Janero stallion complex entrance and far enough away not to be noticed, but close enough to keep a watch out for Redfield.

Horse vans came and went. JD imagined stallions being led out and washed, and maybe one or more of the office staff stepping out for a smoke, and so the few hours till lunch wore on, JD entertaining himself imagining the goings on in the breeding shed.

He knew from his own work at Eden Hill and Hawk Ridge that, come breeding season, the crew often ordered take out for lunch, so Redfield might not leave the premises until quitting time, which could be well after dark, depending on how the third breeding session went. Maybe they had only a few bookings, he thought, and that wouldn't be too late.

JD slouched down in the seat and waited. He called no one, did not respond to non-relevant calls for several hours. He merely waited. Then he called Harper to let her know his whereabouts and she flared a bit, cautioning him about getting fired. She knew how close to the line JD tread with the Chief. Mostly over it. Then she reported that Wes had taken Cass camping, which made perfect sense to JD. Cass would want to put the abduction behind her and what better way than to run towards the nightmare. Totally in keeping with Cass' character, not to mention Wes' comfort zone.

JD said he'd be home when he got home and disconnected, resuming his solitary vigil. Once he stepped out and behind a tree, but other than that, he got out only one other time before the sun set to do some stretches. That was the extent of his activity the whole day, other than downing a protein bar from his stash in the glove box.

As predicted, the crew didn't begin leaving until after dark when the last breeding had been completed, the stallions grained, hayed, and watered. Chad lingered, likely cleaning up, putting gear away, handling the video feeds. The duties were literally endless. But finally, long about 9:30, JD saw Chad's black Infinity come down the drive toward the stallion complex gate. He started his engine, keeping the lights off, and pulled out after Redfield, staying back far enough not to be noticed, then turned the headlights on.

Redfield motored along at an unusually slow rate of speed, which was odd. JD hung with him, watched as the manager then sped up, but still rolled under the speed limit. They were headed toward Versailles, and Redfield continued to do everything right, mile after mile after mile. And then he blew it.

JD smiled as he watched Redfield blast through a stop sign. Gotcha, he thought, hitting the siren and flashers. He saw the driver's side window slide down, and out flew what looked like a glowing ember-tipped smoke, then Chad slowed down and pulled to the side of the road. JD pulled in right behind him.

Redfield didn't smoke, so whatever he'd disposed of, thought JD, it wasn't tobacco. JD felt happier than he had since well before the case began. He stepped out of his vehicle and switched on his body cam.

As he approached the driver's side, he noticed the window was still down. Airing out the car, likely, thought JD, stepping closer and taking in a long, slow inhale as he asked Redfield for his license and registration.

"Oh, for Christ's sake!" yelled Chad, seeing who'd stopped him. He reached into his jacket for his phone, but JD opened the car door and told Redfield to keep his hands visible and step out of the vehicle.

"Have you been drinking, Chad?" JD asked, keeping his voice level and professional. "Or smoking weed? I distinctly smell cannabis in your vehicle."

"I'll get you fired for this, I swear to God." Chad was steaming.

JD turned Chad around and asked him to put his hands on the vehicle. He held the driver's side door open and shown his flashlight around the car's interior, then opened the glove box, finding Chad's registration along with a baggie filled with a few rolled joints. He leaned back and showed the baggie to Chad. "I'll need to look in the trunk," JD said. "You stay put."

He pulled the keys from the ignition and popped the trunk release. He walked slowly around Chad, who turned to look towards the trunk, then his eyes met JD's. They held a look of defeat.

JD continued to the trunk. "Huh," he said, peering around the trunk to Chad, who was now shaking his head slowly, muttering something that sounded like "Shit."

"What do we have here?" JD snapped on a pair of gloves and picked up some hand labeled pill bottles and glass vials of liquid, also hand-labeled, all with no prescribing veterinarian listed, all housed in a segmented plastic container, along with several syringes. The bottles and vials were the same type JD had found in Redfield's secret room. "These warrant further examination," JD said, pulling out his handcuffs. "And I think you'd best come along with me," he finished, gently pulling Chad's arms down behind his back, cuffing him, and walking him to his unmarked truck, all the while happily reciting Chad's Miranda rights.

"You had no right to search my trunk," Redfield insisted, as JD deposited him in the back seat, seized the evidence in

Redfield's trunk, and stepped into his vehicle, drawing the seatbelt around himself.

"Exigent circumstances, Chad," he said over his shoulder. "Exigent circumstances."

28

"Chad, Chad, Chad . . .," JD murmured, entering the light green interrogation room an hour and a half or so later, shaking his head as a father might to a child who'd disappointed him. Seating himself at the Formica table across from a contrite and apprehensive Chad handcuffed to the center metal rod between them, JD opened a file and pretended to read, continuing to shake his head. Chad's left leg extended out straight beneath the table, evidently still injured.

He looked up. "You do know you're kind of a fuck-up, right?"

Chad didn't take the bait. "It's eleven-fucking-o'clock," the stallion manager said, "I think. They took my watch and my phone."

JD closed the folder and clasped his hands loosely on top of it.

"I contacted Edward," Chad sneered. "So kiss my ass. You can't ask me anything."

JD looked around, innocently. "I don't see Edward here, but I would certainly not ask you a thing until he arrives." He smiled warmly. "I will, though, maybe make a few statements."

JD re-opened the folder and scanned it quickly. "For example, it says here that medicinal equine drugs must be prescribed by a licensed veterinarian. And look, here's a list of illegal drugs which cannot be administered under any circumstances . . ." JD tapped his finger on the page and looked at Redfield. "To racehorses. Says that right here. So that's gonna get you into some trouble 'cause I bet that's exactly what I found in your trunk." JD paused, shook his head. "And the syringes, Chad . . . Problematic, buddy."

He continued looking over the report, not looking up. "And I wonder," and then JD looked at Chad and back to the page, "I wonder what our officers are going to find when they search your home." He stared Chad in the eyes. "We definitely have enough for a search warrant now, and you are not going anywhere."

Redfield's rear end wiggled around on the hard seat. He was clearly feeling the heat, his pale brown eyes were troubled. "Lawyer," he said.

"Of course, Chad. Of course. I'm sure Edward is telling his good wife as we speak that he must go to the assistance of his . . . hmmmmm . . . I wonder how Edward will describe you." He folded his hands over the open report. "If he actually shows up." JD let that one sit a while.

"And then there is the problem with the alibis," JD continued. "Mr. Planck did say he was with you when Cassandra Hutchinson was abducted, but he was not present the night Oliver was murdered." JD nodded seriously. "You do see how that is a problem." JD paused. "It's even more of a problem because I have a witness who can put you at the scene when Oliver was killed."

At that, Chad's face flushed its tell-tale deep red. His eyes seemed confused and then JD saw tears welling up. His red, curly hair seemed as if it might actually stand on end.

JD nodded. "Yes, I do have a witness."

"Who?" Redfield demanded. "Nobody . . ." and he trailed off, his eyes going wide as if realizing he'd stepped in it.

"You said 'nobody'? Were you wanting to make a statement, Chad?" JD knew the entire phrase amounted to "nobody saw him."

Chad sat as far back in his chair as his cuffed hands would allow, his mouth set in a hard little line. He appeared nearly to be absent of lips, so tightly were they clamped together.

JD adopted a casual tone, scratched his scalp, and smiled. "I had a lawyer once, in a case I was pretty darned invested in. I'd go off now and then about the unjustness of it all. I was seriously miffed about the case. So anyway, when we got to trial and I had to testify, my lawyer, she says to me 'JD, I want you to bite your tongue.' I thought she was joking. But no, she said it again. 'When you want to pop off, just bite your tongue.' You know what, Chad," JD said, as if advising the stallion manager, "it worked." JD nodded. "It really does work. Surprising, right? I wonder if that's what you're doing now. I bet Edward shared that little bit of wisdom with you over the phone. That's what a good lawyer would do."

JD stopped and glanced at the door, his green eyes squinting, then back to Chad. "Did Edward say he'd be by tonight? Tomorrow?" Then JD caught himself. "Oh, sorry, Chad. Don't answer that. It's a question, so mum's the word."

Finally, Chad spoke. He was clearly rattled, but JD had to give him credit, he mustered up some attitude from somewhere.

"Look, fuckwad," Chad began, "I know what you're doing. You're trying to scare my ass." Redfield adopted a John Wayne pose, or as much of one as could be mustered handcuffed and seated. He turned slightly sideways and narrowed his eyes, looking at JD. "I don't scare easy."

JD belly laughed at that one. "Oh, I know you don't. I can clearly see that is the case."

"You got nothing on me."

JD leaned forward and let the full force of green eyes that had turned hardened criminals to pulp let loose on Chad. "I got you for Oliver's murder. Do not doubt me on that."

"What do you think you've got?" Chad asked, sticking his chin out.

"I'm gonna tear your house to pieces, bit by bit. I'd lay big odds that you kept whatever it was you bopped Oliver on the head with—a tire iron, maybe? A crowbar? I've seen a ton of idiots like you, Mr. Redfield. You think you can clean it up, hide it in plain sight. I bet it's in your fancy garage. Or in your basement on the workbench."

Chad was now visibly shaking.

"And see, what perps like you don't get is you can never, ever, clean it up as good as you think you can. Your prints and Oliver's DNA are gonna be there, Chad. Count on it."

"Could I have some water?" Chad said, his voice quavering.

JD nodded. "Sure, of course." He got up and left, walked to the next door, entered, and viewed Chad through the one-way mirror. Al Walker stood beside him, his arms crossed.

"He's about to shit his pants," Walker said. "He's cooked. Get his water and get back in there."

JD did so, re-entering the room, unscrewing the cap on the water, and uncuffing Chad.

"So," he began, seating himself. "Where are we?" He glanced again at the door. "Oh, right, still waiting on Edward."

Redfield gulped the water and curled a stray curly lock behind his ear. He took a deep breath. "I want to deal. What's on the table?"

"Well, Chad," JD said, "now that may be the first smart thing you've said since I met you." JD smiled. "You're looking at murder one, so not much is on the table, I'm afraid." JD was quiet a moment, as if considering options. "But maybe I could get the death penalty moved out of contention. You're gonna do time. The question is how much, and if there's a chance of parole."

Chad stared, unblinking, at the detective.

"You're a young guy. You could do the time, get out, have a life."

"What do you want?" Chad whispered. "I don't know what I've got you could use. On anything."

"Oh, I'm sure that's not the case," JD said. "Let's put Oliver off to the side. We'll get you either with evidence on that, or your confession. So let's move on. We have a lot of illegal shit going on with the horses. They're dying, Chad. I know that means little to you because, as you've made clear, the racing game is not about the horses, it's about money."

Chad: "So."

"So. The horses. We know their genes are being 'modified.' I think that's the term." JD glanced down at the still-open report as if to refresh his memory, then back to Chad. "And that has terrible consequences for the horses. Plus, obviously, from what we found in your trunk and what I know we'll find in your home, you're squarely in the middle of that and in the middle of drugging the hell out of Janero's racehorses."

JD paused, letting all that sink into Chad's likely horrified state of mind. "I suspect, too, you did a number on Gissendi, that old stallion who dropped dead."

The stallion manager took another gulp of water. Said nothing.

"I figure Isabelle's your contact over at the testing lab. She's messing with the urine race sample tests, maybe she's helping you wiggle the drug concoctions so they're just under the testing limit. And I know she's into gene doping, that's not a question. It's in her employment background."

Still Redfield said nothing. He appeared to be weighing his options, so JD let him sift through whatever micro-molecules of intellectual evaluative brain functions he could marshal. Which, JD surmised, viewing him, would not be a lot.

And then something inside Chad Redfield seemed to collapse. JD observed him as he might an insect being devoured from within by an unseen, deadly agent.

Redfield shook his head. "Yeah, well, you know the thing is . . ." and his voice left him. He glanced at the mirrored wall to his left, his eyes unfocused.

Chad squirmed. "I mean, man . . ." He put his head down, and a curtain of curly red hair fell over troubled eyes. He looked up. "The guy at that shitty double-wide trailer?" Chad folded in upon himself and seemed genuinely terrified. "The guy just answered the door, just opened the fucking door. Bam! Right between the eyes. Dead as a doornail. Shot right between the fucking eyes. Not a fucking word, either." His eyes teared up. "All because he lived in a shithole trailer with a barn in out-of-the way dumbfuck Kentucky within driving distance." He looked horror-struck. "He did nothing. The guy didn't get out one word."

JD let him roam around in the memory. It seemed killing racehorses did not affect Chad, but seeing a person buy it right before his eyes, that was too much. JD shrugged. Not unusual. If you don't see the results of your actions up close and personal, you can just put them in a little box on the mind's shelf, and no one's the wiser, least of all you.

"So who shot Will Mindak? That's the guy at the trailer."

Chad seemed surprised at the name.

"Yeah, we found him."

Quickly Redfield did a mental two-step. Horrified and terrified vs self-interest. JD was curious to see which won out.

"You were there, then. At the second murder," JD said, driving the point home that Redfield was in deep shit.

After a while of mental wrestling, it appeared terror had won out.

"I'm not sayin' another word," Chad said flatly. "I've seen the type back in Oklahoma. They look like good little citizens. Upstanding citizens, when the truth is they're psychopaths." He shook his head. "Lawyer. I'm not saying another Goddamn word." His jaw worked hard. "They'd off me soon as blink an eye."

JD thought about the pronoun. "You said 'They' Chad. Who are 'they'?"

"Lawyer," Chad muttered.

"I can protect you."

Redfield just shook his head and, in his eyes, JD saw the level of fear was high.

"Not from them, you can't." He looked up. "I swear, not from them."

29

T uesday proved to be a very bad day.

Edward Planck had showed up to talk to his "client" long about 9 a.m. They had at first a private and then a very public discussion, the latter as they parted. The Sargent reporting all this to JD said there appeared to be an "unhappy" interchange between the two, after which Chad was deposited back in his cell. The inmate had then turned his back on the world and slit his wrists with a small, filed down, very sharply edged piece of glass, holding his arms in front of him so no one actually saw him in distress until he keeled over and then, well, said the Sargent, then it was too late.

Listening to all this, JD had picked up a pen from his office desk and began twirling it through the fingers of his left hand while staring out his office plate glass walls into the bullpen where uniformed officers were busy at their work. A few stood at desks and chatted, another interviewed a seated witness while typing answers into an online form, and two walked in with coffee. But most were on the phone or staring their computer screens. The place was cranking.

"How did the inmate procure an implement to so efficiently off himself?" JD wondered aloud into the phone, gritting his teeth. The Sargent mumbled a few sentences, which JD asked him to repeat.

Long story short: It appeared, the Sargent felt, as though "someone" had not been watching the pair closely enough. Evidently, either Chad had asked for the glass, or Planck had brought it along, made a suggestion, or upset Chad to such an extent that he'd taken his own life.

"You did not clear Planck before he met with his client?" JD said to the Sargent.

More muttering, then: "Yes, of course we did. But evidently we overlooked something."

JD hung up knowing that a head or several heads were about to roll.

The detective took a sip of his now-cold coffee, frowned, and glanced at his phone. Already close to lunchtime and he still had a ton of research to conduct, the reason he'd gotten to his office early. He dug back into it.

So Chad had killed himself. Well, there you go, JD thought, par for the course on this case. He had no further thought about Chad as a person, since he was distasteful and the world, most certainly the horse world, was better off without him. Harsh, something in JD offered, a slow lob from the frontal lobe. Tough shit, something else offered back, a whack to the brain's backline that skittered out of contention. And that was that.

He had plenty to think through on the case and was not about to get sidetracked trying to nail Edward Planck for whatever his involvement was in Redfield's death. It seemed quite a convenient way the lawyer might extricate himself from a relationship that was about to go very public, this was true. But chasing that down would not garner JD one chess move forward in discovering who was actually pulling the strings, ones that had resulted in Oliver's death, Cass' abduction, and the drugging and gene doping going on at Janero. JD walked to Walker's office, made his thoughts clear, and another detective got assigned that jaunt through the fun house.

Back in his own office, he pulled the blinds and sat in front of his computer. So Chad was out, and it seemed more than one person was involved in all the mayhem JD was trying to sort through. "They," Chad had said, and also that "they," apparently, looked like good little citizens, but in fact were "psychopaths."

JD got a yellow legal pad out and drew a vertical line down the middle. To the left he wrote the names of some "good citizens" he'd encountered and those in the "maybe" category. On the right, those obviously bad actors who got a "no" vote just on the face of things.

Max Sidarus . . . a definite maybe. Gus Pinard, Janero's trainer, another maybe, but leaning hard toward "no"—appeared to be a bad guy, but JD didn't have enough information to be categorical. The vet Jason Williams and his paramour, Cecelia Fournier, a "yes," probably. Isabelle, a "no" in capital letters. Williams' ex-wife; the broodmare manager; Holly, the broodmare night worker; the assistant stallion manager under Chad; Catherine, the woman who prepped the mares going to the breeding shed. All were "yeses." The list was a long one. Certainly a longer one than in the "no" column, which amounted to only Pinard and Isabelle.

Pinard. JD thought through how he'd entered and exited the case. The detective and Wes were summarily dismissed at Janero's racing barn, Pinard calling Sidarus and making a quick get-away. Then he shows up at Eden Hill to quiz Marshall about how he was coming with the case concerning Oliver's death. That was the extent of his presence following the murder.

He seemed a rather dim bulb, JD thought. Pretty blatant to blow off the police and pretty stupid to show up at Eden Hill's training track asking Marshall, of all people, about the case. Like that wouldn't get back to JD. But maybe he was cagey, maybe the dimwit routine was his cover. He had to be a damned good trainer or a farm like Janero would not turn their entire string over to him.

192

Maybe he was laying low and off to the side on purpose. He was worth another run at, JD decided.

And then he remembered the burner sitting next to the computer in Chad's secret room. He called Cheryl and told her to get on that asap, put everything else aside. He bet there were communications between Pinard and Chad, and likely between Chad and Isabelle, and maybe "they" would show up as well.

He came to Isabelle. JD drummed his fingers. He needed to circle back to her. He drew a circle around her name and then some devilish horns.

But both Pinard and Isabelle were obvious—or, in the case of Pinard, somewhat obvious—bad actors. Chad had made it clear that "they" appeared just the opposite. So should he click through the longer list, the "yes" folks, see if he could dust up anything?

In the end, he felt compelled to start with Isabelle. He was about to put the call in, when something tickled his brain, which was the way his intuition sometimes got his attention. Like when he wasn't paying attention to it. He sat with that a moment.

Then JD sat up, suddenly alert. He put his pen on his desk. No, he thought. No, no, no, no. Realization dawned on him. He'd been running away from the case, running away from its center, its origin. Chasing Chad, chasing Cass' abductor, chasing Oliver's killer. Chasing, that was the problem. No. Stop running, he told himself.

Return to the origin.

The key to it all was the drugs and the gene doping. JD went back to the conversation he'd had with Jake McCann, the reproductive specialist at Hawk Ridge's broodmare barn. Back to Tim's experiences at Janero. He needed to follow up on the racehorses. More specifically on Gus Pinard, the trainer in charge of them. Look back further, not just what had happened recently, but Pinard's pattern, his history. See if anything showed up that might shed light on what was happening to the racehorses now.

He got Cheryl on it, and Cheryl got the team diving into Pinard, and into anything they could find on the horses presently in his training regimen.

A few hours later, JD had a big report onscreen. He called Cheryl, thanked her, and told her to get back to Chad's burner. He read through the report slowly.

It was clear that long before Pinard had come to Janero, in his early years, the trainer had an unusual number of horses die in his care. He'd worked at the less prestigious tracks back then, so nobody now was likely interested in that. He didn't have a horse in a stakes race until quite a few years down the road.

The racing public saw horses fall to their knees and not get up during races, but only briefly as the camera crews were clued into quickly panning away from those shots. Bad for ratings. But what wasn't apparent at all to the public, even in the briefest of moments, were the horses, often youngsters, who died on the training track. The stats, JD well knew, were sickening, all across the country. That's why one of the major racing syndicates had quit U.S. racing altogether for years in favor of Europe, where the drug laws were much more strict.

Pinard had racked up enough heart attack and breakdown deaths in his early days to warrant investigation. He'd been exonerated. The racing game had always contended collateral losses, meaning horses dying, were inevitable. And Pinard's early "losses" as a trainer were not unlike other trainers' experiences, some of them major names in the game. So the findings on Pinard didn't shock JD.

But then Pinard's horses started winning, and so did he. He built his career on buying young horses on the cheap—those with less-than-stellar breeding, or whose conformation didn't warrant a second glance—and winning with them. He made a few into stars on the lower tracks and moved up. He got better horses to train, more wins, and continued his rise into the high-dollar world of stakes racing. JD suspected he'd perfected his drug concoctions. He still had horses come back with positive test results, but with more money and an assistant trainer, the suspensions and fines didn't make a dent in his operation, which rolled on without missing a beat.

Then Max Sidarus hired him, and he hit the bigtime. JD scrutinized his record. Since coming on at Janero, the horses under his care were faring worse physically than previously. Though he'd had a history of drug testing infractions, in the last two years, those numbers had gone down but the likely effects of drugs and, from what JD had learned, gene doping, had not—JD found heart attack deaths among healthy two-and-three-year-olds, snapped legs, the anemia that had ended the colt under Bradford's care, and serious injuries that hadn't resulted in euthanization.

Catastrophic breaks could occur for any number of reasons, JD was aware of that, but if the horses were drugged, that could be due to overtraining and racing while on pain killers, or other illegal drugs. Or due to some medication concoctions that were legal, but had deadly side-effects, especially when combined. Or using drug cocktails along with gene modification, which might occur if they were trying to perfect gene doping without taking a hit on their wins. The possible reasons were as numerous as they were disturbing.

All in all, it was a heartbreaking read and JD was well-used to things that broke most people's hearts. He stopped reading.

When he and Harper had married and merged their farms, they'd had a meeting with all the employees. No drugs, no harsh care, no heavy hands on the horses, who always gave their all to you. The broodmare manager clearly stated she'd rather a foal not be handled at all than handled roughly. She had an Australian horse handler in once a year to work with her staff. All the mommas and the babies were happy and healthy as a result. And Marshall did not put up with anyone mishandling the runners. He kept the number in his two-and three-year-old string low so he could individualize their training. They never sent their studs abroad during the U.S. breeding off season, not wanting to take a chance on shortening their lives. They never over-booked the studs. Eden Hill and Hawk Ridge did it the right way. And they proved you could win racing safely and cleanly.

JD picked up the papers. Not so here, it appeared.

The picture at Janero was emerging. Pinard, with the help of Isabelle most probably, was doping the horses. Adding gene doping to the mix would undoubtably exacerbate the danger to their runners. Chad's attitude—that the game was all about money—seemed the way things operated in Pinard's racing barn as well.

That could be because Pinard had inside help from Isabelle at the testing lab. It wouldn't be hard for her to test his drug concoctions so he, or someone else, could adjust them and stay under the testing limits. And with her background, she'd be the one to help him with gene doping. That's what Tim Bradford had suspected when he'd put down the colt with severe anemia. With Isabelle's help, all Pinard's horses could be physically compromised. Some, as was the picture, to the point of death. That's why the horses' tests came back clean, time after time—the drugs flew under the testing limits, and they didn't yet have definitive means to prove gene doping.

But who was behind it all?

Max Sidarus had hired Pinard. And usually the vet was involved, so was Jason Williams in on it, too? Chad, clearly, was the drug delivery boy. He hadn't seemed bright enough, though, to have been much more. Good at following orders—killing Oliver was likely just that. And Isabelle certainly had the expertise and the attitude to mastermind what was apparently going on, plus she'd had a relationship with Oliver. What was that all about?

But Chad had said "they," so it wasn't any one of them. And he'd indicated they put up a great front. Pinard didn't fit that profile and neither did Isabelle. But then, neither did Chad, so who knows what looking "good" amounted to with him. Maybe people like Pinard and Isabelle, people who were accomplished, had a great professional appearance, maybe that amounted to "good citizens" in Chad's book.

And what about Max Sidarus? He sure played the "concerned owner" role to perfection, genuinely shocked by Oliver's murder, it seemed, and convincing in his relief that his racehorses had come back clean when the Racing Commission had swooped in for testing. Was he simply a great actor? Did he have a partner?

JD put in a call to Tim Bradford then sent him all the information he had on the breakdowns, injuries, and deaths of Janero racehorses under Pinard's care. He asked Bradford to analyze it all, consult with McCann if he needed to, and get back to him as quickly as possible.

His next call was to his contact over at the Racing Commission, a guy he'd gone to high school with who worked under the Equine Medical Director. He could wait to make a formal request, but he was tired of waiting. He spoke to his former offensive lineman, sent the racehorse jockey club names over to him and told him he needed all the medical records—with specific emphasis on the medication records—asap.

JD wanted information he could use to nail Pinard, burn him good, and then flip him.

30

After making those two requests, JD turned back to Pinard. Apparently, he had not only been investigated at lower-level tracks but in Lexington, too, and not long before the Commission had ordered the recent tests run on the racehorses, the ones that had come back clean. As before, the reason for the investigation was racehorse deaths, this time at Janero. And, as before, Pinard had been exonerated.

JD finished up all the info he could find on the trainer, then headed next door for a smoked turkey sub and wolfed it down, swilling a Pepsi for the caffeine and sugar rush, then headed back in his office. In his inbox, there awaited the medical records his buddy had procured, and JD shot them over to Bradford, asking him to pair the records up with the deaths and injuries and see what he could come up with.

His next move was to do a face-to-face with Pinard. Time, he figured, to head over to Janero's racing barns and check out what was what on that front. He grabbed his jacket, downed the rest of his cold coffee, grimaced, and was out the door.

At the big barn's entrance, the detective walked past the array of stellar racehorse photos and turned left at the dirt aisle. Ahead he saw one of Janero's runners, a 6-year-old stallion, Hyota, who JD and Harper knew well, having followed his career. The horse had brought home six figures thus far in his racing career and was one of Janero's prized runners. He hadn't won any of the premier races—no Kentucky Derby, no Dubai, but he'd consistently come home with a check over the years, so they kept him running. And because the horse had great breeding lines, sale to a less prestigious farm and stud duties just might be in his future.

The bay was having his feet worked on, the farrier being a guy JD wouldn't hire for any reason, but he didn't have a thing to say about who Pinard had doing plates.

JD approached the farrier, bent over at the waist, the stallion's right front hoof on a stand. Henry Evans was reaching over with a gloved hand for a dispensing gun loaded with a tube of something. He caught JD out of the corner of his eye, set the hoof back down, and stood holding the metal gun.

"What are you doing?" JD asked, though he knew quite clearly what Evans was up to—keeping the stallion's hooves together so he could stay on the track. The bay turned to JD, his eye going momentarily soft until his groom jerked the lead rope and pulled the horse's head around.

Evans focused on JD's police jacket and looked at the horse. "Just getting his hooves in some sort a shape," Evans said, turning back to JD, smiling, running his free hand down his leather chaps. "His feet are falling apart, his hoof condition is crap."

JD nodded. "How long has that been going on?"

Evans looked quizzical, as if unsure about all the questions. Then: "He's been goin' downhill for a while now. I've done all I can at this point." He adopted a saddened look that JD didn't buy.

"What are your thoughts on that?" JD knew that such hoof conditions could be the result of nutritional deficiencies due to, perhaps, to drugging. Might as well probe that angle a bit, see if anything popped.

"He's a money maker," the farrier said, shrugging. "What can I tell ya?"

JD sent a look Evan's way and the smaller man cowered. Seeing he wasn't going to get anything useful from Evans, he nodded, and the man bent to his work.

A voice from the end of the aisle called down the row of mostly empty stalls—Pinard's assistant trainer. He strode toward JD, a stopwatch in one hand, a clipboard in the other, a Janero ballcap on his head. "You here for?" he said, getting to the detective and seeing JD pull out his ID. But the Panamanian assistant recognized him and ignored it. "You want Pinard? He is not here. He takes the fillies to Sarasota. They run."

"Just thought a stop-in might be good," JD said, seeing he wasn't going to get anywhere there either, given the head trainer was in New York. "I'll head back around when he's back. Next week, maybe."

The assistant trainer nodded vigorously and stood there.

JD left, disgusted, thinking he'd hit another dead end. He took a last look at Hyota and wished him well, hoping that big heart and those crumbling feet held together until he went to stud.

JD climbed in his cruiser and headed out. He'd just have to rely on Bradford putting a different set of pieces together.

JD headed home, calling Wes in the process. He and Cass had come back early that morning, spending only one night camping in the woods—too many bugs for Cass, Wes reported, calling her a wuss. She'd headed to the gym then was going over to Keeneland's backstretch. Wes was helping Lucas over at the stallion racing barn. JD told him to stay put, he'd come to him. He put in a call to Bradford, got his voicemail and left a message. He wanted the vet's analysis, it could only strengthen the case.

JD pulled into Eden Hill's entrance and sped up the curving drive, followed the circular roadway to the stone stallion barn, originally built over a hundred years ago but updated through the years. He couldn't do much until he heard from Bradford or

Cheryl on Chad's burner, so hanging out with the horses and picking Wes' brain seemed as good a way to spend time as any.

He walked through Lucas' raked gravel swirl pattern just outside the barn and entered, stopping to brush a hand down Sugarland's chestnut face extending over the half door, the colt's eyes curious. The chestnut nodded, appreciating the attention. JD raised a finger to Lucas coming out of the feed room and saw Wes down by Deacon's stall feeding the black stallion a handful of hay.

The barn held a rich mixture of sweet and sharp scents—horse, hay, loamy manure, and the slight tang of urine. John Henry or Lucas had raked the aisle clean, and in most stalls, sleek, muscled-out runners shuffled around, drank water, or ate their green hay.

"What the hell, Wes?" JD said, approaching him. Deacon liked only two people, how did Wes squeeze in on that?

From the far door, a red bay stallion not working at the moment was being brought in from grazing, his neck arched, his feet prancing, his chain lead going taut. His groom deposited the big boy in his stall and the colt immediately turned to his hay.

JD checked his phone. Still no word from Bradford.

"Let's go," JD said, getting to Wes, and backing away from Deacon, whose amber eyes were as fierce as his own. Deacon towered over the men, sending out monster vibes, and JD was glad the guy was in his stall.

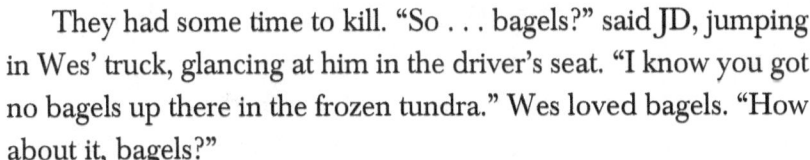

They had some time to kill. "So . . . bagels?" said JD, jumping in Wes' truck, glancing at him in the driver's seat. "I know you got no bagels up there in the frozen tundra." Wes loved bagels. "How about it, bagels?"

Wes started the truck, admired its rumble a minute, backed out and pulled forward, then put his wrist on the truck's steering wheel, his high cheekbones and jet-black hair beneath the battered Justin showing in profile. "I make bagels," he said. "I got skills."

JD checked his phone again. Nothing. He looked at Wes and smiled. "Oh, yeah, I see that neck of yours, would those be bite marks? You got skills, alright."

Wes said. "Huh." He looked over, raised a lip.

"Come on, bagels, man. You know you been pining away for 'em."

"Drinks," Wes said. "Preferably expensive bourbon." His eyes stayed trained on the long drive down to Georgetown Road.

"Naw," JD said. "Got too much in play." He filled Wes in on the developments. Or lack thereof, he thought, finishing up.

They headed out to get some Town Branch bourbon, JD not arguing much. He figured he could down a shot. He glanced at Wes. Maybe two.

JD complained about Pinard's absence as they headed over to the distillery and complained some more about waiting on Cheryl and Bradford.

"And if we don't hear from one or the other by the time we're done, I'm getting on somebody's ass."

The pair walked through the distillery's entrance, past the huge, shiny stainless steel distillation system on display through the windows. They moseyed on to the shop, seating themselves at the small bar. JD ordered a flight of bourbon while Wes got up to peruse the merchandise. The drinks delivered, they set about putting away shots, no talking involved. Halfway through the second set up, Wes spoke.

"Shouldn't be drinking on duty." He held up his glass and stared at the amber liquid in the half-light. "Detective." He smiled slightly.

"Define 'drinking'," JD said. "This isn't drinking." He lifted the shot glass and downed it as if to prove a point.

Wes smacked his lips. "This is fun."

"What?"

Wes looked at JD, his gray eyes in a squint. "Fun."

"Since when are you into fun?"

"I'm into fun. I'm all about fun."

JD downed a shot, stared at his friend. "Murdering fish and wildlife, fun like that?"

"You hunt."

"Not lately." JD turned and scoped out the smattering of visitors in the small shop. Tourists in shorts, the women clutching purses close to their sides, the men handling the bourbon bottles with undisguised fondness.

Wes cracked a knuckle. "Domesticated. That's sad, man," and he downed another shot then nodded to the bartender for another flight.

The bartender suggested full-fledged drinks but backed away when the scowls began.

The two men stared at the array of bottles on the back bar, not talking.

A fat man with hairy arms, a bald head, and curly black hair sticking out of the back of his t-shirt collar laid his hands flat on the bar next to Wes, looked at him.

"Had the rye? Best rye in the state. Peppery, got that bite at the end, know what I'm talking about? You gotta try it, I swear. Right Leo?" He nodded to the bartender.

A talker. Wes looked at JD. "That's just wrong," he muttered, nodding at the collar. He ignored the man, and, disappointed, the guy walked away.

"Yeah," Wes continued, "domesticated. You got a designer pond with designer fish."

JD smirked, his green eyes alight. "Huh."

"Koi—fabulous, man. And a designer dog."

"Don't mess with Kelso."

Wes considered it. "Naw, Kelso's good. I got a wolf."

"You do not have a wolf."

JD and Wes looked at each other. Wes turned back to the bar. "I did have a wolf. Found her with a bullet in her shoulder, dug it out."

"You have her bite on a knife?" JD asked, smiling.

"I got ways. Doctored her, kept her in an old pen out back, then she dug her way out."

"Uh-huh," JD commented.

"Healed up ok."

JD smiled, turned the glass in his fingers, admiring the amber glow. "Dug her way out. Like most of your women."

Wes snorted. "Peace, buddy, leave that shit alone."

"Get out any way they can," JD said.

Wes shook his head. His man bun bobbed.

They were quiet again.

"We had some good times."

"Yeah, we did," JD agreed.

They each knocked one back.

31

H is phone chirped and JD glanced at it on the bar. "Bradford," he said to Wes, then, answering, "Yeah."

"Sorry it took so long," the vet said right off. "Had back-to-backs and a tough time finding McCann. With what you sent over, I think we need him in on this."

JD nodded, circling his finger in the air at Wes who downed the last two shots and stood, easing on his Justin, and pulled a wad of bills out of his pocket. He plunked down enough for the bill and a hefty tip as JD finished up with Bradford then they both headed to the truck.

Bradford said Harper had called McCann on one of their broodmares in foal. She was one of Harper's favorites and she had concerns since the mare, Deayah, was older and she'd had some problems before. The reproductive specialist had carved out some time and was heading to Hawk Ridge at 3:15. Bradford had sent him JD's material, but who knows if he'd had time to look at it.

"At any rate," Bradford finished, "I'm headed that way now, so if you're around, let's meet up. You can see about Deayah and pick McCann's brain."

JD filled Wes in as they headed back home. Though he had other things on his mind, JD spared a moment. "I'd hate to lose that mare or the baby," he said. "This is her last foal, and she's Harper's favorite."

Wes said nothing. He wasn't into the whole broodmare thing.

Once at the barn, they saw two trucks—Jake McCann's and Tim Bradford's—jumped out and headed in. The nights had finally warmed and most of the mares and foals were still out to pasture and wouldn't be in until the next morning, so the barn wasn't heavily populated.

There were some snorts and whinnies among the few big-bodied mares-in-foal still stalled and about to deliver. They circulated through the shavings, shuffling and munching their hay. JD loved the smell and maternal vibe in the mares' barn, an oddity, he felt, borne of his upbringing at Hawk Ridge.

Up ahead, McCann, dressed in stained white overalls, stood behind Deayah's hind end, sutures in hand, while his assistant stood at the mare's head, stroking her and murmuring. On the dirt aisle were blood-stained wipes from McCann cutting away some flesh. The mare didn't appear uncomfortable, though her delivery canal was being stitched closed. She wasn't that far along, and the vet was giving the mare the best chance to carry to term.

McCann turned, hearing them, needle poised, smiled, and nodded to the mare. "Lidocaine, it's beautiful." He turned back. "She's not feeling a thing."

He got back to work. "This'll save her from an infection. These older girls, sometimes they just need a little help. We'll keep an eye on her." He finished up, and clipped the thread, then dipped down into a bucket and cleaned the mare's hind end off. He nodded to his assistant and Deayah was escorted into her stall where she bent to a flake of hay.

McCann turned to his assistant and stripped off his gloves. "Be a moment," he said to her and she began cleaning up, packing McCann's gear.

"Did you get all the documents I sent?" Bradford asked. He was as interested in McCann's take as was JD.

McCann nodded. "Yeah, but if you have 'em on you that would help," and Bradford reached into his portfolio and pulled out the sheets.

"Jason Williams, Janero's vet, is on the medication charts," Bradford said as McCann flipped pages, nodding.

They were all quiet a few minutes while McCann went through the documents.

"Heard he got kicked," McCann said, meaning Williams, and chuckled. "Cowboying it," he murmured, finishing up and Bradford nodded, smiling.

JD and Wes stood by silently, letting the two professionals gossip.

McCann looked up as his assistant went by. "I'll be along," he said and shuffled the pages together, handing them back to Bradford.

"I looked at them briefly when you sent them over," McCann said to Bradford, "but good to see 'em again, thanks. And truthfully, you probably know as much as I do about how to put the meds, the race results, the breakdowns, the deaths . . . how to put it all together. But I'll tell you what I noticed."

"Thanks," JD said, and McCann looked his way. JD continued. "I need something I can go forward with. Something I can use with Pinard, leverage."

The broodmare manager and a few grooms began to head in, the mares sticking their soft muzzles, then their heads over the half-doors, hoping for some hay or grain.

"Let's take it outside," JD said, and they trouped out to the parking lot. The sun was sending slanting afternoon light their way, and JD knew McCann and Bradford's time was precious.

Jake McCann stuck his hand out to Bradford. "Could I see those one more time? Just want to check something," and Tim pulled out the papers again.

McCann nodded after flipping to a page. "Yeah, so here." He looked up, his clear blue eyes locking on JD. "You've got a filly who collapsed and died from," and here McCann looked at the paper and read, "'catastrophic pulmonary hemorrhage and edema leading to heart failure.'" He read a bit more. "It says this occurred during training, a 'routine gallop, not strenuous.'"

He looked up. "So. The horse's medical chart showed she'd received thyroxine in feed, estrone, an anabolic steroid, and Bute. Side-effects of long-term use can be a problem with clotting. So it could be that she ingested this over a long period and that led to the hemorrhage which led to the heart failure." He handed the papers back to Bradford.

Wes spoke up. "That doesn't sound good."

"No worse than what some vets around here do," Bradford said, his expression sour. "And Jason Williams probably initiated and ok'd that, if it was long term."

"I also noticed a colt, dead of a heart attack," McCann said, his tone even more serious. "He was prescribed Ace—Acepromazine—it's a tranquilizer that can mask EPO effects in the bloodstream." He focused in on JD. "The drug reduces abnormally high levels of hematocrits, or the measurement of red blood cells which carry oxygen through the body, which is what the EPO would do, raise those levels. And that would increase a horse's performance."

JD nodded. He knew about EPOs and about Ace, but not about the hazards of this combination.

"EPOs have dangerous side-effects," McCann continued. "That's not news. Side-effects like heart attacks, as in this horse. They increase the blood's viscosity, resulting at times in death by stroke or heart attack."

"You think that's what happened here? JD said.

McCann shrugged. "Dunno. But . . ." He glanced at Bradford. "The whole things smells bad, I'll say that."

JD nodded and Wes looked on stoically.

They all fell silent, each person handling his own private version of disgust.

"Thanks, Jake," JD said finally, and got a salute from McCann.

"I'll give Harper a call, settle her concerns about Deayah." He started out then turned back. "Hope what I offered was of help." He turned back and jumped in his truck. His assistant, who was texting, looked up and waved as they backed out.

"We got something?" JD said quietly to Tim who was putting his portfolio back together.

"Well yeah, I think those two deaths are fishy, too. And there's one more interesting thing I found. It's an infraction so it's something the lab caught. I did a little research on my own. Pinard had TCO2 levels in two fillies who finished first in separate races come back well above the testing limit."

"Jesus," JD said. He knew what that meant—milk-shaking, which had been around forever. He looked at Wes. "TCO2 levels would mean the fillies were likely given bicarbonate of soda, water, and maybe other drugs. They used to stick a tube down their noses into the stomach. But now, a lot of them use a loaded 'bullet' in the mouth from a dose gun."

Bradford jumped in. "Doing that 4-6 hours before a race lessens the lactic acid buildup in the muscles, so the horse can run further longer. These two fillies didn't die, but Pinard did get nabbed on being over the testing limit, resulting in a fine and suspension."

"Which resulted in what, exactly?" Wes asked.

Both Bradford and JD looked at him as if he was a naïve twit, which Wes appreciated not at all. Pinard had assistant trainers, so his operation carried on without missing a beat.

"And on the drugs Jake talked about?" JD said.

Bradford shook his head. "The truth? You likely have the right information—Jake gave it to you straight. But you don't have proof. The Commission was on it, the lab ran their tests, the meds are dangerous, yes, but legal."

JD sighed.

"This case is a fucking merry-go-round," Wes muttered.

32

That morning, prior to Wes and JD tying a small one on and hearing from McCann, Cass had hit the gym, then headed over to Keeneland to meet up with an old trainer friend, Harriet Glover, who'd believed in the young jock when she'd first hit the stakes races. Glover had given her a leg up on one of Cass' favorite mounts back then, a huge chestnut filly she'd connected with like no other until she'd met Deacon and then Memphis. Madame Angelis was smart and cocky, and back then they were perfect mirrors of each other.

"Member Angel?" Cass said, leaning on the track rail beside Glover, who was watching her second set file in and get to their workout. They were on the big track, the sun already well up, and the white and red striped poles brilliant against the greening infield. Cass loved the soft banter among the exercise riders, how businesslike they were moving into their work, how still and quiet they stayed above their mounts.

Glover smiled, her sun-lined, weathered face crinkling with well-earned creases. "She was a piece a work, that one." She turned to Cass. "Come to think of it, you both were," she said, grinning down at the small jockey.

"That big race, she just ran off," Cass said, laughing. "I couldn't rate her to save my life at the first, but I got her." She recalled the head-strong filly and that race clearly. "There was speed in that race, and she wanted to go up there. I finally got hold of her, held her back, held her back . . ."

"Oh yeah," Glover said, nodding, eyes on her set moving into their workout. "I remember that one. Angel was mad as hell."

Cass watched the horses out on the track for a moment, each one taking to the work differently. A large black colt ran with his head held high followed by a bay arching his neck, the intensity clear in his eyes. Some ran with effort. Others seemed to float over the track.

"Yeah, she was pullin' and pullin'," Cass said, turning to Glover, returning to her memory. "So then, in the turn, I let her loose and she was so mad, she took off—I let her think she was running off, I pulled back on the bit so hard and she thought she was takin' off on me," Cass said, laughing. "She'd show me, that's what she was thinking. My arms were ready to fall off when we won."

They both looked down at the rail they leaned on, shaking their heads, nodding and remembering. Two old friends recalling past battles.

Then Cass sobered. She'd ridden Angel in the filly's last race. Cass didn't want to remember, but the image was seared into her. They were in the middle of the turn, everybody was getting ready to run and Cass saw the jock's rear end come up ahead of her. He'd tried to ease back his filly a little, then a little more. It took only a second. Cass tried to get Angel out, but that filly came back on her. Angel clipped her heels, went down. Cass broke her collarbone. Angel broke her neck.

The jockey looked up and the big track came into focus, the horses, the sound of their hooves and lungs, the smell, the riders in their helmets and tasseled-top knit hats. You couldn't dwell on things like that or you couldn't ride. Or you'd ride scared.

Glover watched Cass, ignoring the workout. The trainer had run the same movie Cass had playing in her mind. You don't forget those things. Angel down, gone. Cass broken. She put her hand lightly on Cass' arm.

"Anytime you go out there, you don't know if you're gonna come back," Glover said, her voice unemotional.

Cass nodded, still gazing at the track. Horses trotted by, and down close to the rail a sleek, smooth-muscled gray breezed, his tail furled out behind him. Glover was right. It's in the back of your mind every race, but you can never think of it or you start riding scared. Then you might as well hang it up.

"How many jocks we see ride like that, scared?" Glover said.

Cass nodded. "They make mistakes, overreact. Then they get afraid to move into a spot and you're right behind 'em," Cass said softly, having seen it. "Now you're pulling your horse up and swerving to get around him. Doesn't work, you can't ride scared."

She looked at her old boss, saw the concern in her deep-set eyes.

"That's right, Cass. And right now, you got a major load of scare in you." She shook her head.

Cass took the words in, hard as they were to hear. But she'd ridden Memphis, she thought, she'd done ok on him.

"I was up on Memphis, you see that race?"

"Yeah, I was there, I saw it."

"I won that race," Cass said, a little defensiveness thrown in.

"I know you won that race." Glover paused and stared Cass down. "Doesn't change a thing, now does it?"

The jockey nodded. Glover, again, was right. She'd battled it down that day, but it was there in that ride on Memphis.

"You want to ride?" Glover finished up, looking back to the track. "Get it together or get on the sideline."

The two watched the rest of the set finish their workout in silence. Glover had asked Cass over to see a colt she might want her up on. But Cass realized that wasn't really why she'd invited her. Glover's last comment, that's why. Nobody else would have said it. Cass scuffed her paddock boot. But maybe Cass had known that and that's why she'd agreed to come.

The two old friends stood quietly together, watching the set finish up, Glover's assistant trainer heading over—they'd get the official times from Keeneland's clocker, but Glover's assistant showed the trainer what he'd gotten. Presently, Glover's just-worked youngsters walked off the track and headed up the hill to the barn. The colt Cass had come to see was in the final set, so she stuck around.

She looked at the track and grandstand. Not a lot of people had shown up this morning—a couple of men down the way chatted, drank coffee, and leaned on the rail, while a few others watched silently, jotting down notes. In the stands, a trainer she knew and his assistant watched with binoculars. A casual, focused, workaday feeling settled over the track. These were the caretakers, the masterminds, the teachers, and out on the track were the exercise riders who never saw a moment of glory and would never feel the elation of winning. Still, they did their work, day in, day out, sick or injured.

But not full of fear, Cass knew. She thought about Angel and gazed around.

Sometimes you couldn't avoid the deaths and injuries, she knew that. Sometimes, bad luck caught up with you.

But she'd seen the other side, too. Like now, she thought, thinking about Janero and how she'd ended up a pawn in it all. She looked at Glover. She'd been right about Cass' fear. JD and Wes would figure the case out just like they'd figured out where she was when she'd been taken. And Harper wouldn't let up until the case broke and the horses were safe.

Cass had a different job. And she would do it, get rid of the fear. Whatever that took. Riding was her life, and she'd be damned if she'd let go of it.

Glover brought her out of the deep thoughts, pointing out the bay colt just now moving out of his warm-up. The rider dropped them down to the rail and Cass watched the colt move out smoothly, then pick a fight with the rider, wanting to go. She smiled, having ridden horses that wouldn't check. Hard mouths on some, like trying to pull a table, she thought. This guy looked to be yanking the rider's arms right out of their sockets.

"Takes two to fight," Cass murmured to Glover. The trainer handed Cass her binoculars and the jockey watched the colt round the turn and head out on the backstretch.

"Benny's smart, you watch," Glover said. "Colt'll shift one way, he'll shift the other."

Sure enough, the exercise rider outsmarted the colt. The horse shifted and Benny shifted just like Glover said. The colt cocked his head, and Benny cocked it toward the fence. The rider stopped pulling and the colt settled in, then rounded the far turn and breezed fine coming home.

Cass handed the binoculars back to the trainer. "Yeah," she said grinning. "I'd love to hop on that guy."

Glover laughed. "How did I know you were gonna say that?" Then Glover turned serious. "Look, we go way back. I trust you. Tell me when you're ready. Don't bullshit me and get my colt hurt and you hurt."

"Don't need to say it," Cass said, nodding at Benny as he walked the headstrong bay by them, the colt snorting and breathing hard, prancing, his muscles bunched. Benny was smiling as he ran a hand down the colt's damp neck. He obviously loved his work and loved the big colt.

Glover said, "I got the vet coming to do a lameness check on a filly up at the barn. Come with me, and we'll look at what I got that colt pointed at."

They walked up the dirt walkway lined by white fencing, past the small track on the left and onto the barn, the set coming up behind them. Cass could hear the hollow *clop clop* of hooves and the easy chatter among the riders. Spanish drifted on the air, mixed with a bit of soft laughter.

It felt like family. Like home, Cass thought. She'd focus on that, on the horses. Not on the fear.

Up ahead, she saw the hot walkers slowly making their way around the small dirt track beside three young racehorses, the shedrow to the left dotted with stuffed haynets outside each stall, square bales in the aisles, and exercise riders here and there removing black padded vests and helmets. A groom sprayed off one of the fillies who'd just worked, the young horse's head raised, her ears back, as the water streamed gently over her face.

She and Glover walked into the sparse grass around the cool down track, and they spied the vet up ahead dressed in what Cass thought of as "the uniform"—khakis and a blue oxford shirt. He watched as a groom led a petite filly out of the stall, then walked the three-year-old away from the vet and back toward him. The vet, who Cass recognized as Jason Williams, had on a formidable leg brace, and nodded as he evaluated the filly. He pointed to the left rear leg and the smaller woman with him picked up the hoof and tested it. No abscess, Cass thought, as the assistant put the hoof down.

As Glover and Cass neared the vet and the smaller woman at his side, Cass heard him say he'd put a block in and see where the issue was, and the assistant got busy setting that up. Cass knew he'd begin low, near the hoof and block the leg higher if he needed to until he found the site where the lameness originated.

They arrived at the filly and the trainer waited quietly to see what Williams came up with. Cass stood at Glover's side and Williams looked up, caught her eye and smiled. Cass smiled back, thinking, the guy's got charisma, she'd give him that. And he had quite a few other attributes—hazel eyes, blond hair, and that not-so-subtle sexual allure. He didn't interest Cass, but that was not the case with most all the other women she knew.

She stepped forward to get a better look at the filly's leg, and suddenly her world shifted entirely. On the air, Cass picked up a scent, one she recognized. A wave of nausea and overwhelming dizziness swept through her, then she tried to step back but found herself paralyzed, rooted in place, staring at Jason Williams. That scent. That cologne.

She frantically looked right and then left, confused. There wasn't a man close by other than the groom. She looked back at Williams but saw he was now bent, intent on administering a PD block to the horse's pastern, uninterested in her.

She felt a surge of fear, saw Glover look over at her with concern, an eyebrow raised.

Cass struggled to breathe, took a beat, and tried to focus on that and not the terror welling up inside her. Step back. Breathe, she told herself, trying to go within. In for four seconds . . . she counted . . . hold for four seconds . . . out slowly. She was able then to literally step back, out of the range of that terrifying scent.

Around her Williams was chatting to his assistant and then to Glover, not noticing her, but Cass heard none of it.

How could he act so . . . Breathe, she told herself, in and out. She kept that up for another minute and then tried to take a step, found she could move freely and turned to Glover.

"I need to take care of something," she said quickly, steadying her voice as much as she could. "We'll catch up later on the colt."

Glover's eyes held concern still, but Williams was asking her about the filly, so she nodded at Cass and turned to the vet.

Cass pivoted to the left and walked to the back end of the shedrow as slowly as she could, taking the long way to the parking lot, but not wanting to get near the vet on her way out. She walked through the passageway at the end of the shedrow heading to the next barn and pulled out her phone. Her fingers shook as she hit speed dial, calling Harper, who picked up on the second ring.

"Hey," her friend said, "what's up?"

Cass took a deep breath, let it go slowly, then said, "Jason Williams. The vet. He's the one who kidnapped me."

33

Harper sat up, put her laptop to the side. "What? . . . Williams? Seriously? That's . . . What happened? Where are you?" The questions spilled out. "Did you call JD?"

"No, I called you."

"Are you ok? Do you want me to come get you?"

"No, I'm not ok," Cass said, and filled Harper in on everything.

"I'm coming. You stay put." Harper rose from the couch, headed to the kitchen for her keys.

Cass got to the parking lot, trotted to her truck, and opened the door. "I'm not staying here. I have my truck."

"Come home, then," Harper said, leaning on the counter. "Now. I'll call JD and meet you here."

"Get Wes," Cass said and drove out trying not to break the sound barrier.

Twenty minutes later, she arrived at Harper's to learn that the boys were out on the case and wouldn't get back until after they met with McCann, which was in a little over an hour.

"It'll be a while," Harper said.

"Where are they?" Cass said, her face pale. Harper motioned her into the living room and gestured to the couch. "Where's Wes?" Cass said quietly. Her expression was trying for stoic, but Harper could see how much she needed him there.

Harper filled her in on the meeting with McCann and Bradford, and Cass insisted on heading over to the mares' barn. Harper convinced her that they needed the information the vets could give them, and with McCann's schedule, who knew when he might have time again. Both JD and Wes needed to do this.

"You know JD and Wes have worked on things far worse than this case. They do best together." Harper said. "You know they do. Leave them be, they'll be home soon enough."

Reluctantly, Cass nodded and sank into the leather couch. Harper got her grandma's afghan and wrapped it around the jockey's shoulders. Cass looked so small and vulnerable, thought Harper, heading for the kitchen. She made Cass a sandwich, but her friend wouldn't eat.

Understandable. Harper wasn't hungry either. She sat next to the jockey and asked Cass if she wanted to talk about it, but all she got was a mute head shake. She seemed, Harper thought, in shock.

They sat on the couch quietly, not talking, Harper just trying to be a comforting presence for Cass, though it was clear she wasn't about to be comforted.

They sat that way for a long while, not talking. Cass fell into a light sleep once and woke up with a start. Harper made them both tea and they sipped in silence. The next few hours passed that way, both of them just trying to get through the passage of time, until finally they heard JD and Wes come through the door, Kelso's toenails clicking on the hardwood behind them.

Harper had purposefully not told JD what was going on, she'd just told him to get home right after the meeting with the two vets. Things with Cass would not change in the time their meeting took, so she'd made the decision.

JD wanted to know what was so urgent, and she said she'd fill them in when the pair got home. If she'd told JD, she knew he and Wes wouldn't have taken the meeting and they needed to. She glanced at Cass. She hoped it wasn't a decision she'd regret.

JD strode in, Wes following with Kelso trotting alongside him, glancing up in adoration.

"What's going on?" JD said, seeing the back of Cass' head, the rest of her sunk on the couch with a wrap around her.

Wes picked up on the tension and walked quietly around to the couch. Harper rose and Wes took her place, pulling Cass to him without any words. He took off the Justin and set it on the coffee table, turning clear eyes Cass' way.

She fell onto his chest, closing her eyes.

Kelso plopped down next to Harper who was sitting in a club chair to the right of the couch. JD walked to her and planted a kiss on her head, keeping his eyes on Cass. He straightened and walked to the fireplace, sat on its raised hearth, elbows on his thighs, his eyes taking it all in.

"What happened?" JD began, and Cass opened her eyes, looked at Wes who nodded, then at JD.

She told them what happened, ending with, "It's him, JD. I'm positive."

JD looked at Harper and then at Wes. "Ok, Cass," he said, turning back to the jockey. "Take me through it again, but this time slowly."

Cass ran her hands over her head, fingers deep in her short brown hair. "Ok," she said, and went step-by-step through what happened, beginning with walking up to the backstretch barn.

"And before that," JD said. "Fill me in on all of it, start to finish."

She did, but at the end, she lost it and was not able to go through being in the presence of Jason Williams again. Her brown eyes went bleak, her shoulders bowed. She looked like she was folding in on herself.

Wes looked at JD. "Keep going," and JD nodded. Harper looked on. They all knew Cass had to do endure this, it was the only way to get all the information.

JD: "Ok, Cass. You up to this?"

The jockey nodded, her eyes locked on JD's.

"Let's think about it," JD began. "The cologne that Jason Williams wears is probably worn by how many people, Cass? A hundred? Less? More?"

He watched Cass sit up, lean away from Wes. "I smelled it JD. It was him. I know it was him."

"I believe you. But, Cass, think about it, we can't know for sure."

Anger flared on the jockey's face. "Don't treat me like I'm a child. I know what I know."

"I'm gonna shoot that guy in the fucking head," Wes said, looking at JD.

"And that's why I'm in charge," JD said, glancing Wes' way.

The two men stared at each other, neither one giving an inch.

Wes, mad now, jerked a thumb at Harper. "Some guy takes your woman, what would you do?"

Cass snorted, exasperated. "What the bloody hell did you just call me? Your what?" She looked from Wes to JD. "Seriously, the both of you. Jesus."

Harper stepped in, standing, and moving to the fireplace so everyone could see her. "Let's take it down a notch," She looked at the three of them. "Ok, several notches. Look, we'll figure this out. Come on, we cannot get sidetracked."

JD rubbed his hand over his eyes a few times. He turned back to Cass. "Ok, Cass, think. When did you smell the cologne on the guy?"

Cass threw off the afghan and crossed her legs on the couch. "When he grabbed me. In my kitchen. I smelled it then." She looked at Wes then back to JD. "I distinctly remember that smell. And I smelled it exactly the same today. It's him. I'm telling you, it's him."

JD said, "And any other time? When he put in food, when you escaped?"

Cass thought about it quite some time as she stared at the coffee table. They all knew she didn't want to relive the ordeal, but she was.

"No, not really," Cass said quietly, her eyes at first sad, then fiery.

"So we're back to square one," JD said.

Cass was vehement, "We are not back to square one. I told you. It's him. He took me."

"I'm gonna shoot him in the fucking head. I swear to God," Wes said, looking flatly at JD.

He and Wes had gone at it before like this. Tensions were high, that was certain. But JD also knew that Wes' comments spoke volumes about how he felt about Cass, despite his protests. He also knew Wes would pull it together.

The detective smiled. "Yeah," he said to Wes. "I hear ya. I wanna shoot him in the fucking head, too." He looked at Harper. He looked at Cass and then he said, "But what if he's not the guy?"

Later, JD went into the home office off the living room alone and thought about the whole thing. He sat at the family's old rosewood desk, staring at the racing and stud photos lining the walls amid shiny bits and other remembrances of Eden Hill's long history in the racing game. He glanced out the big window, onto the moonlit pond.

Chad had said the people JD were looking for were exactly what Jason Williams appeared to be—affable, normal, a good citizen. Cecelia Fournier, too. Both of them fit Chad's brief profile. So he wasn't about to dismiss Cass' story. But unless Williams had his scent specially made, which was unlikely, Cass' wasn't a definitive ID. Like everything else in the case, he needed much more proof to go after the vet.

And Cass had been under enormous stress in that little room in that falling down barn in the middle of nowhere, not knowing if she was going to live or die. Could he trust the conviction she had that it was Williams? JD knew that many times, people had much more knowledge about things tucked far below conscious thought than they realized. Was that going on here? Was Cass calling on information she had but didn't know she had?

On the other hand, JD also knew that survivors, like eyewitnesses, often made mistakes in identifying a culprit.

He was very close. He felt the case was about to crack wide open, felt it in his bones. He just had to stay focused, not go down any rabbit holes, and get the job done.

As he always did.

34

The next day was filled with a whole lot of nothing, which frustrated JD no end. He once again reviewed the case but found no next step. He'd just have to wait for events to unfold, which infuriated him.

He and Wes headed to the shooting range, popped off a few rounds, mulled things over. Wes said he was heading back to meet up with Cass, who'd insisted on riding workouts for Marshall—her way, she said, of working through "stuff." Wes got that and gave her space but insisted on meeting up after lunch. The two parted, Wes heading home, JD heading to the precinct. Again to the office, he thought, where there awaited more of the same—a whole lot of nothing.

And then Cheryl called.

"The burner? Chad's burner" she said a bit gleefully in the phone. "You can come read the texts yourself, or I can just tell ya."

"Shoot," JD said, turning down the truck radio.

Cheryl rattled it all off. The gist: Chad's burner had back-and-forth texts to and from Isabelle, detailing adjustments to drugs needed so they'd be under the testing limits, and when what Isabelle termed "those other things," would be ready, which JD presumed meant modified genes. Then there were calls to a number Cheryl couldn't find anywhere, but no texts were made to it, only phone calls. A mystery burner no doubt, thought JD.

JD hung up, checked the time. One-thirty, still time to get to the testing lab and grab Isabelle. He called Walker, got him started on an arrest warrant, and headed that way, not wanting to call ahead and alert her so she could get her lawyer in. Or leave.

JD wanted to eyeball her, see how she took the news about Chad's texts.

A while after, he strode into the lab's reception area, identified himself and was seated. Soon the lab's director opened the door, came in, and sat down next to the detective, his hands gently folded in his lap.

"I'm Isabelle's supervisor," he said by way of introduction, though JD recalled he'd stuck his head in the door during his previous interview of Isabelle. "She's not here. Took off last Wednesday, said her mom was really ill and she wasn't sure she was going to make it. Heart attack, apparently."

He rubbed his hand over his bald head, a hang dog look on his face. He regarded JD frankly. "Tough to lose her. She oversees an entire racing section in the lab, and I don't know when she'll be back."

JD knew Isabelle's mother had died when she was 13. So, she'd felt the heat, apparently, and had taken off. He took out his notebook, flipped through some pages and found it. Isabelle had taken off the day after he'd interviewed her. Interesting.

The director kept his eyes on JD. "I gotta say, though, she was helpful even in her state. She was obviously distressed."

"How so?" JD said. The director seemed positively inclined toward Isabelle, having no clue as to her actual activities.

"I asked her for a suggestion on a sub, and she gave me a name right away. Then I didn't hear from her. Called her cell a couple of times, but no response, so I followed up on her suggestion last Friday." He paused. "I've got names, but I trust Isabelle. Anyway, it was this French woman, Cecelia something she recommended. Spoke to her, she sounded competent, said she can step in in a few days." He looked relieved, then worried. "I'm concerned about Isabelle, though. I still haven't heard from her."

JD sat up straight, ignoring the director's last comment. "Cecelia Fournier? The French woman? The nutritionist?" That was Jason Williams' live in. What did Fournier know about drug testing?

"Yes, that's the one. She's focusing on nutrition now. But Isabelle said she'd worked with this woman in Ireland, at a gene testing company, a commercial one with a world-wide reputation. So the woman knows her way around a test tube. She's a chemist, in fact. She'd been Isabelle's supervisor."

She apparently knows her way around gene doping, too, JD thought.

The director continued. "I was lucky to get her. She was only too happy to step in for her friend. And I checked on her references. She's as good as they come, evidently." The director seemed satisfied.

JD shook his head at how unaware the director seemed, saw his quizzical look, and erased it. He stood, thanked the man and left the lab.

"Isabelle's probably sipping sour apple martinis in Morocco," JD said. He'd picked up Wes and they were headed over to Eden Hill's office to check in with Harper.

"Or pushing up grass down there by the national forest," Wes replied.

Yeah, JD had to consider that. Maybe Isabelle had created a rift of some sort and had to be done away with. And conveniently, she'd recommended or been strong-armed into recommending someone to take her place who knew more than she did. Likely, Fournier had her tentacles in Chad and Pinard as deeply as she evidently had them in Isabelle.

At the office, Pepper said Harper had jetted out half an hour ago, not saying where she was heading.

That was odd, thought JD, checking his phone. No text, no call. He glanced at Wes, and they both exited, hopping in JD's truck.

It was a short drive home, and rounding Grandpa's barn, JD saw a car he didn't recognize parked in the circle next to Harper's Range Rover and Wes' truck—all three sat just in front of the house.

"I'll hang back," Wes said, quietly, seeing JD's jaw set.

"Yeah," JD said, "not sure who that is." A bad feeling swept over him.

JD glanced to the second story as he pulled in back of the truck, so Wes could jump out and get to his truck without being seen. He nodded, and Wes slipped out quickly, went into a crouch and headed to the truck, hit the lock on the key fob, and quickly slid his black gear bag out, taking it around the back of the truck. Wes, too, checked the second story, but no one peered out.

He nodded at JD. They needed no words, having worked missions in country many times—they had uncanny radar and equally uncanny communication. Wes would circle around the back of the house, JD knew, and enter silently. It was a familiar pattern to them both.

JD hopped the stairs where Kelso stood at alert, his golden tail up, his nose pointed at the door, a low growl sounding in his throat. Yeah, thought JD, something is going on. He tried the knob, found the door locked, used his key, and walked into the hallway, making Kelso stay on the porch.

"Harper!" JD called, as he normally would getting home, and walked casually toward the great room housing the living room, see-through fireplace, and kitchen, taking his time, testing the atmosphere.

It felt charged.

Ahead of him, at the granite island, stood Jason Williams, a Glock in his hand, his right arm tightly around Harper. His wife strained against him, a large piece of duct tape over her mouth.

Her eyes were wide with fear, her blond hair damp with sweat.

JD understood the situation immediately. He'd gotten too close, and now Harper was about to pay the price.

He picked up a whiff of William's cologne mixed with the smell of fear. Cass had said she'd smelled something "high-end." JD agreed. He felt rage surge but didn't act on it.

Not yet.

He shut down everything inside except his tactical sense, and the scene slowed down. His peripheral vision picked up nothing, but his mind registered every detail. Jason's heart raced, JD could see the vein in his neck throb. He seemed a bit unsteady, too, given the leg brace, but had a good hold on Harper. The vet smiled, but JD knew he was churning inside.

Nothing had been moved in the kitchen or living room so the vet had likely not been there long. JD didn't look at Harper, he knew she'd hold it together, and couldn't chance any emotion—not from either of them.

JD stared at Jason, his eyes flat and assessing. No telling what Williams would do with that gun if he got spooked. JD left his own sidearm holstered, but it wouldn't take much to draw it and wipe the smug look off that beach boy face.

The detective glanced around quickly, checking more closely for Fournier, but the gene doping queen-turned-nutritionist wasn't visible. JD knew she was there somewhere.

Late afternoon light filtered through the louvered windows to the right, just next to the office door. The kitchen lights were on, illuminating William's white-blond hair, highlighting the sheen on his forehead.

"Hey there, JD," Williams said, smiling, motioning JD forward with his free hand, which held Harper's phone. He had on khakis and a finely striped blue and white oxford cloth shirt—professional garb. "Great timing. Amazing, really."

The vet nodded and his smile got bigger. He seemed to relax a bit now that he had the upper hand. He shifted weight from his braced leg to his right one.

JD didn't wonder that the guy had conned nearly everyone he'd met—that was a mega-watt smile he had there.

"We were just about to text you," Williams said, looking fondly at Harper while holding up her phone.

He pocketed the phone and shifted the Glock to his left hand as he slid behind her. Harper used that opportunity to drop her left shoulder and slam her elbow into his solar plexus. Williams caught his breath and pulled Harper closer to him by the throat.

He chuckled and looked at Harper fondly.

JD had stepped forward in the moment but stopped as Williams tightened his grip on Harper's throat. The detective noticed the vet's huge hands. Huge, but deft with that big Glock.

Williams held his left forearm against Harper's throat, then lifted her right hand and put it gently on the granite counter, patted it, and said, "Let's just leave that there for a minute." He stroked Harper's right shoulder with his Glock.

"That's a good girl you got here, detective," Williams said, looking at JD, speaking as if his wife was a small child. The vet grabbed a chef's knife from the butcher block on the granite island with his right hand. He waved it at JD, its sharp silver glinting in the overhead lights.

"I'd rather you not draw your weapon, detective." He made his point with the Glock and the knife. "Just a suggestion."

JD wondered if Wes was inside yet. The doors were locked back there and so were the windows, but Wes was fast with lock picks, so JD wasn't worried. He knew Wes wouldn't make a move while Harper was in harm's way. He'd scope the situation out and lay low, knowing even a shot to the head was not a good idea, given that Fournier was lurking around somewhere and could get off a shot or move into position should Williams go down.

He and Wes had done this dance before. They'd be patient . . . until they weren't.

"So, here's the deal," Williams said, laying the flat blade of the chef's knife on the top of Harper's right hand. "I know your wife is right-handed." He shifted his arm a bit, loosening his forearm on Harper, and flicked the Glock JD's way by cocking his wrist. It was an awkward movement, yes, but JD saw Williams could get off a shot and retain his hold on Harper, so he stayed put, watching and breathing as a predator would.

"She would have a terrible time getting through life without her thumb," Williams said, a look of grave concern playing over his apple cheeks. "Even worse without a whole hand, don't you think?"

"What do you want, Jason?" JD said, his voice flat. His eyes went to Harper, and he saw her relax just a little.

Williams cocked his wrist again a few times, flicking the Glock JD's way. "No, no, no, we won't have any of that going on, Mr. Detective. You keep those green laser beams on me, sir."

All three of them were silent a moment, the air throbbing with tension. Outside, JD could hear Kelso barking.

Then Williams smiled. "I warned you once," he said, "and look where that got us . . ." Williams seemed oddly delighted, glancing again at Harper.

"Warned me how?" JD said, realizing Williams must be speaking of the threatening voicemail.

Williams shook his head, grinning. "Nope, not gonna bite." He affectionately ran his hand over Harper's hair, smoothing it, admiring it, tilting her head his way. "She's a pretty one," he said to JD, a malicious glint in his eyes.

JD stood rooted in place, still not reacting. If he made a move, Harper was dead.

JD, instead, studied Williams more closely. He'd seen that look before. Chad Redfield had been right. Williams was a psychopath. JD could almost see the vet's mind envisioning how he'd mutilate his wife. And it pleased him. Williams was a scary guy—he enjoyed hurting things, killing things.

But JD had spent his professional life dealing with scary guys. And Williams was an amateur next to some he and Wes had handled in the war.

And, thought JD, Williams had just confessed to sending that threatening voicemail following Cass' abduction.

JD asked again: "What do you want?"

The vet seemed to think it over. Then: "You know, now that you're here," he trailed off a moment, "in the flesh, as it were. I gotta say, that's a really good question." He shrugged as if genuinely perplexed. Then he smiled. He was playing with JD.

"So what, this is revenge?" JD said. "You're going to kill both of us? Then what?"

"Sure, revenge. That works for me." Williams grinned. "I'm assuming you're not going to let us walk. So yeah, let's go with revenge." He shifted his weight again, considering it further. "Or maybe let's think of it as tying up a few loose ends before we get out." He nodded, then looked at JD. "We've got enough, I'm not greedy." He laughed.

To his right, JD heard a door open, turned to see the diminutive, brown-haired Cecelia Fournier enter from the home office to the right of the windows, a small Glock 19 in her hand.

Small, JD knew, but it was a deadly pistol.

She walked quietly up to Jason and stood, studying JD as if he were a lab specimen, her head ever-so-slightly cocked. She didn't smile.

Wes could take her out, thought JD, and he could do the same for Williams. But. the timing would have to be perfect. They couldn't chance that just yet, so JD didn't act and Wes stayed put, too, wherever he was

"You two," JD said, gazing at Fournier then back to Williams, adopting a disappointed tone. He chanced a glance at Harper and saw she was trying mightily not to give in to the terror she obviously felt. Steely, he thought. His wife was opting for steely.

Williams perked up, seemed interested in JD's tone. Fournier hadn't moved a muscle.

"You two," JD repeated, putting his hands in his jacket pockets.

The vet shook his head, a serious look on his face, and flicked his pistol. JD removed his hands, looked at the floor a moment, then up, his jaw set hard. He shifted deeper into tactical mode.

"Obviously, you're not stupid people," he said, keeping his eyes trained on Williams. "Obviously you realize there is no way out of this. You kill us, what do you think happens? You think no one's gonna pick up the ball? You kill a cop? And his wife? You don't think they'll pull out all the stops to find you?" He stared down Williams who, JD sensed, was the weaker minded of the two.

Williams laughed. "We set up this whole operation."

"Shut up," Cecelia said, not looking at Jason, her eyes locked on JD.

Williams cowered slightly, then he inflated his chest and looked at his lover. "I'll handle this," he said and turned back to JD.

"There's nothing tying us to anything. I set up the lab. I got Pinard on board. I hooked up Isabelle, made her the contact for everybody—Chad, Pinard—there's not one text or phone call, there's nothing on us."

Fournier turned her body toward him. "*Tais-toi*, Jason," she said severely, lapsing into French, which got his attention. "I say not to speak."

JD watched the two. He always marveled that, right at the end, the bad guys liked to brag, show how smart they were. Right up until JD slapped the cuffs on, or sometimes until their lives took a very bad turn.

In this case, Fournier was obviously the driver, the brains. JD saw they were both nuts, but Williams seemed the least capable of controlling himself. And there appeared a growing rift between them. That was something he could use.

"Oliver," said JD breaking into their stare down. "Why kill Oliver?"

Williams looked at JD and smirked then nodded toward Cecelia. He glanced back at Harper, set down the chef's knife and caressed her hand, still lying motionless on the granite countertop.

"Well," began Williams, "it was like this . . ." He glanced at Fournier and winced but kept on. "Cecelia here thought Oliver was getting cagey. He was a suspicious sort, or so said Isabelle."

"Chad want to be the big man, he want to move to distribution," Fournier broke in. "So I say, Oliver . . .," and here she drew a finger across her throat. "Then you move up. You get the career . . .," she paused, thinking. "*Quel est le mot?*" She thought about it a moment more, then: "Ah, 'bounce,' *oui*."

She turned back to Williams. "I say shut up, no?" She then casually raised her Glock 19 and shot her lover through the temple.

He dropped, a surprised look on his face. "Not much, this one," she said and shrugged as Harper lunged toward her. Fournier stepped to the side and smiled, her Glock 19 trained on Harper then on JD, freezing them both.

JD sighed. It was over, Fournier just didn't know it yet. How it would end for her—that was the only question.

From the shadows behind the steps, Wes silently crept forward.

"You're outnumbered," JD said quietly. "You could get one of us, but not both."

Fournier smiled, still shifting the gun from one to the other. "You will see. I do this many times." Her French accent seemed more pronounced now that the stakes were higher. She must realize, thought JD, that her odds had just gotten really long.

Wes hung back, waiting on JD's signal. JD knew he had to keep Fournier talking, distract her.

"So it was Jason who kidnapped Cass, right?" The cologne, the message. It had been Jason.

Fournier nodded, then frowned. "Then he get the kick. He send this Chad to feed the woman, and he . . ." She scowled. "She is the tiny jockey. Yet she escape. She kick him good. You explain that?"

JD took a breath and tried to smile. Keep her talking. "You obviously don't know Cass."

Suddenly Wes stepped around her, his M-4 trained on her head.

"Wes, no," JD said evenly, "we need her alive."

JD then watched Fournier raise the gun to Harper's eyes. "Three to one, not the good odds," she said and focused.

Wes tapped her on the shoulder, reflexively she glanced his way, and he shot her between the eyes.

35

JD and Harper surveyed the horrifying bloody damage—two bodies lay in increasingly larger puddles of blood on the hardwood floor. Jason Williams still had that stupid, surprised look on his face, but JD didn't want to close his eyes and disturb the scene. The back of Fournier's head was mostly missing, her brains and bits of red-stained bone splattered the floor as well as Williams' crisp blue and white-striped shirt.

"Problem solved," Wes commented.

None of it bothered JD in a personal way. Where Wes seemed bereft of feeling altogether, JD was simply clinical.

He moved to Harper, who seemed stunned, rooted in place. JD put his arm around her, tried to steer her toward the couch but she didn't move from the granite countertop.

"Jesus, Wes," said JD looking things over, his arm around Harper's shoulder, thinking how tough it was going to be to wind up the case now that his two main culprits were dead.

He looked at Wes. "You coulda just waited a minute, bud." He looked back at Fournier, thinking well here's a freaking mess to clean up.

As for the case, there was still Gus Pinard and Max Sidarus, they weren't in the clear yet.

Wes tapped his holstered gun. "Guess so." He bent and peered at Fournier's head then looked up. "But you know me, you can't take me anywhere."

JD called it in and hustled Harper out of the house.

"I'm going to the office," she said, once on the porch, her eyes stark. She'd ripped off the duct tape and hadn't winced.

"Nope," JD said, pulling her to him, "you're sticking with me." A big mower rumbled by, finished with the day's work of cutting the pastures. Silence settled in after its passing.

Wes trudged out of the house, touched his Justin, hopped down the porch stairs, and blasted out in his truck.

Likely to pick up Cass and head for a few more Town Branch shots, thought JD, wishing a little that they could join the two. He turned back to Harper. But he knew when the shock wore off, Harper would have a tough time. Likely what she'd just been through would call up her sister's murder and the terrifying aftermath of that. It had happened not all that long ago, so she'd need him. No way his wife was handing all that on her own.

Harper pulled back from JD. "I'm going. I need to work. I know you get that."

They stared at each other a few seconds.

"I need to work, JD," Harper said again, her eyes level. She was composed and firm. "That's what I do." She paused. "That's what you do. We work."

JD nodded finally, agreeing but not liking it. He made her promise to check in. Knowing her as he did, he'd be able to tell if she was whirling into the ozone.

So Harper headed to Eden Hill's office and JD headed to the precinct. He'd let Sidarus and Pinard go for the moment and focus on Williams and Fournier, home and vet clinic.

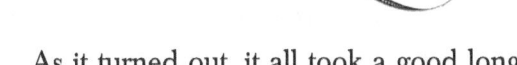

As it turned out, it all took a good long while to mop up. JD waded through all the paperwork at the precinct, the questions, set up his interviews, conferred with Walker, did more paperwork, only heading home well after dark.

He skirted the still-bloody scene and headed upstairs.

He found Harper in bed with a book, jumped in, made her feel better, or so she said, and they both drifted off into a light sleep, JD holding Harper, her head resting on his chest, the beat of his heart the only comfort she could find.

The next day JD was up and out of the house early, hoping he could get the clean-up crew in later that day. He landed at the precinct to find, as he'd suspected, that Oliver's DNA and trace amounts of Chad's as well as his partial fingerprints, showed up on a tire iron found in Chad's garage. JD was glad of that, he didn't need the evidence his illegal search had turned up in Chad's bathroom. He put that case to bed.

The more interesting possibilities, again not surprisingly, came from Williams' large animal veterinary clinic, where the Tyvek-and-glove-clad tech crew had found nothing in the office proper, but figured there was a whale of a haul behind a hidden door inset with a digital key code. When JD got the news of the secured room around 10 a.m., he headed over to the clinic, trusting that the someone on the team would officially break the code and he wouldn't have to call on Wes and his special black-market toy.

Everyone was there, waiting on the specialist who arrived and took her time working on the digital key encoding. Eventually there was a satisfying click, and the heavy door swung open to reveal a fairly large lab lit by bright overhead lights switched on by JD. They all trooped in.

The scene was clinical, clean, and orderly: stainless steel cabinets, refrigerators, and workstations lined the perimeter and, in the center, stood a long island inset with sinks, its surface littered with red and yellow-stoppered test tubes set in blue and red holders, labeled bottles, paper towels, and more paraphernalia than JD could take in at one glance. The perimeter stations housed microscopes, Petri dishes, protective glasses, testing equipment, sliding glass partitions, and computers.

Cheryl was there, supervising, and pretty soon told JD they'd need some special folks to decipher what was going on in the Petri dishes and with some other organic specimens they'd found, though many of the vials and bottles on the long central counter, in cabinets, and in the refrigerators were labeled.

JD called the Racing Commission as that seemed the politically correct thing to do and the director said he'd alert the testing lab immediately. The director, a knowledgeable and conscientious guy JD respected a lot, thanked the detective, saying they'd been funding gene doping research and this cache of evidence would likely take them miles down the road in understanding what the cheaters were up to.

JD nodded as he listened, mumbling he was glad to be of help.

The director paused a moment, then with a bit of mirth said, "Those relationships you build playing ball—I heard you were a damned good QB—they stick around, don't they?"

JD smiled. So the director knew his former offensive lineman had forked over some info. Good to have cooperation, he thought, even if it sometimes came under the table. It seemed the director felt the same. JD chuckled and hung up.

All in all, the team found, bagged, and otherwise secured an array of what appeared to be gene modification paraphernalia, specimens, treated organics, and labeled files on the computer housed in the lab. JD donned gloves and sifted through the computer files, which were organized excel documents of Janero's horses, the name of the gene modified, the expected outcome, the actual outcome, along with dates and other information. There were also excel sheets listing the same sort of information but including combinations of gene doping, drugs, and medications administered. As well, JD located information on testing limit alterations needed for various illegal concoctions—these were from Isabelle—the adjustments made and the outcome.

The files were extensive, detailed, damning, and JD couldn't wait to compare what they'd found to the files he'd sent over to Tim Bradford, the ones he and McCann had reviewed. JD felt the room held everything he'd need to make a slam-dunk case, though the main actors were dead. But he'd sure get a lot of mileage out of the find in the lab, which the Racing Commission and testing lab could use.

As Cheryl had indicated, the team also found caches of illegal drugs, legal drugs, and medications, all labeled. All the collected material would be forwarded to the DEA in the hopes that the investigation would be widened, and the international major players identified. It was quite possible that Jason Williams and Cecelia Fournier were working with folks outside of the United States, and given Fournier and Isabelle's work history, JD would put his money on Europe as the origin.

Max Sidarus was exonerated by notations Cheryl found among the files. Documents were located with clear instructions and workarounds to administering drugs and altered genes outside of Sidarus' awareness as well as instructions about his scheduled absences. Fournier, Williams, and their minions went to great pains to conduct their illegal activities well away from the owner's scrutiny.

There were a lot of additional documents to pour over, so JD put Cheryl in charge of collecting and sifting through it all, asking for a call should something astounding come up. Otherwise, he'd wait for her full report as soon as the review was finished.

That, thought JD, left Gus Pinard. The detective rose from the files he'd been scrutinizing. Pinard. The last weasel to find. The slippery one, JD mused, stacking the paper files into a pile, always lurking about the corners, disappearing when JD showed up, slipping in to pick Marshall's brain at the training track.

But there was no hard evidence JD could use to arrest Pinard. He hadn't shown up in the texts on Chad's burner and nothing incriminating had yet turned up in the lab to tie the trainer to the operation. The only solid evidence JD had was Williams bragging that he and Fournier had set up the whole thing. Williams had mentioned Gus Pinard, so he was clearly in on it, but they weren't around so that info was not going to nail Pinard. And though Harper and likely Wes had heard Williams' confession, that wasn't enough for an arrest warrant for the trainer, not the way this case was going.

JD needed proof, substantial, irrefutable proof, to bust Janero's trainer.

A confession, for example. JD smiled. Wes was very good at extracting confessions.

Walking to the Range Rover, JD opened to feelings of vengeance—for what had been done to Cass, especially for what had been done to Harper, and for the deaths and injuries to the horses. He focused it all on Gus Pinard. It wasn't fair, he knew that. But the trainer was left and as so often had happened during the war, who was left bore the brunt.

But JD indulged in those feelings only a moment. That was a dark abyss into which too many soldiers had fallen, some under his command. He'd seen their vengeance, felt it himself on occasion, he'd understood it, but had never let it have the upper hand. Wes, it wasn't a part of him. He'd separated himself so completely that the acts he'd committed caused him neither pleasure nor pain.

JD thought about all this in the few seconds it took him to reach the SUV. Then a coldness settled over him. He'd get Wes.

And then they'd get Pinard.

36

If the trainer was smart, thought JD on the way to Janero's racing barn with Wes, Pinard would be long gone. Surely, he'd heard the news—everyone involved was dead. Or, in the case of Isabelle, vanished to parts unknown, possibly of the type below ground.

Beside him, Wes studied the landscape flying by, not talking, obviously going within, then turned his attention to his M-4 pistol. A quiet and stealthy menace stole over him—he geared up externally and internally. He'd always been that way.

But as he and Wes exited the Range Rover at Janero's big racing barn, entered and inquired about the trainer, it appeared Gus Pinard was not clued into the noose tightening around his neck.

JD flashed his ID at a groom walking a hingey-shouldered bay colt back in from a bit of grazing and was told the trainer was at the training track.

JD glanced at Wes. "Let's take a look . . ." and he headed to Pinard's office first, just next to the barn door's entrance.

As they made their way down the aisle, young racehorses walked easily beside their grooms, nodding their finely featured heads, heading out for a bit of grass after workouts. Other stalled youngsters stood quietly as grooms secured white leg wraps and loaded hay into nets at each stall.

Nobody paid any attention to the detective and Wes.

"He would not be that stupid," commented Wes on the way to the trainer's office.

JD smiled. "Well, there's been some idiots in charge so far."

Wes tugged the front of his Justin and strode alongside JD.

They entered the office door and found themselves in an entryway lined with a ceiling-high stainless-steel rack of shelves. JD set about picking through the contents, thinking Pinard might have hidden something incriminating among the supplies.

Wes stood by looking skeptical.

"Providerm, baby oil, vet wrap, Brasso." JD read off the labels. "Raplast, DMSO, Blu-Kote. Iodine, Chlorhexidine, turpentine," JD murmured in disgust. He turned to Wes. "The usual."

Wes smirked. "Surprise, surprise."

"Smart ass."

They walked into the office, which was, oddly neat and tidy. And clean. On the wall hung black-framed portraits of famous runners, Pinard and others in winner's circles, and assorted racing shots, on and off the track. Along the back wall, beneath the window, hung an array of training gear—bridles and reins, shiny chifney bits, stud chains, all orderly and well-cared for. Not the usual for a busy trainer.

They heard a low growl and, in a moment, a scruffy old black dog limped out from behind the desk. Seeing JD and Wes, the old guy began wagging his tail slowly and JD smoothed the sleek head. He and Wes sifted through the papers on the desk, opened drawers, and found nothing.

"Ok, the track," JD said, and they headed out.

Again, thought JD, Wes couldn't resist the smirk.

Whatever. They hoofed it out of the barn.

Janero had two training tracks. JD and Wes headed to the first one, a dirt track some distance from the main racing barn. Pinard was at the rail with his assistant and a finely dressed couple JD didn't recognize. The detective glanced at his phone. It was late for training, so JD was curious about what the foursome was up to.

Wes and JD quietly approached the chatty group and overheard the trainer speaking to the couple. His assistant stood nearby looking obsequious.

". . . like your filly here," Pinard continued, nodding to the well-muscled filly making her way around the track. "She looks good. Very well made, good turn-of-foot, looks to have a good head." He smiled, watching the couple nodding appreciatively.

JD and Wes were quiet, observing.

"Sometimes," Pinard said, pulling on his long chin, ever the thoughtful trainer, "sometimes you gotta start over." He looked at the filly. "She'll be fine here. She didn't do good on the track? We're gonna go back to the beginning. First, we settle her in, then we walk, then we go a little more, we jog, then we breeze." He paused, waiting for the head nods. "We go slow."

JD had to admire the façade. Pinard, the caring, wise, knowledgeable trainer only looking out for the best interests of the filly. And the wealthy couple.

Wes snorted in derision, which caused Pinard to turn his head. Seeing the pair, he slapped his clipboard on his thigh and scowled, his long face a mask of displeasure.

The couple, dressed to the nines—obviously a pair of rich, hopeful owners—looked quizzically at JD and Wes.

JD began to pull out his ID, which stopped Gus Pinard in his tracks. He held up his hand. "Just let me finish up, ok? Then we'll talk." He turned to the couple and smiled. "I think you've made a wise decision. I'll let her be a bit, think about the best regimen for her and we'll talk."

The couple, feeling dismissed, looked at each other, then at the detective and Wes. JD had on his Hawk Ridge jacket, so Pinard likely figured he'd get rid of the couple before they caught a drift of what was really going on.

Janero's trainer stuck his arm out and shook the husband's hand. The wife extended her hand, evidently used to being an equal partner, and Pinard quickly gave it a perfunctory shake.

"We'll just see our girl settled in her stall," said the man and the couple pivoted as the exercise rider exited the track at a walk. They all headed toward the barn leaving the trainer alone with JD and Wes.

Pinard pulled out his phone.

"Nope, not this time," JD said, putting his palm out for Pinard's phone. He wasn't about to let him call in Sidarus and slink away again.

"We can talk here or at the station," JD said quietly, and Pinard pocketed his phone.

"In my office," the trainer said and stomped toward the barn, his shoulders slumped.

Once inside Pinard's private sanctuary, the trainer sat at his desk, ran a hand over his dog who then slunk away to the corner and plopped down on his bed.

JD and Wes stood, there being no other chairs in the office.

"You got piss-poor timing," Pinard said. "This is the busy season, you know that." He shook his head. "I got nothing for you."

JD and Wes stood by silently, Pinard glancing at Wes then, seeing his eyes, swiveling to JD.

"Chad is dead," JD began.

"Yeah, I heard."

"And Williams and Cecelia Fournier."

Pinard's long face went white. "What about 'em?"

Wes said, "Dead, both of them." He stared at Pinard, who could not then look away.

"How? What, wait." Pinard shook his head. "They're dead?"

Wes and JD looked at each other and then at Pinard. JD watched the trainer struggle for composure, his mind likely reeling. The pair stayed quiet, watching Pinard wrestle with the facts. Then the trainer's mental turmoil settled a bit, but there was no calm, no methodical, smart processing going on that JD could see.

But Pinard was putting two and two together. He was realizing they'd come for him now that everyone else involved was dead.

JD looked at Wes who also studied Pinard, then watched his buddy walk to the wall and lean against it, crossing his arms. What would the trainer do? Run for it? Go on the attack? Call a lawyer? If they were taking bets, Wes' look said, he'd vote for the run. It was the stupid move.

They waited a minute more. JD figured the run, too. Idiots always made the dumb move.

But Pinard surprised them. "So you think I'm the only one left, you're gonna pin this all on me?" He sat back in his chair, folding his hands in his lap, his pock-marked face resuming its normal gray hue. "That's your big move?"

His phone rang, and Pinard pulled it out of his pocket, didn't answer, and set it on the counter. He looked at JD with hooded eyes. "So you come for me, huh?"

"We did."

Pinard laughed. "Well, you woulda cuffed me you had anything."

So, thought JD. All those years coming up on those lower tracks had taught Pinard something after all. Cheat and CYA. Obviously, the trainer was not going to go easily. And he was right, they didn't have anything on him. Nothing definitive.

So, a stand-off.

He looked to Wes, the confession king.

Wes slowly walked to his right, gently fingering the racing gear hanging along the back wall behind Pinard. The trainer strained to turn, but then snapped back to JD.

Wes gently lifted a thick pair of rubbery reins, thoughtfully considered them, ran his hands lightly along them, then tested their elasticity. He nodded and looked at JD, who glanced toward the wall of photos. He knew exactly what Wes was up to.

Wes quietly moved behind Pinard who seemed rooted, and whipped the reins around the trainer's neck twice, pulling them taut. No words were spoken.

Pinard's sunken eyes went wide, his mouth gaped open, his hands flew to his throat as he began sputtering and choking.

JD turned back, expressionless, and watched Pinard gasp and twist in terror. Wes hauled the trainer up, walked him to the wall. From his bed, the old dog picked up the tension and began a low growl.

JD watched a moment more, then murmured "Take it easy, Wes." He didn't need another Fournier episode. They needed at least one perp alive to tell the tale.

But Wes did not take his eyes off Pinard, he slammed him hard against the wall, his gray eyes inches from Pinard's face. The trainer became frantic, which was not helping his cause, as it only pulled the reins tighter.

Pinard coughed and struggled to get his hands inside the reins. "Call your damn dog off," he choked out, closing his eyes so as not to see Wes.

Then Wes let go and the trainer quickly fell to the floor. JD smiled. It was one of Wes' signature moves.

"I think you might want to be a little more forthcoming," JD said. He studied the trainer dispassionately and shrugged. Just a suggestion, his manner conveyed.

Pinard rubbed his neck, glanced at Wes then cowered. He looked at JD but stayed on the floor. "You had anything on me, you'd a used it." He looked up at the window as if contemplating launching himself up and out, which, JD saw, was a measure of his desperation.

Pinard then opted for unconvincing anger and shot back at JD, "You got nothing."

"You're right, we don't have anything at the moment we can arrest you on," JD said, mildly, walking over and squatting down, eye to eye with Pinard. "But we're just starting to sift through all of the documents at Williams and Fournier's lab, and you do know we'll find things that clearly incriminate you." He watched Pinard squirm, which confirmed JD's suspicions.

He stood. He had Pinard in the crosshairs. "And we'll get a search warrant, we'll tap your phone, and I'm pretty sure we'll find more than enough to hang you."

Pinard glanced pitifully around his office as if considering all he was losing.

"You're done. I know it and you know it."

Wes had retreated to the wall of photos, and now walked slowly from one to the other, his black hair glistening in the light streaming through the window. He was totally disinterested in the goings on with Pinard and JD.

From the floor, Pinard glared at Wes' back, then to JD who now loomed over him. The trainer seemed to consider his options.

"Tell you what," JD said, seeing Pinard waver. "We've got everything we need to clean up the mess Jason Williams and Cecelia Fournier made—that operation is shut down for good. I've got Chad on the murder of Oliver. And Williams on the abduction of Cass. Doesn't matter, of course, the three of them being dead."

He looked at Wes and smiled. "Fournier, that was his doing," JD said.

Pinard got the message.

Wes walked to Pinard's desk, perched on it, pulled out his gun and fingered it, showing it to Pinard to drive the point home.

"You can't do this," Pinard yelled from the floor, finally finding his voice. He sounded angry but his face held a look of fear. "This is assault, and you're threatening me. That's not gonna fly in a courtroom."

"Huh," JD said. He knew Pinard was not going raise a fuss as that would call attention to himself and pull down some heavy heat.

"Tell you what," JD said again. "Here's the offer. We've got pretty much everything we need. And we'll get you, too. There's no doubt about that. But you could help yourself out here. If you know anything about where Fournier and Williams got their drugs, and everything else they needed for the gene doping—you give me that? I'll definitely have a few words to say on your behalf."

Pinard's old dog lumbered over to him and sank down, putting his head on the trainer's thigh. Pinard stroked the dog's head and back slowly and with some affection.

"I hear ya," Pinard said, finally, not taking his eyes off his old dog. And then more softly, "I'll get you what you need."

Gus Pinard was as good as his word. He gave them three names, two in France and one in Ireland, and the contact information for each of them, identifying the three people as linchpins to the whole operation—they provided Williams and Fournier with everything they needed for their gene doping and drug operations.

All of that went immediately to the DEA and its offices in Europe. And, as it turned out, once the documents at the lab were fully examined, they didn't need anything else on Pinard, so the trainer would be going away for a very long time. There would be no deal.

The DEA had taken over the case, and the trainer was now involved in an international conspiracy. It was out of JD's hands. He couldn't say he was sorry not to have cut a deal for Pinard. He would at least get his cases closed and one major cheater away from the horses.

One cheating scheme down, countless to go.

37

The next week, after a long workday, JD entered the kitchen to find Harper opening the mail.

"Hey," she said, looking up and slitting open an envelope. She picked up an unopened letter and handed it to JD, a slight smile on her face. "For you."

JD turned it over in his hand, noting the stamps and the letter's origin—Morocco. He opened it with a good idea about what he'd find inside. He pulled out a photograph of Isabelle in a flimsy, tie-dyed dress, holding a bottle of clear liquid labeled "*Mahia*" in one hand and a glass of it in the other. She was toasting and smiling, and behind her was a table with an array of food, and behind that a vibrant light blue wall studded with flower-laden planters, small shop openings with colorful ware sitting here and there on the rising, deeper, blue-painted steps leading up to an arched doorway.

JD headed over to the living room's bar and poured himself a finger of whiskey, then looked over to his wife gathering the day's envelopes into a pile. She shuffled the letters and bills together, stuffed them in her briefcase, and looked up briefly feeling JD's eyes on her. She threw the envelopes into the trash.

JD headed over, adding Isabelle's envelope to the bunch, and tucked the photo in his back pocket.

He looked out the kitchen window over Buck's Creek to the barn beyond and lifted a toast to his absent adversary. "Well played, Isabelle," he murmured aloud, and knocked back the whiskey. No wonder she'd gone through the hassle to set up banking there. Morocco had no extradition treaty with the U.S.

Not long after, Wes decided to pack it up and head back to the woods. Neither he nor Cass were teary-eyed about it.

"It's a work in progress," Cass quipped to Harper one afternoon, standing on the bridge over Buck's Creek. The cool April weather had finally broken. The days were warm, the nights full and close, the fields green, the horses kicking and bucking, and running from fence line to fence line.

Harper sat down on the bridge, patted a seat next to her and Cass sank down. They both swung their legs out and back like little kids. Harper's blue eyes followed the water softly running over the greenish brown rocks, and she stayed thoughtfully quiet.

Cass spoke. "It's ok. He'll be back."

"I know. He's connected to you, I get that."

Cass lay back on the bridge, gazed at the cloudless sky. "I still got some stuff to deal with."

"Yeah. The fear." Harper understood that more than most, having herself been abducted and nearly killed. Once in a lifetime was more than enough, but she'd endured near-death twice now. "You don't work it through all the way . . ."

"Yeah."

"Takes a while," Harper said, pulling a round stone out of her pocket, one smoothed by millennia of water washing over it. "Here," she said, leaning back and placing it in Cass' open palm. "Just hold it. Keep it with you." For Harper, the stone had been a reminder that letting her own anguish go was possible. It could be washed away. She'd carried the stone since her sister had died. It was a great gift, especially given recent events, and the only one she could think of to give Cass.

The jockey sat up, leaned her head on Harper's shoulder.

They didn't say anything for quite a while, then they got up and walked to Grandpa's barn.

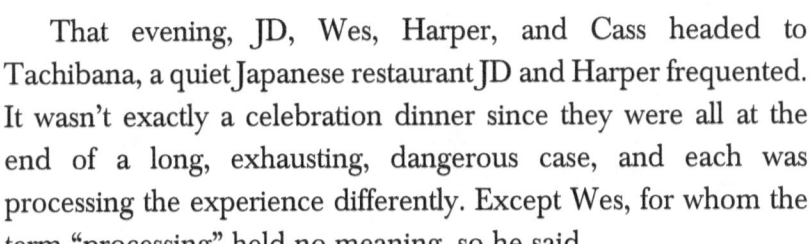

That evening, JD, Wes, Harper, and Cass headed to Tachibana, a quiet Japanese restaurant JD and Harper frequented. It wasn't exactly a celebration dinner since they were all at the end of a long, exhausting, dangerous case, and each was processing the experience differently. Except Wes, for whom the term "processing" held no meaning, so he said.

No one spoke about him leaving in the morning.

The four of them slowly entered the restaurant's spare taupe and cream interior, complete with a polished expanse of hardwood dotted by four-tops spaced for conversation. Wes pulled out his man bun and shook his head, evidently feeling the ancestral vibe.

Harper had JD's arm, and visibly sighed walking in, then let go of her husband and smoothed back her high ponytail. JD turned an admiring eye to his wife dressed in an aqua satin shirt, jeans, and boots. Simple and elegant, he thought, as she'd always been. As for Cass, she'd tucked her shirt into her jeans, the only concession she made to the restaurant's toney interior, and they were all seated near the window.

JD unbuttoned his sports coat and sat last of all, his back to the window, his green eyes scanning the restaurant out of habit. They chatted about nothing, looking over the menu, then Wes ordered an array of sushi for the table, never mind that Harper and JD were regulars and had their favorites. Wes ordered a dragon roll for himself, which caused JD and Harper to laugh and Cass to turn a "Seriously?" eye his way. Wes grinned, saying dragons were his totems.

"Primordial power," he added, giving the table two thumbs up, then flipping them to himself.

And this is why I want you here, JD thought, shooting a smile Wes' way. Light and easy even in the face of hellishness—that had always been Wes' MO.

The women, both of whom had nearly died, said they felt fine, glad to have the ordeal behind them. They were, they insisted, moving on, no harm done.

The sushi was served, and they all dug into the eel, spider, and Negri-Toro rolls, not touching Wes' dragons, nobody speaking, everyone savoring the hand-cut beauty of each roll and every bite. They sipped green tea in silence.

JD and Wes looked at each other amid the quiet enjoyment, both of them knowing the "no harm done" was not going to be the case for Harper and Cass. Both military men had been through aftermaths of intense missions many times and knew there'd be anguish, nightmares maybe, certainly some PTSD to live with or work through.

They ordered dinner. JD and Harper selected Tem-Jyu and Yakisoba to share, Cass had grilled salmon and Wes ordered Unaju, freshwater eel, to which the rest of the table scrunched up their noses. The conversation turned to racing, everyone making an effort to get back to some sort of normalcy.

The meal finished, they all headed home, Wes and Cass retiring first, while JD and Harper stayed up a while.

They walked out onto the porch, and Harper took hold of the tall, white pillar to the right of the steps. The night was moonless, dark and brooding beneath the cloud cover, with only a few stars lighting the mares' far pasture, a hint of rain in the air.

Harper and JD stepped down the stairs, crossed Buck's Creek, and turned left toward the broodmares and foals Harper had just brought over from Hawk Ridge. The pair leaned on the pasture fence and watched the shadowy mothers, some picked out by starlight, their babies at their sides or trotting away into darkness, a small group investigating their new home.

A solitary mare just ahead moved slowly, her velvety muzzle nuzzling the grass then grazing, then stepping forward slowly, her baby at her side.

Harper looked at JD, who put his arm around her shoulder. The horses asked for so little, Harper thought, watching the mares startle and move as one to the left toward the fence line along the drive.

Harper gazed up and out into the universe lit with a smattering of stars, where among them, she imagined, her family and all the horses they'd bred and raised and raced and buried gazed down on them. She and JD stayed quiet, Harper resting against her husband, the moon's eerie light oddly comforting.

Harper watched as the last mare lifted her head and turn a luminous eye her way, then she and her baby ran off into the darkness.

They ask so little, Harper thought again, and we demand so much. She caressed her husband's hand on her shoulder.

JD squeezed her and moved behind so she could lean against him. He wrapped his arms around her and Harper's hands came up to rest on them, taking in the strength of his presence.

Quietly, they watched the mares and babies nearing the far fence, disappearing into the deep, sheltering shadows of her grandpa's century oaks.

Then the pair turned back to the house, leaving the mares and foals to the comforting darkness, and the cleansing rain to come.

For tonight, that was enough.

Catch Up on *The Bluegrass Horse Racing Series*

Blood in the Bluegrass

Action packed from the get-go and filled with unique characters, this book is hard to put down as it races headlong at full speed to the finish line.

~Barry Irwin, CEO/Team Valor International

Harper had put the past behind her. Or so she thought. Fleeing the flashy, high dollar world of Kentucky horse racing for NYC, she'd been content living the life of a successful painter. But escape isn't an option after the accidental death of her sister sends her back to the Bluegrass, a horse racing world filled with hope and heartbreak. As the body count rises at Eden Hill, Harper becomes convinced her sister's death was no accident. Probing more deeply, Harper realizes Paris' death is tied to a dark and deadly secret, one she discovers is why her racehorses are dying. Solving her sister's murder and saving her family's stud farm will take every ounce of Harper's wit and courage. When seven skeletons are discovered on the grounds, and the barn with her best Kentucky Derby prospects is set on fire, Harper bears down to find the killer. The problem is, the culprit could be anyone: Is it JD, her childhood sweetheart, Marshall, their long-time trainer, or is it their nasty neighbor Red Cole, in partnership with her family for generations? Someone is on a killing spree, and though Harper doesn't know why, she is sure of one thing—the murderer is someone she's known and trusted her whole life.

Betrayed in the Bluegrass

A rapid-fire thriller filled with captivating characters, Betrayed in the Bluegrass is a must-read for all horse and horse racing lovers. Set on Keeneland's backstretch, with a brilliantly executed feature race, this action-packed whodunnit packs a punch that will keep you guessing till the end. Betrayed is a riveting addition to Slachman's Bluegrass horse racing series.

~Adrian Beaumont – Director of Racecourse Services
for International Racing Bureau

Lexington Thoroughbred racing's "power couple" Harper Hill and her husband, Detective JD Cole unite in this, the second in Slachman's "Bluegrass" horse racing series. When a mysterious man, beaten and tortured, stumbles into the police precinct asking for JD, then dies before he can divulge his secret, a series of events are set in motion that will put the couples' detecting power to the test and Harper's life in grave danger. Soon after, Aubrey Lowen, Harper's second cousin, is found severely beaten by the side of the road. Hospitalized, he hovers between life and death as Harper heads to Keeneland's backstretch to keep an eye Lowen's head trainer, Henley Smythe, who seems up to no good. As Harper tries desperately to uncover the culprit and help Aubrey's wife Millie save their once-successful Thoroughbred farm, a dangerous character from Harper's past shows up on the backstretch. Amid the dark pool of danger swirling around Harper, JD announces that the Feds have stepped in, preventing the couple from continuing their investigation. Undeterred, the two work under the radar to stop a killer bent on destroying the Lowen legacy and anyone who gets in the way. As murder and greed haunt every step they take, the couple knows that buried deep in Keeneland's chaos the killer lies in wait—but uncovering the murderer just may cost Harper her life.

Also by Virginia Slachman

The Lost Ode

When the owner of Brookfield Stud, Gray Burke, is arrested for homicide, amateur sleuth Julia is left to solve the murder and prove his innocence while following the trail to a lost fortune. Solving the murder may lead to love and treasure, but has Julia backed the wrong horse by believing in Gray Burke's innocence?

Many Brave Hearts

Many Brave Hearts is an unblinking, eloquent, deeply felt memoir of how war can shatter emotional lives and undermine our deepest bonds, redeemed–in the only way possible–with love.

~Kurt Brown

World of Mortal Light

Slachman moves with remarkable skill in long, musical lines creating a richly textured poetry that vividly paints the "real world."

~Allison Funk

Inside Such Darkness

A poetic collection that fiercely engages the reality of loss in poems whose brilliance cuts through the darkness.

~Don Bogen

About the Author

Virginia Slachman is a devoted advocate for retired racehorses as well as for outlawing drugs and inhumane treatment in racing. In addition to continuing her writing and university teaching career, Slachman has worked for years with ex-racehorses in one way or another—caring for them, rehabilitating or retraining them for new careers, and writing about them. Her work in rescue led to her adoption of Corredor dela Isla, her own ex-racehorse who continues to be her loved companion. You can read about their journey here: https://www.virginiaslachman.com/. She's a certified EAL practitioner, a Masters-level Reiki practitioner, the author of three collections of poetry and her memoir, as well as four novels set in the Thoroughbred racing world.

www.ingramcontent.com/pod-product-compliance
Lightning Source LLC
Chambersburg PA
CBHW032025240626
47154CB00003B/787